CW01082574

ALSO BY KIMBERLY MULLINS:

Notebook Mysteries ~ Emma (Book 1)

Notebook Mysteries ~ Decisions and Possibilities (Book 2)

Notebook Mysteries ~ Changes and Challenges (Book 3)

Notebook Mysteries ~ Unexpected Outcomes (Book 4)

Notebook Mysteries ~ Haunted Christmas (a novella)

Notebook Mysteries ~ Suspicions (Book 5) -Released March 2023

Notebook Mysteries ~ Parisian Intrigue (Book 6)- August 2023

Notebook Mysteries ~ To be announced (a Christmas novella) September 2023

Notebook Mysteries

Notebook Mysteries

Parisian
Intrigue

KIMBERLY
MULLINS

NOTEBOOK MYSTERIES ~ PARISIAN INTRIGUE

Notebook Mysteries Series

Copyright © JKJ books, LLC 2023

First edition: July 2023

Mailing address for JKJ books, LLC; 17350 State Highway 249, STE 220 #3515 Houston, Texas 77064

Library of Congress Control Number: 2023901491

ISBN (paperback) 979-8-9871148-9-6

ISBN (hardback) 979-8-218-914190-5

ISBN (ebook) 97908-9871148-8-9

This is a work of fiction. It is based on historical events within Chicago during the time period of the 1880s.

Edited by Kaitlyn Katsoupis, Strictly Textual

Cover Art by Miblart

To Claudia, Jonathan and Joshua, who I am sharing this amazing journey with.

PROLOGUE

PARIS JAIL 1889

"You just had to get us involved," Jeremy muttered from under his hat, not stirring off the bench where he was reclining.

Emma turned toward him and leaned back against the jail cell bars. "Me? I wasn't the one who threw the first punch."

"Calm down," called Dora's voice from the adjacent cell.

"Calm down? You were the one who punched the police officer!" Emma said, straightening.

"That's how I heard it," Tim said from the hallway outside of the cells.

Dora rushed toward him. She pressed against the bars and held out her hand. "Can you get us out of here?"

He took it and said, "Not me, but I brought someone who can help."

A man in a black suit, black tie, and white shirt walked up.

"Cole!" Emma called.

Jeremy lifted the hat off his face, showing a black eye. He sat up and moved it to a jaunty angle on his head. "Hey Pops, here to spring us?"

"That remains to be seen. There's some confusion about the events you were involved in," Cole said drolly.

"What could be confusing?" Emma asked. "I found a dead body in a trunk. The husband slapped me, then the whole room joined in." Frowning, she looked at Jeremy in search of his support.

He shrugged and said wryly, "Yeah, anyone would have known to check the trunk for a body."

Cole laughed. "Most people come to Paris for shopping and sightseeing."

"Well, not us," said Emma firmly.

CHAPTER 1

FOUR WEEKS EARLIER IN CHICAGO

*E*mma walked into the dining room where the family was enjoying a late Sunday lunch. Tim, Dora, Emma, Jake, and Jeremy sat around the table with the children. They had gone to church that morning and were enjoying a lazy afternoon.

"Delivery," she said waving an envelope in the air.

"What is it, Emma, a telegram?" Jeremy asked, setting down his fork.

"No, an invitation," she responded, not looking up from it.

"To a party?" Dora asked curiously as she continued to cut up three-year-old Lottie's food.

"No," Emma said, glancing up suddenly. "It's an invitation to the Paris Exposition!"

"Paris!" everyone said together.

"Someone invited you to Paris?" Dora asked. She felt envious. Her sister was always doing exciting things.

"Not just me. All of us," Emma said and gestured to everyone at the table.

Everyone was silent as they digested the information. Finally, Jeremy spoke up. "Can I see that?"

"Yes," she said as she handed him the invitation.

"Who sent it?" Tim asked.

"It says it's from the Art Curator's Society. Have you heard of them?" Jeremy asked Emma.

"No. I can't say I have. It mentions that reservations are in place for us at the hotel and that the tickets for the train and steamer are prearranged." The name of the steamer was *La Bretagne*. *What a coincidence,* she thought. She had been to Paris previously on the *La Bretagne*.

"When are we expected to go?" Dora asked. She was thinking about the kids, the boarding houses, and all that needed to be done to keep things running smoothly.

Jeremy handed the invitation to her without commenting.

Dora read the note quickly. "But this says tomorrow!" she exclaimed. "How can we get organized to leave by then?"

Tim was already thinking ahead. "We have the help here for the boarding houses and our other businesses. But it's the kids I worry about."

"I think we can do it," Emma said in a firm voice. "We just need to get organized. The first thing I'd like to do is confirm the tickets are authentic." *Paris,* she thought. *This time it will be with Jeremy.*

"Agreed," Jeremy said. "We won't be able to firm up the hotel, but we should be able to confirm the train and steamship tickets."

"I can go to the train station and confirm the tickets if you want to handle the steamship," Tim said to Jeremy.

"I think I can handle that," Jeremy responded.

"What about the hotel? Shouldn't we make sure we have somewhere to stay?" Dora asked worriedly. Papa and Abbey were in Paris, and they had heard from them that the area had millions of tourists and the hotels were overwhelmed.

Emma reviewed the letter for the name of the hotel—The Grand Hotel Terminus. It had been constructed specifically for the event. "I know this hotel," she said, "but with this short notice, we won't be able to confirm our rooms."

Tim said, "Let's meet back here this evening and discuss our plans for moving forward."

Everyone agreed and Tim and Jeremy started out of the room.

Dora halted them. "Hold on. You need to stay and help clear the table first."

The two men turned back to her. Tim smiled sheepishly, "Of course." He went back to the table to retrieve the empty plates.

Jeremy followed his lead and took an empty platter from the table. With everyone pitching in, the dishes were carried into the kitchen quickly. Amy and Ethyl, the housekeeper and helper, had the day off, so everyone had a job to do—scraping, washing, drying, and putting away.

After the tasks were complete, they moved back into the dining room. Jeremy and Tim got ready to leave.

Emma hung back and talked to Dora. She teased, "Won't Papa and Abbey be surprised to see us."

Papa and Abbey had traveled to Paris a few weeks prior at the behest of Gustaf Eiffel. The two men were good friends and Eiffel had wanted Papa there for a final walkthrough of the tower that was to be the centerpiece of the Paris Exposition. The celebration was in place to commemorate not only technological advances but also 100 years since the revolution that had changed France's ruling class from a monarchy to a democracy.

Dora smiled as she hid her concern at being away from her kids.

"What's the hubbub?" they heard from behind them.

Savannah and Ethan walked into the dining room, their appearance slightly disheveled. Savannah Woods worked backstage at a local theatre and was between shows at the moment. Emma used her expertise in makeup and costuming when she needed to be in disguise. Ethan Worthington worked with Emma at James Pennington's law office.

"Savannah, Ethan. Just getting in or going out?" Emma asked with a smile.

Ethan colored in embarrassment. "I just dropped by last night to see how Savannah was doing and lost all sense of time."

"Sure, you did," Emma teased. She was pleased that the duo was dating. There had been hints that big plans were in the future.

"So, what's going on?" Savannah asked again. "Where's everyone rushing off to?"

"Oh. We've been invited to the Paris Exposition. We're finalizing the details," said Emma.

"Sounds exciting. When are you leaving?" asked Savannah.

"Tomorrow," answered Tim from the doorway, where he and Jeremy stood in their coats.

"Tomorrow? Isn't that kind of fast?" asked Ethan.

"It is," Emma agreed. "But I think we can get ready in time. Ethan, I plan to drop by the office and leave a note with Mr. Pennington."

"That should be okay," Ethan replied. "We're a little slow right now."

"Savannah," Dora spoke up, "Lottie is staying here and Amy is going to look after her. I hate to ask, but could you check in with her from time to time?"

"I'd love to," Savannah said.

"Are you going to be okay staying by yourself?" Dora asked. The boarding house was a little empty at the moment. The last family had moved on a few days before.

Savannah slated a glance at Ethan. "Oh, I have a feeling I won't be that lonely."

Ethan turned redder as everyone else laughed.

Jeremy walked over to Emma's chair. "Want to go to the telegraph office with me?"

"Yes," she said and held out her hand to him. He took it, pulling her up. They left the dining room and entered the foyer. Jeremy got her coat out of the closet and, as he helped her put it on, he asked, "Telegraph office first to send a note to the steamship?"

Emma nodded and pinned on her hat as she called, "Tim, are you coming with us?"

"Yes," he called back from the dining room. He leaned in to give Dora a quick kiss goodbye.

"Just a moment." She moved to the sideboard and pulled out some paper. She wrote quickly, folded it up, and said, "Don't forget to give this note to Amy on your way," she said as she handed it to him.

Before taking it, he moved his fingers to the worry lines showing on her forehead. "This trip will be good for us," he murmured.

"Will it?" she asked, leaning into him.

"Yes," he said firmly. "I have to go, they're waiting for me."

She pulled back and slid the note into his pocket. Patting it, she said, "Don't forget."

"I won't," he promised, kissing her again before jogging into the foyer to meet Jeremy and Emma.

"Trolley?" Tim asked as he put on his muffler and buttoned up his coat.

"Yes," Jeremy said, and Emma nodded.

As they exited the house, they found the cool breeze had picked up. The group held their hats as they descended the stairs and turned toward the trolley.

Dora crossed to the window and watched them leave, her frown back in place. Her preference was to stay right where she was. *The occasional trip to New York is fine, but this trip...* she thought. *Paris sounded wonderful but this trip will be so much longer than I want to be away.*

At that moment, she heard a scream and turned toward it, it

was a happy scream from Lottie. The girl had found her doll. She ran over to her mom and said, "Up!" Dora picked her up and swung her around, listening to her squeal.

Five weeks away, Tim wants this. And so do I, she admitted to herself, *I want to see Paris with him. I'll go.* She hugged Lottie tightly. "I'll make sure you're safe while we're gone," she promised.

CHAPTER 2

$\mathcal{E}$mma hung on to the strap on the trolley and turned to her brother-in-law. "Do you think she'll go?"

Tim shrugged. "I'd like her to go. I'd like to see Paris." Emma had talked about it after her first trip, and he wanted to see it for himself. Dora's opinion mattered to him and he would listen to her concerns but he hoped to be able to convince her to go.

"We'll see you back home," Jeremy called when Tim jumped off near the train station. He waved as he left. Jeremy and Emma stayed on for a few more stops.

After they jumped off the trolley and walked the few blocks to the telegraph office, Emma tapped the letter in her hand. "What do you think this is about?" she asked.

"I think someone wants us in Paris," he said in a contemplative voice.

"Nefarious reasons?" she asked. Emma was always up for an adventure.

"Probably. Would that be a problem?" They'd had many adventures but had never traveled to Paris together.

"No, not really, but I do worry about Tim and Dora coming

with us on this trip." She thought about what could happen. There was always an unexpected nature to their adventures.

He mulled that over then said calmly, "They can handle themselves."

She looked thoughtful. "Yes, I believe they can."

CHAPTER 3

a knock sounded at the kitchen door. Dora glanced over and saw it was Amy and waved her in. Amy held up the note.

"This sounded like you needed to see me immediately. Is something wrong? Tim was in a hurry and didn't say much."

Dora smiled. "Nothing is wrong but we do need your help. We're going to Paris."

"Paris?" asked Amy, confused at the news. She pulled out a chair and sat across from Dora at the kitchen table.

"Yes. Lottie and Patrick will be staying here. I'd like you to move in and take care of them for us."

"I can do it. It will be a lot less work with all of you gone," Amy teased.

Dora bit her lip. She was still reeling at the idea of being away from Patrick and Lottie. Amy reached over and placed her hand on top of Dora's.

"You know I care for them like they're my own."

Dora wiped a tear away with her free hand. "I know. I'll miss them so much. We'll be gone four to five weeks with all of the travel time included."

Tim heard her last comment as he came into the kitchen from the dining room. He bent down next to her. "I'll miss them, too, but I'd love some time alone with you."

"Yes, that would be nice," Dora said as she turned in his arms. Amy smiled and discretely left the room.

"Will you go?" Tim asked his wife.

"Yes, I think I will," she said and kissed him.

CHAPTER 4

"So, we're a go?" Dora asked as they sat down at the kitchen table. Sunday nights were informal and tonight they were eating sandwiches.

"We are," Emma stated, shaking out her napkin to place in her lap.

"The tickets are real and we're expected to be on the train tomorrow," Jeremy stated as he built his sandwich.

"Can we get organized and be on that train in time?" Dora asked. Now that she had a plan for the kids, her thoughts moved to the things that must be done before they left.

"We should be able to make it. It's the tight timeline in New York from train to ship that has me concerned. We'll have to go directly to the steamship when we get there," Emma said.

"Paris. Will you be happy to return?" Dora asked. Emma's trip to Paris had involved a close friend's kidnapping and an eventual takedown of an art thief.

"Definitely. Especially with all of the new things there for the exposition. Papa's letters describing all of the new structures, the Eiffel Tower."

"He mentioned there are two sides to the exposition?" Tim asked.

"Yes. The main site is located on the Champ de Mars on the Left Bank. That's where we'll see the Eiffel Tower, the Palace of Machines, Fine Arts and Liberal Arts buildings. The other site is located on the Esplanade des Invalides. There'll be pavilions of the French colonies. We'll also be able to eat there."

"There'll be so much to see," Dora said as she thought about their trip.

Tim heard the wonder in her tone and was glad she had decided to go with them. It wouldn't have been the same without her.

"We'll have to practice our French on the way there," Emma reminded everyone. "They prefer it to English."

They nodded.

"We just need to get the phrases down," she reassured them.

Jeremy hated to interrupt the excitement, but he needed to remind them of a few things. "We need to talk about who may have sent the invitation."

Dora was confused. "What do you mean? It wasn't a group that wanted to reward Emma for her efforts to save the artist's work?"

"We stopped by the museum today and talked to Philip. He didn't recognize the society's name," said Emma. Philip Johnson was the curator of the local museum and a longtime friend.

Dora interrupted, "Does that mean the society doesn't exist, or it didn't before this?"

"We don't know," Jeremy admitted.

"We're still going?" Tim asked, shifting his gaze to Dora.

"We are," Emma confirmed.

"Dora, Tim, we don't want you to go if you're uncomfortable," Jeremy said. He and Emma had decided they should know what they might be walking into in France.

Dora hesitated and took in the picture Patrick and Lottie

made as they played together on the floor. She glanced at Tim. "No, we want to go."

"Yes," Tim agreed.

They continue to discuss the details through dinner. After they split up to begin packing, Emma and Dora filled the trunks in their rooms with dresses and hats. The men would bring smaller bags. Each couple didn't sleep much, anticipating the trip in front of them.

Early the next morning, Emma made her way downstairs. The trunks and bags were staged in the foyer, waiting to be taken on the trip. She heard talking in the kitchen and headed toward it. The closer she got, she could hear Amy reassuring Dora. She pushed open the kitchen door and saw Amy holding Dora's hands.

"I have them," Amy said earnestly. "I brought my things over and I have extra help coming in a few days a week to help with the cleaning. I'll be with Patrick and Lottie the whole time."

"Remember, Patrick will want to spend some time with Uncle Otto's grandkids," Dora reminded her.

"I have that written down," she assured her.

"Nearly ready?" Emma said from the doorway.

Dora gripped her bag tightly and almost said no. Instead, she took a steadying breath. "Yes."

"Well, come on." Emma waved to her.

Dora hugged Amy and they followed Emma into the foyer.

Tim came downstairs. "Amy, both kids are still sleeping."

"All right, I'll get breakfast going and get the kids up after."

Jeremy came in from the stoop. "The cab is here."

The assembled group made their way out of the house. The men they had arranged to transport their trunks were in place behind their carriage. The luggage was moved and the four made their way to the train.

A dark figure crept from the alleyway near the stoop and watched as the wagon and buggy pulled away. The figure went up the stoop and tried the door knob. When it opened easily, they entered. The four must have left it open in their haste to leave.

Once inside, they spotted what they had come for. They retrieved it and exited quickly out the same door.

CHAPTER 5

ON THE TRAIN TO NEW YORK CITY

"I'm tired of practicing French," Dora said. "Tell me about what we'll see when we arrive in Paris."

Emma pulled out a stack of letters. "Papa said the design Eiffel built has passed its inspections."

Tim put down his book. "Weren't there some concerns about his initial design?"

Emma reviewed the letter, "Well, mostly from Jules Bourdais, the architect. He called it a 'vulgar' iron structure. He stated that stonework was superior in every way to Eifel's tower."

"He was in competition with Eiffel, wasn't he?" Tim asked.

"Yes," she said dryly. "And that would explain why he'd question the design that was selected. Papa was on the committee that reviewed both designs to help make the decision." His expertise was as a structural engineer and was in demand to review designs of new buildings. He and his wife spent half of their time in New York and half of their time in Chicago.

"How did Bourdais react to Ellis' review?" Tim asked.

"Bourdais was evasive and issued vague assurances that his structure would undoubtedly stand. He was upset that Papa supported Eiffel's statement about structural changes that needed to occur. Masonry had been pushed to its limits and to go higher they would need to use iron and steel. Furthermore, Bourdais had made no provision for the foundations of his masonry tower. It would rest directly on the ground," said Emma.

"What was Eiffel's experience?" asked Tim.

Emma continued, "He has worked all over Europe on some enormous arched bridges. They became the basis for his design for deep foundations supporting heavy structures. Also, given the height of the tower, the force of the wind would be a major consideration. He said, 'It's the wind that determined the basic shape of my tower.'"

Jeremy was reviewing some of the hand drawings Ellis had included in the letter and said, "The initial design appears to be an unadorned iron architecture."

"It's a different design for Paris," Emma conceded, thinking of the grandeur of the old stone buildings, cathedrals, and palaces. "I'm not surprised people this structure was ugly, at least initially."

"When did Ellis pick sides?"

"I think after the great fire. Papa wants the buildings and structures to have the proper support. Preventing collapse has been his goal since then. He was happy that it appeared the first battle between iron and stone was over with Eiffel winning a resounding victory."

"The main attraction will be the Galerie des Machines; the building is said to be of similar design to that of the Eiffel Tower," Jeremy commented.

"It will be something to see," Tim said. "Didn't Ellis mention it contained fifteen acres of exposition space and was filled with sixteen thousand machines?"

"Sixteen thousand," Dora repeated, awestruck. "What types of things will we see?"

Emma flipped through her letters and found the one that listed the displays. "Here it is," she said. She began reading. "Daimler and Benz gasoline-powered motor cars. The telephone and telegraph will also be there."

"Didn't I see where we'll be able to climb the tower?" Dora inquired, reading over Emma's shoulder.

"Hopefully, more than that. I'm hoping Papa can take us higher up."

"What a view that will be—of the entire exposition grounds," Dora said, wondering about the sights they would see.

"It sounds so big. What else will be there?" Jeremy asked.

Tim spoke up. "I read in the paper that Buffalo Bill's Wild West Show featuring Annie Oakley will be there. There are also Egyptian temples and Aztec palaces."

Jeremy shifted his gaze to Emma. "There'll be something that should remind you of our first trip to New York."

"What's that?" she asked curiously.

"Remember the park?" he asked. "The statue?"

"The Statue of Liberty? They finally got it set up in the New York Harbor."

"Yes, we'll see a miniature version of it on the Seine."

They spent the rest of the trip practicing their French and discussing the sights they'd see. They didn't discuss who might have invited them.

CHAPTER 6

ON THE STEAMER LA BRETAGNE TO FRANCE

"We can slow down now," Jeremy said as he restrained Emma and Dora from a run to a walk. He motioned to the ship with his hand. "It appears there's a line at the gangplank."

Tim caught up to them. "I got the steward to take the bags and trunks on board." He took Dora's hand and they got in line to ascend the gangplank onto the ship. When the line started to move, he moved with it, he didn't get far. Dora wasn't moving. "Dora, come on, this is the beginning of our trip."

She was turned away from him. He knew she wasn't thinking of the view in front of her. "Lottie and Patrick will be fine," he assured her.

"Yes, I know," she said, studying the city one more time before turning back and following him. They caught up with Jeremy and Emma as they stepped off the gang plank and onto the ship.

After checking in and getting their door keys, Tim, Dora, and Jeremy were examining the features of the ship. They had never been on a steamer before this. Emma remembered her last time on this ship and hoped it would be a trip with less excitement. She gave them time to survey the area.

"Emma!" a voice called.

She turned toward the voice and saw the ship's captain coming toward her. She smiled broadly and took the hands he extended to her.

"How wonderful to see you," he said. "Will you be with us on this trip?"

"I will," she confirmed.

He leaned in and asked softly, "No excitement this time, I hope?"

"Me, too." She laughed, knowing he was referencing her last trip to Paris by steamer. She had uncovered a plot that involved a wife and her boyfriend who killed her husband and threw him overboard.

Jeremy walked over to Emma and the captain. Emma introduced him. "Captain De Jousselin, this is Jeremy Tilden. We're traveling together."

"It's nice to meet you," De Jousselin said sincerely. "I'd like to have you both in my cabin after dinner."

"We'd like that also," Emma said warmly.

A young ship officer walked up to the captain. The man spoke softly to him and he told Emma and Jeremy, "I must leave you now. We'll be on our way soon."

"It was nice to meet you," Jeremy said.

"You, also."

As they watched the captain leave, Jeremy took her hand. "We should find our rooms and get settled in."

"You're right." She called out, "Dora, Tim, we need to go to our rooms."

Dora frowned but took Tim's offered elbow and followed them up the staircase. "You will have time to see the ship once we are underway," Emma promised her.

They stepped into a long hallway with a red carpet running its length. They went about halfway down and Emma pulled out her notebook. She pointed to the room on the right, "That's your room. Ours is further down."

Tim and Jeremy pulled out their keys and opened the doors. Emma heard Dora exclaim, *"These are our rooms?"*

Emma smiled. She had been in similar rooms on her last trip and her reaction had been the same.

Dora rushed to Emma's door. "Emma, is yours as big as ours?"

"It is," she confirmed, opening the door wide to show her the room. "

"Aren't they wonderful?"

"The rooms are nice," agreed Emma. She raised her eyebrows at Jeremy. He nodded and moved around the room opening and closing the various doors in the room. Dora went back to her and Tim's room; she was ready to enjoy her vacation.

Emma walked around the living area, dropped down on the couch, and shifted her gaze to Jeremy, "What do you make of this? So far, first-class accommodations."

"Yes. I guess whoever's behind this wants us happy. At least, until we reach Paris."

"Do we worry all the way to Paris or do we enjoy ourselves?"

"Enjoy ourselves."

"I'd agree to that."

He dropped down on the couch next to her and teased, "What would you like to do now?"

She stretched out her arms. "I could use a long nap."

He stood up and pulled her to him. "Now, that can be worked out," he murmured. He kissed her for a long moment before he walked her to the bedroom. They closed the door and had a very long rest.

A few hours later, both couples made their way downstairs and entered the dining room. Dora and Emma were dressed in evening gowns; Emma in red and Dora in dark blue. Jeremy and Tim stood behind them in their black suits.

"Would you like a table?" asked the steward.

"Yes, please. Our names are under Emma Evans," Emma responded.

He moved his chart and tapped it a few times before he said, in surprise. "We have a request from another gentleman to join your group. Would that would be all right?"

Emma moved her gaze to each person in her group. When they nodded, Emma said, "That should be fine."

The steward's face cleared and he smiled. He was relieved that there weren't any arguments about the addition to their table.

He moved from behind his podium and motioned to them with his hand, "This way, please." He guided them through the dining room. When they reached a large round table, they saw one person was already seated.

"Must be him," Emma muttered. Dora nodded.

Jeremy and Tim held the chairs out for Emma and Dora.

Once they were settled, the unknown gentleman said, "I hope you don't mind my request to join your group." He spoke with a French accent.

"No, of course not. Welcome," Emma replied. The others nodded.

They sat quietly reviewing the menus in front of them.

"I'll start the introductions," the man said jovially. "I'm Julian Bernard and I'm traveling to the exposition in Paris. "

"So are we," Tim commented for the group.

"Wonderful. Please introduce yourselves."

Tim took the lead. "I'm Tim Flannigan, and this is my wife,

Dora. We're also traveling with Emma, Dora's sister, and our friend Jeremy Tilden."

"So nice to meet you all," he said, to everyone at the table. "What do you want to see at the exposition?"

They talked throughout dinner about Paris and the exhibits they planned to see. When the conversation moved to questions from Julian Bernard about their lives in Chicago, the quieter Emma became. The others laughed at something Julian said, but Emma didn't respond. Jeremy sent her a questioning look. She slowly moved her eyes from Julian to Jeremy.

What has she seen? What am I missing? he thought, watching Julian. Tim and Dora filled in the gap left by Emma and Jeremy.

After dinner, Dora and Tim excused themselves to go dancing. Emma and Jeremy stayed at the table with Julian.

Coffee and desserts arrived and so did more questions from Julian.

Questions. Questions about where we're from, where we're going, and what we do for a living. Why? Emma thought.

Rather than answering the multitude of questions, Emma began, "Mr. Bernard…"

"Julian, please," he interrupted.

Emma smiled slightly, "Yes, Julian. What do you do for a living?"

"Oh, this and that," he said lightly, avoiding her question.

"This and that what?" she asked, trying to pin him down.

"Business, it's very uninteresting; I'd rather talk about you," he said, his voice smooth.

"Have you been to Chicago?"

"Maybe. A long time ago."

Jeremy reached for her hand under the table and squeezed it lightly in a warning.

She ignored him and stated firmly, "Julian, you've been asking us a lot of questions."

"Have I?" he countered, his pleasant expression not changing.

"Yes," she said firmly.

"Well, I find you interesting," he said and smiled at both of them.

"Why is that?" *What does he know about us?*

"Oh," he said leaning in, "I know that you have a more interesting job than the temporary business you mentioned."

Emma and Jeremy tensed. Jeremy took the next question. "What do you know?"

"I know you're both detectives," he said simply, sitting back in his chair and sipping from his coffee cup.

"That isn't exactly a secret," Emma said. *And,* she thought, *we're not currently on a case.*

"No, but I think it's something you don't share openly and with strangers."

Jeremy leaned forward. "Why the interest in us and our work?"

He smiled. "Oh, I was just fascinated. I have been following your career since you were in France. And," he said as he moved his gaze to Jeremy, "you're with the Pinkerton Detectives."

"All of these questions. Is it just interest?" Emma asked. She clearly didn't believe him.

"Yes, of course." Julian took a drink of coffee, checked his watch, and placed his cup on the table. "Why don't we meet tomorrow and talk some more?"

With that comment, he stood and disappeared into the crowd of people.

Emma shook her head. "That was odd."

Jeremy continued to focus on the direction Julian had gone. "Yes." He moved his gaze back to Emma and asked, "Could he be behind the tickets?"

She took a long moment, thinking about Julian. Finally, she said, "Maybe. He was certainly eager to spend time with us." She glanced at her watch. "We should go. I believe the captain is expecting us in his cabin."

They headed out, passing the dance area where Tim and Dora had gone. "Before we go, should we mention our suspicions to Tim and Dora?" Jeremy asked, nodding toward the room.

Emma glanced around and saw them with another couple, laughing. "No, they seem to be having a good time." *Who was that couple?* she wondered.

"Ready?" he asked.

She nodded and took his elbow. As they walked off, she had to pull her gaze away from them. She continued to think about them as they made their way to the captain's cabin. The steward assigned outside the door held up his hand to stop them, "Just a moment." He stepped in briefly and returned to tell them, "You may go in."

"Thank you," Emma murmured and stepped in. As the two entered, they saw the room was set up with drinks and desserts.

Captain De Jousselin came into the room from a door in the back. He was more casually dressed and had removed his jacket and hat. "Please, come in. Sit down."

"I assume things have been quieter on your ship since my last trip?" Emma asked.

"Yes," he said, "thankfully."

Jeremy leaned forward in his chair, taking the glass the captain offered. "Do you know the passenger, Julian Barnard?" he asked.

De Jousselin's eyebrows rose quickly. "Julian Bernard? Why yes. He travels often with us." He watched Emma closely. "Is there something I should be concerned about?"

Emma quickly assured him, "No, no. We were just curious. Do you know what business he's in?"

De Jousselin sat back and stroked his beard. "I believe he buys and sells merchandise."

She wondered about what the merchandise might be. "Does he normally have crates with him?"

"No, not that I know of," he replied.

They let the conversation about Julian come to an end and instead talked about their plans for Paris.

CHAPTER 7

The next morning Dora, Tim, Emma, and Jeremy walked down to breakfast. Dora stole a glance toward Emma. "I hope you don't mind, but the couple we met last night wants us to join them for breakfast."

Emma shook her head. "No, of course not, go ahead. We're supposed to meet Mr. Barnard."

"Julian," murmured Jeremy.

Emma smiled and didn't comment.

Breakfast was served on the deck. As they approached the sunlit area, both couples split off to find their breakfast companions. Emma hesitated at the door and watched as Dora and Tim moved to their breakfast table. The couple they were joining appeared to be a little older than Dora and Tim. They smiled broadly at them, even standing to hug them as they approached. *Fast friends*, she thought. *I'll have to keep an eye on that as well. No one is above suspicion on this trip.*

"You know you need to be more trusting," Jeremy commented, seeing where Emma's eyes were directed. "It's good for them to have friends."

She let out a long breath. "I know I should, but it's hard to trust people to care about them as much as we do."

"Especially with people you love."

"Especially," she confirmed as they made their way to their table and sat. When Mr. Barnard did not appear, she asked, "Do you think we should wait?"

Jeremy leaned back in his chair, enjoying the feel of the early morning sun on his face, and said, "For a few moments." They relaxed breathing in the sea air.

Several moments later Julian walked up to their table. "May I sit?" he asked.

"Of course." Emma's voice was less severe than the night before. She and Jeremy had talked and had decided that they needed to find out more about this man.

"And where are our other companions this morning? Sleeping in?" Julian asked.

"No," answered Emma. She indicated the table across the room from them. "They met another couple and wanted to spend some time with them this morning."

He turned in the direction she indicated and, when he turned back, she thought she detected a brief frown on his face. It disappeared quickly. She wondered about that as they ordered their breakfast.

"Do you know the couple Tim and Dora are eating with?" Emma asked, wondering how he'd respond.

He looked her in the eye and said, "No, I don't think so."

Jeremy narrowed his eyes at her and she let the topic go. They moved on to talk about their day. To Emma's consternation, Julian brought up more questions about their trip. She tried to match him question for question.

"Where are you both staying in France? At the Grand Hotel Terminus?" asked Julian.

"How did you know that?" Jeremy asked. He was starting to

think Emma was correct and Julian knew more than he letting on.

He answered quickly, "Oh, it's a special hotel. It was built specifically for the exposition. It's lovely and very grand. You will enjoy your time there." He didn't wait for a comment and moved onto another question. "You mentioned you'd be there for how long?"

"I don't think we did mention that," muttered Emma, not quite answering the question.

Jeremy looked over at her and then back at Julian before he replied. "We'll be in Paris for three weeks. We'd like to spend some time at the Galerie des Machines. We're interested in all of the advancements in technology. We especially want to see the new light display. It sounds amazing."

Julian sat back in a contemplative manner and said, "Yes, you know not everyone is happy that things are progressing. Some people are against change and progress."

"I have seen some articles. I thought their response has been mostly nonviolent demonstrations," said Jeremy.

"That could be changing," Julian responded.

"Why are they against electricity?" Emma asked curiously.

"They believe the dangers outweigh any benefit it could provide," Julian said.

"But we're hearing residential homes will soon have lights. If it were truly dangerous, that wouldn't happen," she protested.

Julian's eyes squinted for a moment before he answered. "Yes, there are those who would rather we stopped moving forward."

"Do you think they'll create a problem at the exposition?" Emma asked sitting forward.

"It's something that should be considered," Julian allowed.

Emma thought about that. "Should the police be notified?" she asked.

He waved his hand in dismissal and said smoothly, "I'm sure

they have everything under control. The security is being handled by the Parisian police."

They moved on to lighter topics. After breakfast was finished, they excused themselves to go back to their respective cabins. Emma realized she still knew nothing about the man. She mentioned this to Jeremy.

"You don't need all of his secrets," he teased.

"I know, but a few would be nice. Do you think there's a concern about these anti-electricity people he mentioned? Could they be dangerous?"

"I can't be sure, but it sounds like the French police are aware of them."

"Yes," she said contemplatively.

He took her hand and suggested, "Let's walk around the deck and enjoy our time together."

"Okay," she said softly. She sent one last look at Dora and Tim's breakfast partners.

"They're allowed to have friends outside of us," Jeremy commented softly, watching where her gaze drifted.

"I know. They want to have other friends," she said softly, "but I would like some time with them."

"Tell her. Maybe ask for their new friends to join us," he urged.

"I will," she promised.

That evening, Emma went to Dora and Tim's room. She knocked softly on their door. Hearing "Come in," she opened the door and saw Dora braiding her hair and pinning it to the top of her head.

Tim walked out of the bathroom. "Hello, Emma. Ready for dinner?"

"Yes. I was wondering if we could all eat together tonight," she suggested.

"All?" Dora asked, pausing in her dressing preparations.

"Yes, your new friends are welcome to join us," Emma offered.

Dora chewed her lips and glanced at Tim.

Tim explained, "Lenora and Michael don't like big groups. We've asked them before this and I think the question made them uncomfortable."

Odd, thought Emma. "Okay, then will you both meet us for dinner?" she asked.

"Of course, we'd love that," Dora replied.

Emma started out of the room and asked in an offhanded manner, "Do Lenora and Michael know what we do back home?"

Dora glanced over. "Yes, I mentioned it. I didn't think it was a secret."

"Oh, it's not. I just wondered." Emma smiled and said, "Come down to our room when you're ready."

"We will," Dora said as she watched her sister leave.

"What was that about?" Tim asked, putting on his tie.

Dora smiled, walked over to him, and brushed his hands away to take over his tie adjustment. "I think we've been spending time with our new friends and they're missing us."

Emma walked slowly to her door and, when she reached it, instead of opening it, she lay her head on it. It opened suddenly and Emma found herself in Julian's arms. She yelped and struggled before she realized who it was.

"My dear, I'm sorry. I stopped by to see if I could join you for dinner."

Emma pulled herself upright "That's okay. I was thinking about something just now. You're welcome to join us."

"I told him I needed to confirm with you," Jeremy said.

"Now we're confirmed. I'll meet you there," the other man said.

"Dora and Tim will be joining us also," Emma said, watching his expression.

She saw that that bothered him. She continued to watch him closely.

"Will their companions be joining us?" he asked in a curt tone.

"No," she said slowly, wondering what the concern was. "They prefer to be on their own."

That cheered him up considerably. "Good. I'll head out now."

"Julian," she said, stopping him with her hand, "do you have a problem with Dora and Tim's new friends? Should I be concerned about them spending so much time with them?"

"How could I have a problem when I don't know them? I'll meet up with you in the dining room," he said and excused himself, closing their door softly on his way out.

"Hmm," she murmured.

Jeremy sat on the bed, buttoning his vest. "Julian evidently did not want to spend time with Lenora and Michael."

"No, he didn't," she observed.

Jeremy stood. "I wonder why? Are you worried he knows something about them that we don't?"

"I think we need to keep our eyes on Julian, Lenora, and Michael. There's something there."

"Have you ever seen the three of them together?"

"No. Julian seems to be there just before or just after the time they could meet."

"You need to hurry. Tim and Dora will be here soon," Jeremy reminded her.

She nodded and ran quickly to the closet, pulling out her dark red silk gown. The lace was dyed in black and attached to the front of the bodice neckline. She slipped her skirt and top off revealing her combinations. The gown went on and Jeremy came up behind her and started working on securing the closures as she quickly put her hair up. Just as she was adding some lip color, a knock sounded on their door.

"They're here. Are you ready?" he asked as he finished the last closure.

"I am," she said, patting her hair.

Jeremy slipped on his gray suit jacket and opened the door. "Welcome."

"Are you both ready?" Dora asked.

"I believe we are," her sister stated as she searched for her bag.

"Looking for this?" Jeremy tossed the bag at her.

Emma caught it deftly, opening it quickly to check for her clutch knife. She closed it with a click. "Ready."

They started out.

"Oh no!" Dora exclaimed.

"Did you forget something?" asked Tim.

"Yes, I'm sorry. I need my hair clip." She reached up and felt her hair falling in the back. She inquired, "Can we meet you in the dining room?"

"Yes, do you need help?" Emma asked.

"No, I can fix it. We'll meet you." Dora and Tim hurriedly went back to their room.

Jeremy offered his elbow to her. She took it, and as they walked around the corner, they saw Julian down the corridor. They started toward him but noticed he was not alone. He was with Lenora and Michael. Jeremy pulled them to a stop.

"I thought they didn't know each other," Emma murmured.

"It appears they do know each other, but they don't appear to like each other."

"Yes," she agreed. The three seemed to be arguing.

Jeremy tapped her arm to indicate they should turn back. They moved slowly in the opposite direction of the three, trying to not be seen. As they walked, Emma turned to Jeremy. "Do we confront him?"

"About what? A conversation with people we don't know that well?"

She shrugged. "Okay, maybe we don't need a full confrontation."

"Let's go to dinner," he suggested. They walked on and saw the doors to the dining room. They were etched glass, they sparkled from the lights inside. The steward pushed them open to allow them entry. The host stood at his stand and asked, "Would you like to be seated?"

"Yes, please," said Emma. The host took their name and escorted them to their table, they were the first to arrive.

Julian appeared at the entrance and, when Jeremy spotted him, he turned to Emma. "Let's not mention what we saw."

"Maybe just a comment," teased Emma.

Jeremy raised an eyebrow, and stayed silent, he knew she'd make the right decision.

Julian walked over and pulled out his chair, looking like his normal jovial self.

Emma couldn't help herself and asked him, "Did you have a busy evening?"

Jeremy tapped her leg in warning.

"Not really," the other man said. "After I left you, I was able to get some reading in."

She watched him and thought that he didn't owe her an explanation. He was mysterious, but she didn't think he was dangerous. There was something about him that kept her on her toes. She'd keep an eye on him and his relationship with Lenora and Michael.

Dora and Tim arrived.

"Two very lovely ladies for the table. What more could I have asked for?" Julian said suavely. Both women smiled in response to the compliment.

Emma turned to Tim and Dora as she kept Julian within her sights. "Were Lenora and Michael all right with their loss of dinner companions tonight?"

Julian went still, waiting for their answer.

Tim didn't notice. "I believe so. They weren't at their cabin when we went by, so we left a note."

No, they wouldn't have been there, thought Emma. *They were with Julian.*

The evening settled and the five stayed together after dinner, talking about France.

"Emma, you mentioned this is your second trip. Did you enjoy Paris the first time you were here?" Julian asked. He didn't mention that he knew why she had been in France.

Emma played along with the deception and stated, "The initial reason for the trip was to help a friend, so sightseeing wasn't the main priority. I'm hoping this trip is more relaxed."

"Hmm," Julian commented. He seemed to have no response to that.

∼

The rest of the trip was quiet, with Tim and Dora splitting their time between the two couples.

Emma tried several times to have the other couple join their group, but there was always a reason they couldn't meet.

Emma walked with Jeremy and looked at the water. She turned to him. "They aren't even willing to meet us. Isn't there something odd about that?"

Jeremy looked over at her. "Yes, but it might be just as Dora says—they prefer small groups. Tim and Dora are enjoying their new friends; let's just let it lie."

Emma gave one more glance and said decided he was right. But she continued to think about the argument they witnessed.

CHAPTER 8

SHIP DOCKING IN HAVRE, FRANCE

They had arrived in Le Havre, a port city in France. Their trucks and bags had been picked up that morning and would be moved to the train that would take them to Paris. It would be a day until they arrived in Paris.

Emma and Jeremy were waiting in the lobby for Dora and Tim. She turned when she heard Dora's voice. Tim and Dora were accompanying Lenora and Michael down the stairs.

"Where are you staying?" Dora asked the couple.

When they answered, Emma realized they would be staying in the same place as their group.

Jeremy waved to Dora and Tim and called over, "Our luggage is being moved to a wagon as we speak."

Dora and Tim said goodbye to their friends and moved to Emma and Jeremy. The four started to the gangplank.

Boom!

They started at the loud noise and turned toward it. The sound was a large, empty trunk falling onto the deck. The men picking it up must have misjudged its weight. As they watched a young woman rush over and yell at them to get moving. Her much older husband trailed after her. The beleaguered men followed her direction and picked up the trunk. Jeremy, Tim, and Dora turned back to continue down the gangplank.

"Emma?" Jeremy asked, realizing she was still watching the couple with the trunk. "Are you ready? We need to get to the train."

She gave one last long look at the trunk and the couple before heading to join him on the gangplank.

They found the wagon and their carriage waiting to take them to their train. As they climbed in, a voice called out; it was Julian. "Mind if I get a ride in with you?"

"Yes, we can make room," Jeremy said. Emma raised an eyebrow but scooted over to allow him a place to sit.

"Thank you. It has been a marvelous trip and I'd love the company for the final leg to Paris." The trip over to the train was fun with Julian pointing out sites for them. They arrived quickly and were settled into their room just as the train was pulling out of the station.

A knock sounded on their door. When Emma opened it, she saw it was Julian. *Of course, who else would it be?* she thought. She asked in a wry voice, "Julian, what a surprise. Would you like to join us?"

Surprisingly, he declined. "No, that is fine, I have my own cabin. I'll see you all once we get to Paris." He turned and walked down the hall. Emma closed the door behind him and the group stared at it.

"If he weren't so entertaining, he'd be irritating," Jeremy observed.

"It's hard to turn him down when he wants something. Is it the accent?" Dora asked.

"Do you fancy him?" Tim teased.

She smiled softly and said, "I prefer redheads."

Tim grinned broadly in response and his face turned as red as his hair.

The trip was short, and they were in Paris in just under a

day. As they exited the train, Jeremy and Tim located the luggage and arranged carriages. Julian once again joined them.

"Do you have any additional luggage?" asked Emma.

"Just this bag," he said, indicating the carpet bag he was carrying.

"I don't think I could travel with so little," Dora commented as they watched the trunks being unloaded.

Julian commented, "I bet those hold the lovely dresses I saw you wearing on the steamer."

Dora's face turned red.

"Ready?" called Jeremy once all of the luggage was on the wagon.

They headed toward the carriage, climbed in, and headed to the hotel. Emma spoke to the driver. "108 Rue Saint-Lazare, s'il vous plaît."

"That is located in the 8th arrondissement," Julian explained. "The areas are broken up by their numbers. Arrondissements with higher numbers spiral out clockwise from the center. Its shape is like a snail shell. Most of these were former small villages annexed by Paris earlier this century."

"How far is our hotel from the exposition grounds?" asked Tim, thinking of their travel time each morning.

"About 3,701 kilometers. There should be carriages lined up to go to the exposition. What will slow us down, is the traffic. It's reported that Paris has more people here than ever before."

"Papa also indicated there's a train once you get to the exposition grounds," Emma said.

"It's needed. The entire complex is 220 **Hectares** and the Galerie des Machines you mentioned is at the back of the exhibit," Julian supplied.

Emma muttered, "I should have brought my bike."

"We'll walk if we can't get transportation," Jeremy assured her.

"There is a lot to see on the way; the distance will not feel so long," said Julian.

Dora, Tim, and Jeremy were leaning out of the carriage windows and looking around. As they got closer, Julian continued to point out the sites.

"The arrondissements I mentioned previously are all different. Each one has a feeling with different cultures melding and having their own shops, bakeries, and history."

Emma watched from her seat and enjoyed her family's response to their first time in Paris.

"The hotel we're going to, have you stayed there before?" Jeremy asked him.

"No. It's newly built for the exhibit. It just opened in May. I believe Eiffel himself announced the opening from his tower."

They stopped in front of their hotel, a large brick structure. It was four stories and appeared to take up an entire city block.

They climbed out, and Jeremy paid the driver. He looked around, "What type of facade is that?"

Emma answered. "It's a Haussmannian facade and very elegant. Those," she pointed out, "are Corinthian columns."

The group entered the hotel's main door and were surprised at the opulence—chandeliers, balustrades, hand-painted frescoes, and marble and mosaic tiling.

"I understand there is a bar here that we must frequent for a glass of wine," Julian commented.

They looked around and took in the crowds that were in line for rooms. Emma muttered to Jeremy, "I hope we have a reservation."

"Shh, we don't want to worry Tim and Dora. It'll work out," he said, hoping he was right. "And if not," he continued in a low voice, "the couches look comfortable down here."

She gave him a look but didn't comment. She turned to Tim and Dora, "Have a seat. We'll go check in." The two of them found a space and sat down, continuing to observe the grand room.

Emma and Jeremy approached the desk. There was a line and, during their wait, several people in front of them were turned away with no reservations. Emma squeezed his hand and he squeezed back. When it was their turn, she stepped up and said, "Bonjour, monsieur."

Before the clerk could respond, the young woman who they had seen on the steamer with the empty trunk stepped up. "We need a room!" she demanded in English.

The clerk answered in perfect English, "I'm sorry, madam unless you have a reservation…"

"We have a reservation," the woman interrupted.

"That is fine, but these people," referencing Emma and Jeremy, "were next. You will have to wait your turn."

"But… but I'm…" the woman tried again belligerently.

He looked down his nose at her and said quite firmly, "It does not matter who you are. You will get in line."

That statement finally got through to her and she and her husband stepped back into the line. She was not happy and seemed to turn her anger on her husband. He visibly shrank as she spoke.

"Bonjour, monsieur," Emma began again.

"Bonjour, madam. You may speak English," the clerk stated. His tone was softer than before.

"Thank you. I have a reservation for Emma Evans and family," Emma, sincerely hoped she did indeed have a reservation.

He didn't check his book, instead, he said quickly, "Yes, madam, we have that here. You are on the 3rd floor."

That was quick, she thought. *He didn't check his book. He already knew to expect them.*

"How many keys will you require?"

"How many rooms do we have?" she asked, thinking ahead.

Again, without looking he said, "It is a suite with 3 bedrooms."

A suite? In Paris and at the time of the exposition? "Four, please," she answered. "Could you tell us who made this reservation?"

He squirmed and didn't answer. Instead, he moved some paperwork around on his desk.

Emma started to lean in with more questions when Jeremy put a hand on her arm and leaned down to whisper into her ear, "We can do this later. Let's get to our rooms for now."

She nodded and stepped back.

When there were no further questions, the clerk pulled over a large sign-in book "Please, sign here."

As she signed in, he motioned to a bellhop. "Take their luggage to 319."

The boy's eyes widened in surprise at the location and he hurried to get the baggage cart. He called another bellman over to help with the heavy trunks. Emma watched them and turned back to the clerk, "Merci."

He replied, "You're welcome, enjoy your stay." He watched as they made their way to the elevator and headed up to the room.

Another bellman waited by the elevator while they got organized. Emma retrieved Tim and Dora and joined Jeremy when the doors opened. They entered, and the bellmen followed them. He motioned to the men with the luggage to come up on the next elevator. The doors closed, and they watched the operator take them to their floor. The door slid opened, and the bellman waited for everyone to exit before he said, "Follow me, please."

They followed and noticed the custom etchings of iconic Paris scenes hanging on the walls. "These are lovely," Dora said as she stopped to examine them. As they continued to their room, they stopped several more times to admire the wallpaper and wood floors with beautiful braided rugs.

They stopped and the first bellman opened the large double

brown door for them to enter. The four stepped into the doorway and a large open space in front of them.

"Wow!" Dora exclaimed. She was impressed with everything she saw in the hotel.

"Yes, wow," Emma agreed. *Whoever is behind all this has money,* she thought. She looked at the large area; there were couches, a dining room, chandeliers, and multiple doors leading off of the main room.

Jeremy was unsure if this was usual for Paris. "Was this similar to the hotel you stayed in on your last trip?" he asked Emma.

"That one was nice, but nothing like this one," she murmured as she took in her surroundings.

The bellman approached a door at the far end of the room and pushed it open. "Just the one room?" asked Dora. She was confused about where they'd sleep.

"No," he said in stilted English. "There are three." He walked quickly to open the door on the far end.

Dora noticed he didn't open the third door. "What is that one?" she asked, motioning toward it.

He didn't answer but, instead, opened it for her to review. She stepped up and said, "There are three bedrooms off the main room and on-suite bathrooms?"

They didn't choose their rooms; the bellman chose for them, Each couple went to examine their assigned rooms. Jeremy called out, "Is your room acceptable?"

Tim stuck his head out of their room and called back, "It's exactly right." Jeremy nodded. He and Emma were also happy with theirs.

The bellman arrived with their luggage and Jeremy directed the bellman to place them in each room. He walked the bellman out and paid him a tip. With the door closed behind him, he moved back to the living room to relax with Emma.

Tim and Dora joined them there.

"Well, I guess the question of 'will we have a room' has been answered," Tim said dryly and the group laughed in response.

"Do we want to stay in tonight?" Jeremy asked. He was thinking about food.

"Well, I was thinking about a walk to see what is in the area around the hotel, " stated Emma hopefully.

"And a snack here," Dora suggested as she held a hand to her rumbling stomach. Though the train trip offered food, the selection was limited.

"Now that is a plan," indicated Tim.

Emma said, "First, I think we need to let Papa know we're here."

"Do you have his address?" Jeremy asked. "I can have him notified that we have arrived."

She pulled out her notebook and showed it to him. His lips quirked up in response to the ever-present notebook.

She quickly wrote a note to have him send to Papa. She handed it to him.

"I'll be back," he said. "While I'm out, would everyone like me to place the order for food?"

Tim and Dora got up and Dora said, "Please. We'll unpack. Let us know when the food is here."

"I'll do the same," commented Emma.

The two groups had their tasks and moved to get them completed.

Dora and Tim took a moment to look out of the tall windows in their room. The stone buildings around them were old but so lovely.

"We should have another hour or two to see some of the areas around the hotel," Tim commented.

Dora sighed. She wanted to stand at that window for a while longer but knew they needed to unpack. She moved to her trunk and Tim followed to open the lock for her. Once it was opened, she shook out her dresses and hung them up. Next came her combinations that acted as her undergarments. When she started folding those to add to her dresser. Tim said teasingly, "I can help with that."

"Oh, you, get your own bag unpacked."

As they were finishing up, there was a knock on the door. "The food has arrived!" called Jeremy. That got Tim and Dora moving quickly toward the living room.

Emma was already in the living area, having finished unpacking her trunk. "Turns out it wasn't food," Jeremy said as he walked into the room.

Emma frowned. "Then who was at the door?"

Jeremy stepped away and revealed who was behind him. It was Papa and Abbey.

"Papa!"

She ran to him; he caught her and hugged her tightly. She closed her eyes, enjoying the moment. She opened them again and stepped back to allow Dora and Tim to say hello. She went over to Abbey and hugged her also. Her affection was genuine for her papa's wife. She had been so good for him.

"Abbey, hello," said Emma.

Abbey hugged her back, "We got your note and had to come right over. What a nice surprise. When did you decide to come to France?"

Jeremy came over and hugged Abbey tightly. "Hello, Mom." He looked at the group and said, "Why don't we sit down and we can discuss the circumstances of our trip."

Papa frowned at the wording Jeremy had used but followed them into the living room. As they made their way over, Abbey glanced around and commented, "This is a lovely suite."

"Yes, and that is part of the story," Emma said.

Everyone sat down on the couch and two side chairs.

"What circumstances?" Papa asked. "Is there something going on?" He turned an intense gaze toward Emma. "Are you here on a case?"

"Papa, we didn't decide on this trip; the decision was made for us," she said.

Papa frowned and started to ask another question when he was interrupted by a knock at the door. Jeremy stood up and went to answer it. This time, it was the room service order. He stepped aside to let the waiters bring in the assorted trays.

"Where would you like these?" the waiter asked in broken English.

"The table would be nice, merci," Dora said.

They moved to the dining table and deposited the trays onto the surface. Jeremy walked them out and tipped them for their service.

"Join us," Tim encouraged Abbey and Papa.

"Yes, thank you," Abbey answered for herself and Papa.

They all sat together and passed around plates with fruit, bread, and cheese.

Jeremy walked over to the side table and pulled out wine glasses. "Wine, everyone?"

A resounding "Yes!" sounded from the group, followed by laughter.

Papa sent a serious expression to Emma and said, "Now, tell me about this trip. How did it come about?"

She explained about the letter, the tickets, and the hotel.

"Should you have made the trip? Not knowing if there were actual reservations once you got here?" he asked, concerned for them.

Jeremy explained, "We did confirm the train and stream-liner tickets. We all decided we'd take the rest on faith that we would have a place to stay once we got here. How could we pass up an opportunity for an all-expense-paid trip to Paris?"

"Have you had any trouble on the trip so far?" asked Ellis.

"Not so far." Emma squeezed Jeremy's hand as a warning not to mention Julian.

"Keep your eyes open," he said. *A mysterious benefactor?* What could they want with his family?

"Papa, we will," Emma said. "We're going to check out the Art Curator's Society first. Then we're going to see if we can track down who sent the tickets to us."

Abbey decided to change the topic. "Would you like to hear about the things we've seen?"

"Yes, please," said Dora, eager to hear more about the city they were in.

Abbey started. "The crowds are rather large—so get out early. The bakeries are called Boulangeries. They open very early and the bread is not to be missed. You must try the croissants and pain au chocolat."

"Yum!" said Tim. The others nodded in agreement.

"Also, the sourdough bread we have here is called pain de campagne. The bread has a particular method to eat it. Let me show you." She picked up a round loaf of bread and tore it into pieces with her hands. "Like these."

"I like that," Tim said and picked up another round loaf and tore off a large piece for himself. "Dora, we need to find out how they make this."

Abbey gazed at them thoughtfully. *I'll have to do something about that.* She had several friends who were bakers and would not mind an extra pair of hands to help with the morning baking. She also had a surprise for both Dora and Emma for the next morning. "Please keep your morning free tomorrow. I have an appointment set up for you," Abbey stated. She had acted quickly when she found out they were in the city.

"What kind of appointment?" asked Emma.

"It's a surprise. I'd like to pick you up at 8AM if that is okay?"

"That would be lovely," Dora answered for them both.

"Tell us, more," Jeremy suggested.

Abbey smiled at him and held out her hand for him to take. "I have had plenty of time with friends."

"What she's saying," Papa said, taking her other hand, "is that I have been busy with inspections at the exposition."

"And playing with the toys," she commented.

When the group frowned, not understanding her reference, he said in a self-mocking voice, "Yes, she calls the machines toys."

She smiled, forgiving him for leaving her. "He's forever over there tinkering and asking questions, but I get to see him in the evenings. I'm happy with that."

While they talked about the exhibits Abbey had seen, Papa stood and motioned to Emma. She nodded and walked with him over to the balcony.

"What are your plans?" he asked, his voice serious.

She answered the surface question. "We plan to see the exhibits and explore the city as much as we can."

"Emma," he said, his voice low. He knew she was dodging the question.

She looked him in the eyes and said truthfully, "Yes, Papa, I understand what you're asking. We, Jeremy and I, are going to investigate the group that may have sent us the tickets."

"How do you expect to start? And what do you expect to find?"

"Initially, we thought Philip could tell us the organization was real. He indicated it didn't exist when he was in Paris, but it could have formed later. I have several of Philip's contacts in the area. We'll stop by and find out if the organization exists. If it does, we'll thank them for the trip."

"And if it doesn't exist?"

"I'd have to assume we have been brought here for a nefarious reason. I'd like to know why here and at this time. What is it that makes us so valuable to them?"

Papa frowned at the way she phrased that question. "Why indeed?" *What was it that Emma, Jeremy, Tim, and Dora could provide that no one else could?* He continued to mull that thought over when Abbey walked up and slid her arm into his.

"Ready to go?" she asked.

He leaned down to kiss Emma's cheek and murmured, "Send me a note when you get the information about who paid for the trip."

"I will," she said softly. "Goodbye, Papa. Goodbye, Abbey. We'll see you in the morning." She watched as they walked back to say good night to everyone.

Abbey said, "Just a moment." She rushed back to Emma and whispered, "I'll arrange a morning in a bakery for Dora."

"That would be perfect," she said and kissed her cheek.

Abbey rejoined Papa, while Dora and Tim walked them out. Emma turned back to watch the scenery from the window. Jeremy came up to Emma and pulled her back to him. "Everything okay?" he asked.

"Yes, Papa was just concerned about who might be behind this trip."

"Aren't we all? Would you like to check Philip's contacts out first thing tomorrow?" he asked.

"It'll have to wait until after the surprise trip in the morning," she said regretfully.

They stayed there for a few more minutes, enjoying the view.

"Are we going out?" Dora asked impatiently from across the room. They had eaten and she was eager to see some of Paris.

Emma turned to her. "I think we can manage that. Though we should stick to this neighborhood for tonight."

They put on their coats and hats and made their way to the elevator. They exited the crowded lobby and walked down to the Avenue Montaigne, Rue du Faubourg Saint-Honoré, and Élysée Palace enjoying everything they saw.

They walked for a long while and when it started getting late

Emma said regretfully, "We should head back. We don't know the area that well."

The group agreed and they headed back to the hotel. It was about the time the exposition was closing and a huge boom could be heard.

"What was that?" asked Dora, looking panicked.

"I heard about that," Jeremy said. "At each opening and closing of the exposition, they set off a cannon."

"Every morning and evening?" Dora said faintly.

"We'll get used to it," Emma assured her.

CHAPTER 9

The next morning came around quickly. Jeremy and Emma heard a soft knock on their bedroom door.

"Emma," Dora called through the door.

Emma called, "Come in." She and Jeremy were lying in the bed.

"We want to get going early to the bakery. Would you like to get dressed and join us?"

Emma looked at Jeremy, then back at her sister. "Our first trip to a boulanger? Of course, we want to go."

"We can't miss that!" Jeremy said and sat up.

Dora excused herself to allow them some privacy as the two got dressed. They were ready quickly and met Dora and Tim in the living room. The group headed out.

"We should have plenty of time before we're supposed to meet Abbey," said Dora. The sun was just coming up as they made their way downstairs to the lobby.

"Do we need to stop and ask the concierge for a recommendation?" Tim asked.

"No," Dora replied. "Abbey gave me the name and location of

several of her favorite boulangerie. She said the first one is about two blocks from here on the right."

The area was quiet in the early morning. They strolled along the sidewalk, looking in the windows of many small shops. When Emma delayed a bit in front of one, Dora called, "We need to hurry; there'll be a line."

"Oh, of course, let's keep going."

They turned the corner and saw why they had to arrive early. A line had already formed, though it moved quickly with persons exiting the shop carrying delicious-smelling pastries.

They waited patiently, leaning close to the window as they tried to get a view of the varied pastries available.

"What should we get?" Emma asked.

"Croissants, they're buttery goodness and Abbey said not to be missed," said Dora.

"What about some pain au chocolat?" Tim asked. He remembered the description from the night before.

Jeremy nodded. Chocolate was also a favorite of his.

They entered and the smell of bread washed over them. Emma paused in the doorway, thinking of Mama and her bakery. *She'd have loved this,* she thought. their turn had come and as they stepped up to the counter, the clerks were in a rush, their morning spent baking and then selling. She asked, "Dora, would you like to order for us?"

Dora looked nervous but asked for the croissants and pain au chocolat in French. The baker smiled and handed her the pastry bag in exchange for their money.

"I hope you enjoy it," he commented in accented English.

Dora blushed and they shuffled out so the next person in line could get their order.

They stepped out with their wonderful-smelling treats and could not wait for a second longer to take a bite. The pastries were handed out. Emma took a minute to pull her croissant apart.

"Dora, look at these layers."

Dora mimicked her move. "I'd love to find out how they can do that."

Emma took a large bite and moaned. The butter and the layers were lovely. Dora reacted the same way. They glanced at the men, their hands were empty. "Where are your pastries?" Dora asked.

"We have a problem," Tim said.

"A problem? What kind of problem?" Dora asked worriedly.

"Our pastries are gone," Tim said sadly.

"Already?" Emma asked.

Jeremy answered for both of them. "Yeah....we didn't take the time to investigate the pastry; we just ate it."

Emma finished her pastry. "How was it?"

"We should have gotten two," Tim answered unhappily. He looked longingly back at the bakery but the line had grown even further.

"Why don't we walk to the Arc de Triomphe?" Jeremy suggested.

Emma teased Tim. "We might find another boulanger on the way."

Tim grinned and instantly cheered up. They began their walk. It was easy to spot the boulangerie; the lines were long. They waited in one more line to get more pastries. This time they waited to eat them.

Their destination stood at the western end of the Champs-Élysées at the center of Place de l'Étoile. Signs in the area stated that this was the meeting point for the 17, 8th, and 16th Arrondissements. They counted as they went around it and saw there were twelve radiating avenues. After they went around twice, then found a bench to sit on. The boys ate croissants this time and the girls ate Pain au chocolat. All agreed both were delicious.

After they finished, they walked around and read the writing on The Arc de Triomphe. Emma read aloud, "It honors those who fought and died for France in the French Revolutionary and Napoleonic Wars, with the names of all French victories and generals inscribed on its inner and outer surfaces."

"Doesn't the exposition also honor the revolution?" Dora asked.

"Yes, the 100 years since the event occurred," commented Tim. They were silent thinking about how many deaths occurred during that event. The four continued around the structure.

"I believe you can go to the top of the structure and look out at all of Paris," Emma said.

Jeremy walked around until he located the stairs and called, "It's over here." The monument had opened for viewing a few minutes earlier.

A man stood at the entrance and directed them to the top. "The area you're walking in changed only thirty to forty years ago. Napoleon III changed the tree-lined boulevards and wider streets were added."

The group made their way to the top and took in the view. Paris was laid out in front of them. It was a wonderful site, a fashionable avenue with trees on either side that formed rectangular groves. There were also footpaths, fountains, and gas lighting.

Dora nudged Emma. "We'll have to come back and shop here."

"I'd also like to see the Élysée Palace," commented Emma.

"Countries with monarchs are staying away from the exposition," commented Jeremy, continuing to look out at the sites.

Emma said, "They don't want to foster the idea that it's a good thing to dissolve their countries' political systems."

"The revolution was also quite violent," Tim mentioned, "I'm pretty sure the kings and queens left in Europe would like to keep their heads in place."

The rest of the group laughed and Dora punched him. "None of that, we don't want to be rude."

"Who me?" he teased back and grabbed the hand she had punched him with and kissed it.

"Emma," Dora asked, trying to change the subject, "what is the architecture we're looking at?"

Emma said, "It's an old city. You'll see examples of architecture from every period, from the Middle Ages to now. Paris was the birthplace of the Gothic style and has important monuments of the French Renaissance, Classical Revival, and the flamboyant style of the reign of Napoleon III. We're also lucky to see new landmarks that will be around for a long time, like the Eiffel Tower and Grand Palais. I do wish we had a map; we could explore more of the area."

"I got one from a man at the desk downstairs," said Dora as she pulled it from her pocket. "It's called the chromolithographic tourist pocket map. We should be able to use it to get around."

"We could have used this earlier," teased Tim, reviewing it.

"I forgot I had it," she admitted.

They studied it and pointed out sites that appeared on the map—the Eiffel Tower, the Pantheon, and others.

Jeremy noticed the time, "We should get back. Mom will be picking you up soon."

The four of them headed down the stairs, being careful of the tourists passing them on their way up.

"Our surprise," Dora said happily.

"Yes, of course, the surprise," muttered Emma.

Dora caught her by the arm and pulled her to a stop. "Aren't you looking forward to it?"

"Not really. I just had some things I needed to get done this morning," Emma said. She was thinking of the questions she needed to ask the museum curators.

"But you will try to have a good time?" Dora asked, feeling a little disappointed.

"I will," she promised and smiled at Dora. She appeared cheered and they continued to walk arm and arm to the exit.

"The exposition will be opening soon," Emma commented.

"Oh, yes, we'll have plenty of time to go once you return," Tim told her.

They walked through the tree-lined streets, admiring the magnificent homes made of stacked stone. Emma stopped and commented, "I'd like to see the inside of some of these."

Jeremy looked around. "Mom may know some of the residents; we could ask if it's possible." Abbey had lived in France for many years.

Emma nodded and said a bit dreamily, "That would be amazing." *What a dream*, she thought, *to be able to live in this amazing city.* She thought of something else. "You're sure she knows them, right?" she asked Jeremy. His mother was a very skilled cat burglar and had been known internationally for her skills.

He smiled. "I'm sure the visit will be conducted through the front door and not a window."

They got back to their room and freshened up. When they heard a knock at the door, Emma rolled her eyes but got her hat and headed to the door with Dora.

It was Abbey, and she was smiling brightly. "Are you ready for your surprise?"

Emma smiled, understanding this was family. "Yes."

"Me also," Dora said.

They followed her down to a waiting carriage. Abbey instructed the driver to go to an address that was in the opposite direction of the exposition. When they pulled up in front of a very elegant clothes shop, Emma sucked in her breath. *Definitely a surprise*, she thought.

"Emma, it's clothes," Dora said excitedly.

Abbey saw their reaction and grinned. "A good surprise?" she asked.

They grinned back and then climbed quickly out of the carriage.

"We have appointments for you both. Let's go in," Abbey said and they followed her into the shop. The garments hanging in the room were so beautiful. Emma would have loved to look at the structure of each one. *How are these wonderful gowns put together?* she wondered

"Abbey," a woman's voice called. "Are these your two daughters?"

"They are. This is Dora and Emma. Girls, this is Madam Sucrest, she's an amazing designer."

"Hmm," Madam Sucrest said as she walked around the girls. "You're right, they have lovely figures. But the foundation garments. Tsk tsk. Ladies, you need support. It makes the dresses fit so much better." She clapped her hands loudly. Two assistants appeared and escorted Dora and Emma to the dressing rooms. Madam Sucrest followed and commented, "First, we'll need to fit you for corsets. We may have some we can adjust for you to take home today."

"But," protested Emma, "we don't wear corsets."

Everyone stopped at once and Dora ran into the assistant in front of her. "And why not?" Madam Sucrest asked.

"Mama said they'd be bad for us and lead to medical problems," Emma responded.

"Bah! Medical problems only occur if you put them on incorrectly or use the wrong materials. A good corset will fit and provide structure."

Emma continued to offer facts. "Isn't whalebone used to stiffen it? Won't that cut into me?"

"No, if anything, whalebone is flexible and will fit better with the heat of the body." The woman reduced her voice level.

"Will you give it a chance? We can put you in one and show you what a difference it will make to the dress."

Emma was still worried and looked at Dora and said in a low voice, "Mama didn't approve of these."

Dora was more reasonable and answered her in the same low tones. "But, Emma, that was over fifteen years ago. Let's see what has changed."

Madam Sucrest studied Dora. "You have had a child?" she asked.

"Yes," Dora said. She was embarrassed that it was visible on her figure.

"The corset can offer support, especially during the time of heavier breasts."

Both girls were resigned to trying the corset and moved into their dressing rooms. Once they undressed, they stood in their combinations while the assistants measured both women and went to get a corset that would fit.

Emma's assistant said, "The fasteners are in the front now, so you may dress yourself. I'll show you how to put it on. Do not overtighten; we can pad you out to make your waist look smaller." The assistant tightened the stays in the back. "I will only tighten it to give you a shape, we want you to be able to move around and do things you'd normally do."

Emma paced and realized it did offer support to her chest and back. *This does feel pretty good,* she thought. She moved and kicked out with her leg. She lunged forward and then tried to lean back. "Okay, so there are limitations," she murmured.

The assistant frowned. These were not the moves normal customers did to check to see if they could move in a corset. "The dress is next."

Emma watched as the assistant went to the beautiful gold dress hanging in the room.

"That one?" Emma asked, holding her breath for the answer.

"Yes," the assistant said as she took it off the hanger and walked it over to Emma. "Arms up, please."

Emma placed her arms through the dress and the assistant pulled it over her head. The dress settled on her hips and was fastened in the back.

"You may turn around now."

She turned and saw her image. "Oh, that is lovely." The gold and brown tones were deep with a square neck. She looked at the structure of the garment and saw that the corset did its job. It didn't impede her breathing.

The assistant saw her examining the garment and said, "The stays give structure to the top, and padding attached inside the skirt and top help to fill out the garment."

"Emma! Come out," called Abbey. "Dora has come out already."

She walked out of the door and Abbey said, the satisfaction clear in her voice, "Perfect."

Emma turned and saw Dora standing on a wood block to allow her assistant to hem the skirt. She was wearing a dark blue color that was similar in style to her own. A full skirt with a structured top. The difference was the necklines. Dora's was scooped and Emma's was a bit higher and square.

"Oh, Dora, you look lovely," Emma said.

"So do you," her sister responded

"Do you approve?" Abbey asked them.

"We do!" they said at the same time and grinned.

Madam Sucrest came out and walked around both girls and nodded her approval. "We need to do some fitting on these, but we have some day outfits you may take with the corsets."

They changed into the other outfits, which were quickly fitted to them. An hour later, they were having tea and cakes while they waited for their dresses to be finished. Madam Sucrest called, "They're ready." They went back and put on the suit dresses; they were perfect.

They exited the shop and hugged Abbey. "Your other dresses should be ready later in the week."

"How long have you known each other?" asked Emma.

"Oh, for a long time," Abbey said, not sharing anything else.

"Was Madam Sucrest always so talented with her hands?" Dora asked.

Abbey unexpectantly said, "She had to do something after retiring from stealing jewels."

"She was a..." exclaimed Dora.

"Yes, she was once a famous thief. Almost as good as me," Abbey said, then laughed.

"Did you work together?" asked Emma.

"We have," said Abbey. She changed the subject. "Now, tell me, did you like the dresses?"

"Thank you, these are so lovely," Emma said.

"I'm glad you enjoy them. I need to get you back so you can start your investigation."

They returned to the hotel close to noon and Dora asked Abbey, "Would you like to eat lunch with us?"

"Thank you, but no. I'm meeting Ellis and going to see some of the exhibits with him this afternoon. We'll see you soon," she replied.

"Abbey, thank you," Emma said. "We had a nice time and the garments are gorgeous."

"You're welcome," she said as she watched the two women climb down. She told the driver to take her to her apartment.

They watched her go and Emma turned to Dora. "That was amazing. Who would have thought corsets could be comfortable?"

"I agree," said Dora. "This really helps my back. Since I had Lottie, I've felt strained."

"I didn't know. I hope it helps, but don't wear it too often; your muscles need to be allowed to work without it," Emma suggested.

"I will. Ready to go up and let the boys see the new dresses?" Dora asked.

"Yes, let's go up."

They headed into the crowded hotel and waited for the elevator.

"Will you head over to the exposition this afternoon?" asked Emma.

"Yes," Dora answered. She mentioned lightly, "Lenora and Michael will be meeting us here."

"When was this arranged?" asked Emma, carefully keeping her tone even.

"As we were leaving the ship."

"They must be close by," Emma said, not revealing she knew where they were staying.

"They are staying in the same hotel we are."

As they entered the hotel lobby and heard a voice call, "Dora!" They looked over and saw Lenora and Michael calling her.

Dora raised her eyebrows at Emma, who commented drolly, "I'll wait here."

"Thank you," Dora said softly.

Emma watched as her sister hurried over to them.

They hugged and talked animatedly. *Plans for the exposition*, Emma thought. She continued to watch Dora interact with the couple.

When she didn't come back, Emma walked over to the elevator. Just as the doors opened, Dora rushed up. They gave their floor number to the operator.

"Just caught it," Dora said, out of breath.

"Plans all worked out?" asked Emma. She tried to keep any emotion out of her voice, looking at the top of the elevator.

"Yes," Dora said, smiling. She didn't realize Emma was unhappy. "They have a carriage and we'll start over as soon as we have lunch and freshen up."

Emma continued to dwell on that sudden friendship. There were too many unanswered questions about these people. They were both silent as they waited for their floor. The doors opened, and they stepped out together and made their way to their hotel room.

They opened the door and called out, "Tim, Jeremy!"

"We're in here and we ordered lunch; chicken and vegetables with bread and fruit. Come on in."

They walked in and the men viewed the outfits for the first time.

"Wow, those are nice," Tim said.

"Do you notice anything different about us?" Dora asked.

"No, not really," both men said.

Emma and Dora laughed. Dora said, "We'll show you later."

"Hmm," Jeremy teased, "now I'd like to know what's different."

Emma laughed and said, "Later."

They started to eat and Emma grew quieter.

"Is anything wrong?" asked Jeremy.

"I am just thinking about the people we need to meet this afternoon." Philip had given her a letter of introduction to meet with several museum curators. *The investigation into who brought us to Paris must come first,* she thought.

They ate quickly and got their coats and hats from their rooms. "Is everyone ready to head downstairs?" asked Jeremy, pulling on his coat as he exited the bedroom. Like Chicago, the weather during September could be chilly.

"I just can't wait to see the tower and the opening into the exposition; there are supposed to be fountains and statues the entire distance from the entrance to the far central dome," commented Dora.

Emma wanted to go see it but knew they needed some answers first. "We'll get there as soon as we can," she said, "I can't wait to see it also. Will we be able to meet you for a late tea?"

Tim cleared his voice and Dora said apologetically, "I'm not sure. We promised the rest of the day to Lenora and Michael. How about dinner instead?"

Jeremy nudged her and she responded begrudgingly, "That will be fine."

The two couples headed out of the room and down the elevator into the lobby, where they immediately saw Lenora and Michael. She noticed they didn't approach their group but called to Tim and Dora to join them. *Why do they avoid me and Jeremy?*

Jeremy watched them leave and turned to Emma. "Okay, let's have it."

"They don't want us around," she stated.

"Yes, they do, but their new friends want some alone time. It's not that unusual," he reasoned.

"I know, I just thought we'd be with them at the exposition. That was the plan."

"We'll have two weeks," he pointed out. "Just let Dora and Tim know how you feel. I'm sure they'll make time for us."

"You're right." She knew he was right but she turned to stare at the group of four.

He wanted to stop her from dwelling on Tim and Dora's new friends. "Do you have the curator's name and address?"

"Yes, we'll need directions."

He looked around and saw the concierge at his desk. "Over there," he said, indicating the desk.

They made their way over. The man spoke English and gave them directions to the museums. "You will need a carriage to get there."

"I hope it isn't in the direction of the exposition," Jeremy said as they exited. The crowds already forming in the streets and traffic didn't appear to be moving.

"Me, too!" she said, looking around.

"Do you have the letters Philip wrote?" asked Jeremy.

"Yes, I have them here," she said, tapping her pocket.

"We need to walk a few blocks to get away from this crowd," Jeremy said.

"You're right."

They crossed the street and walked to a less crowded location to locate a carriage. They found one and gave him the address. It was located in another arrondissement. They looked around as they traveled and enjoyed the view of the different neighborhoods going by.

The carriage pulled to a stop in front of a large stone structure. The building's appearance was that of a palace. A large number of the monarchy's homes had been turned into buildings for the public good. They paid the driver and got out of the carriage. He drove away as they turned and stared at the large building with many different floors.

Management will not be easy to reach in an establishment this big, Emma thought. They needed to speak with the top person. She hoped her letter would get them to the person they needed. She took a deep breath and they ascended the imposing stairs.

The museum had been open since 10 am that morning. They entered through the main double doors and into a large entryway. There was a security station there; they paused and inquired about the manager. The guard said he was unavailable. They weren't getting anywhere with the large imposing man.

"The letter," muttered Jeremy.

"Oh, yes." She pulled it out and said, "I have a letter that might help."

The security guard took it from her and carried it over to a closed door on the opposite side of the gallery. It seemed like an eternity, and then the door opened again. This time, the guard was accompanied by a man of about fifty.

"Bonjour!" the man called to them. He had white hair and a full beard. His suit was burgundy with white lace at the cuffs.

"Bonjour," they replied.

"Je suis, François Le Burke, le réalisateur."

"Je suis Emma Evans et Jeremy Tilden," Emma said.

"You may speak English. Would you like to come to my office?" the director said, indicating the way with his hand.

"Thank you," Emma said gratefully.

They walked through several exhibits. Emma had to concentrate on why they were there and not get distracted. They entered the director's office. It was a large space that was different from the main museum in that it had windows. Normally, museums didn't like natural light; it could wash out the art. Gas lights were used to illuminate the areas.

Le Burke moved behind the large desk and indicated the chairs in front of his desk. "Sit, please. I read your letter of introduction. I have known Philip for years. What can I do for you?"

"Yes, we met with Philip because of an invitation we received." Emma handed the invitation to him.

"Hmm," he murmured as he read it. He said in a distracted manner, "Yes, Philip, was tied up with that mess a few years ago —forgeries involving paintings." He looked at her in surprise when he realized with whom he was speaking. "You said Emma Evans?"

"Yes," she responded.

Le Burke got up and came around the desk and took her hands in his. "My dear, we're so grateful to you! So many artists' works could have been lost forever."

He went back to his chair and picked up the invitation again. He studied it carefully and said, "You'd like to know if this is authentic."

"Yes," Jeremy said. "We haven't received any follow-up and we're concerned about the reason for wanting us here."

"I can tell you this. This is not an authentic organization. I'm involved on the boards of the main art societies here in Paris. I'd have at least heard of it if it existed."

Emma let out a long breath. "So, the reason given for our being here is fraudulent. But why?"

"Have you seen anything suspicious since you arrived in Paris?" he asked.

Emma thought of Julian, Lenora, and Michael, but said, "No, but we're concerned that we're being manipulated."

Le Burke picked up his pencil and started writing. "I'll keep the name and ask around to see if anyone else has heard of it."

"We'd appreciate it," Emma said. "We're staying at the Grand Hotel Terminus."

He wrote that down and thought he'd have to send notes to other museum curators in the area. He asked, "Have you been to the exposition yet?"

"We'll be going after this. We wanted to see you first," said Jeremy.

"I'm honored. You must stop by the central dome. It's at the far end of the fountains after you get through the tower. Inside of it are arches and murals that are wonderful in their detail and artistry."

"We'll keep an eye out for them," Emma assured him. "Thank you for taking time for us today."

"I'm pleased you brought this to me, and I'll follow up as soon as I know something." With that, Le Burke stood and accompanied them to their carriage. "Au revoir," he called.

They climbed into the waiting carriage and requested to be taken to the exposition. As they started moving, Jeremy looked over at Emma.

"Who are you thinking of for this?"

"The same as you, I'd expect," she said, glancing over at him.

"Julian, Lenora, and Michael," he confirmed.

"Yes," she said contemplatively. "They've shown up seemingly out of nowhere, and now they've interwoven themselves into our lives."

The trip to the exposition grounds was indeed taking a long time. The driver had warned them that the trip would be longer as the streets were very full.

He was correct as they got closer to the bridge, they were surrounded by other carriages and people walking. The Eiffel Tower, the main entrance to the exposition could be seen from where they were. The anticipation took Emma's breath away and suddenly she couldn't wait to get there.

Jeremy felt the same and looked around. "It would be simpler to walk," he pointed out. Emma agreed and started out of the carriage.

Jeremy laughed and stopped her. "I think we should tell the driver first."

"True." She called to the driver, "We'd like to get out here."

He nodded and told them their price. It was not necessary to pull over; the crowds had brought them to a stop. They paid him, climbed down, and took the footpath across the bridge. Walking up to the entrance, they stood for a long moment and marveled at the size of the structure. It distracted them from anything around it.

"Jeremy, come over here," she said, moving through the crowds to get to the tower. She moved until she stood where one of the interlocking joists connected to the ground. Spinning in a circle, she took in the four massive pillars that held the tower's shape. "It's tall!" she said.

"You know, it's 57.64 meters just to the first level," commented Jeremy. "Give me your hand." She gave it and he pulled her back out of the crowded entry into the Exposition.

"We just got here! Where are we going?" she asked, laughing at his excitement.

He kept pulling her and she realized why; he wanted to get a view of the entire structure. "It's rather like a triangle," said Jeremy.

She studied it, "Except that it appears to be curved on its sides. It has different levels and different platforms."

"Didn't Ellis say Eiffel designed it because of how it would handle the wind?" Jeremy asked.

"Yes, the design causes the air to flow through and not push or pull on it. The actual placement of the supports and platforms took this into account."

"How long does something like this take to build? Was it being constructed when you were here last?"

"I believe the pillars were going in when I was here, but I don't remember seeing it in person at the time. I think I just wanted to get home to you." That period was full of personal turmoil for Emma and Jeremy. Each had faced challenges that required them to act without each other.

He leaned back, shielding his eyes to see the top. "How far is it to the top?"

"At its highest point, it's 324 meters. Papa says there's an apartment at the top for Eiffel."

"I'd love to see that!"

"Me, too," she said. She'd have to ask Papa if that were possible.

They continued to look around the base and Jeremy said, "Didn't Ellis say there were only stairs?"

"Initially," she confirmed. "The elevator didn't work at first, so only the stairs would be utilized to climb to the top. Papa wasn't thrilled; it was 328 steps to the first floor and 674 steps to the second floor. In total, there are 1,665 steps from the esplanade to the top of the tower. "

"What's on each level?" he asked curiously. "Is it just empty?"

"No, each level is something special. The first level has four majestic wooden pavilions designed by Stephen Sauvestre. The second level has an observation deck and, finally, the summit where Eiffel's office is located."

Jeremy laughed. "I'm not so sure I'm that good with heights. Did you want to go up today?"

They looked at the long lines for both the elevator and the stairs. Though the lines were significantly shorter for the stairs, Emma shook her head and said regretfully, "No, maybe next time. Why don't we wander around the exposition ground and see what else is here first? Plus," she said, sending a grin his way, "we have an in."

When he raised his eyebrows at that, she answered the silent question. "I'm sure Papa can get us up faster."

"And probably higher," he said and laughed. "Okay then, we're going to the exposition."

Though it was her suggestion to leave, it was hard to tear her eyes away from the iron structure. Jeremy had to tug at her hand as they made their way through the crowds.

The tower had taken up all of her attention and she hadn't noticed anything past it. But now, as they made their way through, she saw the large white fountains surrounded by lush grass. The water feature had numerous statues around it and at the main water supply. There was a wide walkway on each side and buildings boarding it.

"It's wonderful."

"Let's move away from this crowd," he suggested.

The entire world seemed to be trying to get into the exposition that day. They walked to the grassy area and paused to take it all in.

"Before we go any further, we should review the map," Jeremy suggested. The concierge had given it to them when they mentioned they'd also be attending the exposition. He pulled it out of his pocket for them to examine.

She looked down at it and then glanced around the area and the many buildings. "That must be the central dome is there," she said, pointing toward the far end where a gold dome could be seen.

"What are the ones on the left of the dome?" he asked, looking over her shoulder at the map.

She read it out loud, "The Palaces of Liberal and Fine Arts, each with a richly decorated dome, facing each other across a garden and reflecting pool between the Eiffel Tower and the Palace of Machines. Both were designed by Jean-Camille Formigé. Both buildings had modern iron frames abundance of glass but were completely covered with colorful ceramic tiles and sculpted decoration." She studied the grand structures. "What will they do with it once the exposition is over?"

"I don't know," he said honestly. He studied the map and said, "The crowd seems to be coming in through this one point. According to this map, there are twenty-two different entrances to the exposition around its perimeter."

"Good to know if we need to get out quickly," she teased. She looked at the map and around the area and asked, "How long do we have to view everything?"

"They're open from 8AM until 6PM for the major exhibits and palaces, and until 11:00 in the evening for the illuminated greens and restaurants."

"What is that there?" she asked, pointing to the map.

He looked on and said, "They're certainly ornamental. It says it's Les Invalides. It's the major ceremonial entrance. The two tall pylons with colorful ornaments, like giant candelabras."

Emma continued to review the map. Suddenly, she frowned, looking down and then up again, and drummed her fingers on her lips.

"What's wrong?" Jeremy asked. He knew she only did that when she was planning something.

"I don't know where to start; there's too much to see."

"Now, that is a good problem," he said with a wide smile. "Why not start at the back and work our way forward?"

She squinted at the map and said, "Galerie des Machines." She looked back at him. "Excellent idea."

As they started out, a voice rang out. "Would you like to take the trains? They're supposed to be very efficient."

They stopped when they heard the familiar voice.

"Julian," she muttered, with a frown on her face. She put a smile on her face and then turned. "Julian, how nice to see you again. How did you find us?" she asked lightly, but there was a bit of steel in her eyes. She really wanted the answer to that last question.

"Oh," he said, "I just happened on you. May I accompany you?"

When Jeremy started to say no, Emma bumped him with her hip. Instead, he said, "Yes, please do."

She leaned in and said in a low voice, "It'll give me a chance to question him." She looked over at Julian. "You mentioned you were here for business. Is it at the exposition?"

Julian wasn't forthcoming and instead murmured noncommittally. When he didn't continue, Emma pulled herself together and decided this would take some time.

"Have you had a chance to see anything yet?" Julian asked.

The question was broadly asked, but Emma decided it involved the exposition. "Oh, not yet. We just got here."

"I just got here myself."

She didn't believe him; the man had too many secrets.

"Where are Tim and Dora this afternoon?" Julian asked curiously as they started to walk further into the exposition location.

"They left for the exposition after lunch," said Jeremy.

"Alone?" he asked lightly, seemingly uninterested.

"No," replied Jeremy. "They're with Lenora and Michael."

"Hmm," he commented. "They have formed a friendship and are continuing to see each other?"

"Yes," Emma said. She tried to not let her worry show in her voice.

Jeremy wanted to pull her out of her thoughts and took her hand. "Let's look around," he suggested.

"I heard the cultural areas are interesting," she mentioned as they walked.

Looking at the area around them, Julian commented, "A separate, smaller site is located on the esplanade of Les Invalides, which is where the pavilions are. The exposition is showcasing villages inhabited by natives of the colonies. That is where you can go to a large number of outdoor restaurants and cafes with foods from Indochina, North Africa, and other cuisines from around the world."

Emma forced her gaze away from Julian. The three continued to stroll toward the central dome. The fountains were turned on and the water flowed and the sound drowned out the noise of the crowds around them. They paused and took in the area. The water flowed from a large white statue; other statues were lined up around the water.

They moved past it and climbed the steps up to the gold dome. As they entered, they immediately stopped to view the amazing sight in front of them. Even Julian seemed affected; his questions stopped as he took in the interior.

The people that entered behind forced the three to move further into the building. Julian pulled them over to the side to allow the others to enter. They continued to gaze at the murals and the gold that seemed to engulf the room. The artistry of paintings and panels located on every wall fascinated them. The sun shone in through the high windows and the chandeliers caught it and gleamed, throwing halos around the room.

Julian seemed to have found his voice and said, "We should move along."

Emma and Jeremy continued to look around. The dome was

the entry hall for the Palace of Fine Arts, Liberal Arts and was the axis and entry for the Galerie des Machines.

"It appears this is only the beginning and opens up into other areas." Emma turned her gaze away from the ceiling and realized what was in front of her. It was the Galleries des Machines. At that moment, she could only marvel at what she was seeing. The structural supports pulled her in; she looked back to motion to Jeremy and saw he was distracted by the fine arts wing.

"Tony would have wanted to go there first," he commented. Tony was someone they were both friends with. Her first trip to Paris was to help him with an art heist/kidnapping case. He studied art and was the assistant curator of the museum in Chicago.

"Yes," she agreed. "We'll have to go through it so we can describe it to him later." She desperately wanted to go into the gallery of machines but understood the draw of the art.

"I just hope we have enough time to see it all," Jeremy said.

"We will," she said confidently. They had two full weeks left of their trip.

They moved forward, not looking back to see if Julian followed them. "The construction from the tower is being used throughout this building," Jeremy commented.

"I think Papa mentioned the design was initially used in bridge construction and this is the first time it's been used like this."

"Think about how many more things are displayed here; so many new inventions, so much new technology has been evolving."

"It doesn't seem that it's unpopular." They walked into the gallery; again, the crowds wouldn't allow for long observation and they had to move to the sides.

"Edison's lights are being used to illuminate the whole thing," Emma said in wonder at the bright interior.

"I didn't expect the area to have decoration," Jeremy said, pointing out paintings, mosaics, and ceramic bricks that formed part of the cladding on the walls.

"Yes, the decoration continues from the dome," she marveled, spinning around. "It's so big."

Julian's voice startled them when he said, "It's 370 meters long."

So big, thought Emma and she continued to review the space. *It's difficult to know where to start; there are three separate walkways surrounding the machines.*

"So many new things. What is that up there?" Emma asked as she pointed toward the platform located far above them.

"That, I believe, is a train track," Jeremy commented, watching it move up and down the gallery. They walked up to the stairs that lead to the train. Jeremy read aloud from the display. "Bon and Lustremont Paris are builders for the rolling carriage over the Gallery des Machines."

"It's so high up in the air!" she exclaimed, anticipating the ride. *It really is the best way to see everything,* she thought, continuing to study the sheer size of the space. The trolley appeared to roll the entire length of the gallery, allowing people to see things from a different angle.

"I understand that Edison's inventions are displayed here and in some of the other pavilions," said Jeremy, as he looked around.

"We'll have to get over to the different exhibitions after we finish this gallery," stated Emma. "Though this one feels like the one where we will spend the most time."

"Yes," said Julian, his voice going low. "It is an important exhibit, one that will change the world. Too many people are trying to fight the use and expansion of electricity. Without it, none of these marvelous inventions would exist."

Emma was distracted for a moment and said, "You

mentioned that before. Do you think we have cause for concern at this event?"

His face went dark momentarily. He laughed, trying to cover, and said, "How would I know? I know only as much as has been in the paper."

She looked at Jeremy, and he shrugged his shoulders. They needed to keep an eye on him; something was going on here. He seemed preoccupied with the anti-electric group.

They had only passed a few exhibits when they saw Tim and Dora. *And of course*, thought Emma, *Lenora, and Michael.*

Emma called out to her sister, "Dora!"

Dora heard her voice and turned toward her. She smiled, quickly running over with Tim following closely behind. Emma noticed Lenora and Michael stayed back.

"Isn't it just marvelous, all of these new things?" Dora asked.

"It is," Emma agreed.

"Julian," asked Dora," how are you?"

"I'm good. I heard you both were here already," he said. "Have you been in the exhibit all since you arrived?"

Emma, too, noted the question and her response. Julian's questions were clues. She needed to start documenting these and reviewing them with Jeremy.

"We started after lunch and then we meant to come here first but Lenora and Michael wanted to see the lighting display first," Dora answered.

"Which part in particular?" Julian asked.

Tim answered, "Oh, the layout and where everything was being managed from. That sort of thing. It was interesting to see how the electricity has been brought into the exposition."

"Really," Julian murmured.

Emma sent him a sharp look at that question. *What is he implying?* Another voice distracted her. She glanced over Dora's shoulder and saw Papa. "Papa," she called and went over to him quickly to give him a hug and a kiss on the cheek. Dora followed closely behind and also kissed him on the cheek.

"Emma, I thought I'd find you here—among all of the new technology."

She grinned, "It's marvelous."

"Jeremy, is she wearing you out?" Papa asked as Jeremy and Tim walked up.

"Not just yet." He smiled broadly. "How much time have you spent here since you arrived in Paris?"

"I think that the answer given by me would be different than that given by Abbey," Papa said in a self depreciating voice.

Emma looked around, "Is she here with you?"

He smiled, "She said she's spent all of the time she'll ever spend in here."

"So, you have been here a lot?" Emma teased.

"Yes, I find it infinitely fascinating," he admitted. His gaze moved to Dora and Tim. "I didn't expect to see you both here. Is there something that interested you in particular?" Emma wondered about that; it was almost like a warning.

"We're enjoying everything," Dora commented. "We'd probably be spending more time in the other exhibits, but our new friends really wanted to see the Edison exhibit and the Galerie des Machines first."

"Try to see other things as well; the time will fly by," Ellis commented.

"Yes, Papa," said Dora. Tim had been thinking along the same lines. He enjoyed their new friends, but he and Dora had a list of things they'd like to see.

Papa looked around and said to their group, "Would you like to go to the highest level and ride the suspended carriage? It will give you a bird's eye view of the entire gallery."

That was exactly what Emma wanted. Her eyes lit up and she said, "Yes, please." She put her hand out to Jeremy's and he took it; they were eager to see the gallery from the height of the suspended carriage.

"Dora? Tim?" Papa asked as he noticed them hesitate.

"Please include us in that. Let me check with…" Dora's voice trailed off as she turned. She looked back at them and said, "I'll be just a moment." She walked a distance from their group. When she came back, she was wringing her hands, "They aren't there. I hope they don't think we left them."

Tim frowned, "I'm sure they'll find us later." Though he continued to stare in the direction Lenora and Michael had gone.

Emma said, "We also have someone with us." She turned and called, "Julian!"

He wasn't there either. "Jeremy, do you see him?" she asked.

Jeremy observed, "I guess our company has also disappeared."

"Should we…" She let it go as she followed her family up the stairs to the carriage. She continued to look around as they climbed, trying to see everything. They made it to the top and stood in line to take their turn.

She spotted someone familiar in the crowd. *Is that Julian?* she thought as she leaned across the railing. *It is him. What is he doing?* She could only see his back; the persons he was talking to were blocked by the machines. Two people stepped closer to Julian and she could see who he was talking to. *It is Lenora and Michael. Just like the last time, they're arguing again.* Whatever the topic, both sides were taking it seriously. It almost came to blows until Lenora stepped between them to separate the men.

"What are you looking at?" Dora asked hugging her from behind.

"Over there," she murmured.

Dora followed her direction and said, "Isn't that…?"

"Yes, it is," Emma commented quietly, not wanting to share her opinions about her new friends.

"That's odd. I didn't think they knew each other. I never saw them interact before this."

"We saw them have a similar conversation on the ship," Emma said.

Dora turned her around. Once they were face-to face, she said, "You did? You didn't mention it."

"No, I wanted you to enjoy your new friends. One argument didn't seem pertinent."

"No, one wouldn't have been a concern," said Dora as her eyes moved back to the argument. It seemed to have no resolution and they stormed off in different directions.

"Should I be worried?" Dora asked.

Emma was quiet for a long time before saying, "I don't trust them."

"Which ones—Lenora, Michael, or Julian?"

"All three. I feel they're involved in something. I'm just not sure what," she admitted.

"It doesn't appear that they're on the same side."

Emma looked over at her. "You don't sound too disappointed that there may be something up with your new friends."

Her sister smiled, "It's getting to be a little too much. They're always around."

"I thought you liked them."

"I do but in smaller amounts. It's like strudel; I like it, but I don't want it for every meal."

Tim and Jeremy heard that last part as they walked over to where Emma and Dora were standing. Tim pulled Dora to him, "Are you talking about Lenora and Michael?"

She nodded.

"You told them?" Jeremy asked Emma.

"Yes, it was time. And Dora and I just witnessed another fight between the three of them." Dora quickly explained to Tim what they had just seen.

Tim asked, "This has happened before?" He didn't know if he

should feel upset that they had left him and Dora out of the conversation.

"Yes," Emma admitted.

"We didn't know if they were arguing over something petty on the ship and we didn't want to influence you about your new friends," Jeremy said.

Dora frowned, knowing how Emma could keep secrets from her. Her sister tended to make too many decisions on her behalf.

Tim watched the expressions on his wife's face and knew where her mind was headed. He leaned down and whispered in her ear, "Don't be upset. They told us when a second event happened."

She nodded but felt she needed to ask another question. "Is there anything else we need to know about?"

Emma hesitated and Dora saw it. "Well?" she demanded.

Emma looked at Jeremy and then back at Dora. "We..." she began, only to be interrupted by Papa.

"We're next," he called.

They hurriedly moved toward the opening of the trolley and, while they were waiting to board, Dora took Emma's arm and turned her until they could see in each other's eyes. "We'll talk about this later."

"We will," Emma replied softly. The line started moving and their group boarded the trolley. They headed toward the far side to take their seats until it was full.

The trolley engineer said loudly, first in French, then in English, "To ride safely, please do not stand or rock the vehicle."

They listened to his instructions and prepared themselves for the trip. The excitement removed all thoughts of Lenora, Michael, and Julian from their minds. She held Jeremy's hand tightly as she observed the sheer expanse of the gallery. "So many new things," she said.

Papa heard her and started pointing out the machines below.

"Little girl, look over here." That was something he had called her since she was a small child.

The trolley made its way down and back again. It just wasn't long enough for her, and Jeremy could see she was disappointed at having to get off.

"We'll come back. I promise," he said softly.

"Yes, definitely," she responded.

As they exited the trolley and made their way downstairs, the group agreed that they'd spend the rest of the day together —eating at the exposition grounds and heading home that night. Papa enjoyed the day with his daughters and their husband/companion. No one had mentioned that Julian, Lenora, and Michael had disappeared. Each felt relieved that they were together as a family.

After the long afternoon of walking, they had a late dinner with Abbey and Papa at their hotel.

"It's getting late. We must go," said Abbey. She noticed Ellis looked tired and thought it best to get him home for some rest. The hours he was keeping on this trip were strenuous, up by 6AM and usually down at the exposition grounds with Eiffel until late in the evening. She wanted to make sure he didn't do too much.

They made their goodbyes and the door closed when Jeremy said, "Emma, didn't you mean to ask Abbey about something?"

She glanced toward Dora, "Yes. I forgot."

"I think you can still catch her if you take the stairs," he suggested.

Emma thought quickly, "I'll do that." He held the door open for her and she dashed to the stairs. As she exited the door into the lobby, she looked and saw the elevator was standing open. *Where are Papa and Abbey?* she thought to herself, glancing around. Not seeing them, she went to the main entry doors.

Papa's outline was seen easily through the glass. *There they are,* she thought and put her hand on the door and started to pull them open when she saw them speaking with someone. She released the door when she saw who it was. *It's Julian. Do Papa and Abbey know him?* She decided to find out, but before she could, a crowd came through the door, pushing her further into the lobby. She untangled herself and made her way back to the door and opened it. *Gone!* She ran down the street, but there was no sign of them.

Odd, she thought. She didn't think Papa and Abbey knew Julian. Had he just happened to be in the area? *Unlikely,* she thought. *I'll need to ask Papa about this.*

She glanced again toward the front desk, wondering if the crowd that had pushed into the lobby had gotten rooms yet. She studied the people in line and saw a lovely young lady and what was perhaps her mother, though she only saw her back. The daughter appeared to be of negroid descent. They both looked tired, the older woman with her back to Emma was leaning onto the younger woman. A long trip probably. *Hopefully, they have a reservation,* she thought and headed back upstairs.

She knocked lightly and Jeremy opened the door. He asked, "Were you able to catch her?"

"No, I wasn't," she said, meditatively. "Where's Dora and Tim?"

"They went to get ready for bed but said they wanted to talk when you returned."

He could tell something was bothering her as she took a seat on the couch. He sat down next to her, took her hand, and asked, "What's wrong?"

She looked forward for a long moment, "When I found Papa and Abbey, they were talking with Julian."

"Julian! I didn't realize they knew him."

"I'm not sure they do," she said thoughtfully. "It's possible they ran into each other."

"That's a lot of coincidences."

"I agree. I'll follow up with Papa tomorrow."

She continued to be preoccupied and Jeremy asked, "Was there something else bothering you?"

"Yes, we have so many new people in our lives; people who seem to keeping secrets from us."

Dora and Tim walked in and heard the word secret. Dora had gotten ready for bed and was in her robe, her hair loose on her shoulders.

"Yes, secrets. Emma," she started, "I'd like to know what's been kept from us."

Emma jumped up and said defensively, "That isn't fair. We were trying to give you some space and time with your new friends."

"Who you didn't trust," Dora accused.

Jeremy stepped between the sisters, "Dora, I discouraged her from interfering in your new friendship. We really only had some suspicions."

Tim, always the peacemaker, said, "Let's sit down and discuss this calmly."

After they sat, he looked toward Emma and Jeremy and asked, "Can we hear the suspicions so we can make our own decisions?"

Jeremy's mouth quirked when Emma pulled out her notebook. She reviewed her case notes, "It's a lot of little things. The fast friendship, not just yours with Lenora and Michael, but also Julian's with us."

"We also had the added issue of us being brought here for reasons we're not sure of," added Jeremy.

"And the confirmation from Philips' friend that the organization that brought us here does not exist," she explained.

"When did you see the first argument?" Dora asked, remembering they had mentioned another altercation.

"It was the second night on the trip when your hair had come down. You went back to your cabin and we continued on," she said.

"Could you hear anything?" Tim asked.

"No, unfortunately, we only saw them talking," Emma replied.

"What else?" Dora asked.

"There isn't a lot more," admitted Emma.

"Well…" started Jeremy.

Emma nodded, encouraging him to go on.

"There is the electricity thing," he finished.

"Electricity?" asked Dora.

"Yes, we have nothing solid, but Julian has mentioned the anti-electricity people more than once, and when coupled with the arguments…" Emma explained.

Tim glanced at Dora. She nodded, and he said, "We might have something to share."

Emma frowned and leaned forward. "Tell us."

"Today, we mentioned the time we spent at the Edison exhibition?" Tim explained.

"Yes," said Jeremy.

"We didn't just look around. We also got special access to the rooms where the electricity comes into the building," Dora explained.

"How did you get access to that?" Emma asked, knowing how tight the security was around the technology exhibits.

"Papa," admitted Dora. "We used his name and we were allowed into all of the secure areas."

"What were Lenora and Michael doing during this time?" asked Emma.

"They were extremely interested in where the electricity came in and how it could be turned on and off," Tim admitted.

"They also explained all of the security to us," commented Dora.

"But we still have no real connections of anything bad to any of them. We just have conjecture," Emma said,

"What do we do?" her sister asked.

Jeremy stood and walked to the mantle. "For now, we keep a watch for anything suspicious."

"I'd recommend you curtail your exposure to Michael and Lenora for now," Emma said firmly.

Dora frowned, "I'd like to make my own decisions, but yes, I think you're right."

There was a knock at the door and the group jumped in response. Jeremy walked over and opened the door. It was a bellhop. "Yes?"

"I have a note for Dora Flannigan."

Jeremy held out his hand, "I'll take it."

He handed it over, and Jeremy pulled out some coins and tipped him. He closed the door and went back to the living room. He walked over to Dora and handed her the note, "It's for you."

Emma frowned. She watched as Dora opened it slowly while the group waited.

She read silently and laughed abruptly. "Abbey sent me a note; she's arranged for me to work in a bakery in the morning."

Wonderful, thought Emma. *She didn't forget.*

"Early?" Tim asked, knowing baker's hours because of the family bakery back home. The dread in his voice was evident.

"Yes." She laughed. She knew Tim was not looking forward to being up with her at that hour.

"What time?" His tone hadn't changed.

"It says 3AM," she supplied.

Emma lay her head back on the couch, "I'm glad I wasn't included in this 'surprise'. What will you learn to make?"

"The rounded bread and croissants. The types of bread we've had since we have been here," Dora said, looking at the note and thinking about the bakery.

"You must make those once we get back home—since we tried them here, I don't think I can live without them," Emma said with a laugh.

Tim stood up holding out his hand to Dora, "We need to go to bed. If you have to be there at three, we'll have to be up earlier."

"You're right," she said, taking his hand to help her stand. "Can we meet you at the exposition tomorrow?" Dora asked her sister.

"Are you sure you won't be too tired?" Emma asked, concerned that she'd wanted to do too much.

Tim answered for her. "She should be back in time for a nap before we head over. We can meet you after lunch." *And I'll also be taking a nap*, he thought.

Jeremy poured himself a glass of wine and brought one to Emma. "Knowing Emma, we'll be at the Galerie des Machines or in the science pavilions," he said smiling at her.

"This's true—I also want to see the new telephone demonstration and lighting exhibits," said Emma.

Dora thought again of Lenora and Michael's fixation with that pavilion. "You might want to watch out for Lenora and Michael," she commented.

"We will," Emma promised.

Before the conversation could continue, Tim pulled on her arm and reminded her of the time.

"I'm being reminded we must go to bed. Goodnight," she said, allowing Tim to lead her to their room.

"Goodnight," Jeremy and Emma called, watching them leave.

Emma took a drink of her wine, "I enjoy baking, but not that much!"

He laughed. "I'd much rather wake up at a reasonable hour."

She thought about how many people were still arriving for the exposition. "So many people," she said, "in one place."

"Yes, the hotel has stayed busy."

"I noticed that. While I was downstairs, there was another large crowd checking in."

"People from all over the world are in Paris."

"Yes, I'm finding the people as interesting as the exposition," she said, drumming her fingers on her lips.

He knew that meant she may have seen something and asked, "What did you see?"

"I don't know," she said but continued to drum her fingers.

"What was it?" he asked, prodding her.

"It was a young girl of about sixteen and a companion—her mother, I believe," she said and didn't add more.

"What bothered you about them?"

"The girl seemed to be worried and anxious."

"It may have been the crowds or from traveling," he said reasonably. "Did the mother seem anxious?"

"No, I didn't see her directly. She was facing forward the entire time."

They let the silence settle around them as they finished their wine and went to bed.

Emma woke from a sound sleep and looked around the dark room. She heard Dora's voice next to her. "Emma, can you get up? I need to speak with you."

"Yes," she said softly and got up, careful not to disturb Jeremy. She followed Dora into the living room. She could see Dora was dressed and ready to leave for her bakery job.

Emma rubbed her eyes, "What's wrong?"

"Tim is sick. He needs to stay here."

"You can't go on your own," Tim said from their bedroom door. Emma could see him pulling up his suspenders. His face had no color and he seemed to be swaying on his feet.

"Tim, go back to bed. I'll take her," Emma said firmly.

He was conflicted but knew Emma could handle herself. "You don't mind?"

"Of course not," she assured him.

He started to object and opened up his mouth to say something. Immediately he regretted it. He covered his mouth with his hand and ran to the bathroom.

Dora bit her lip, watching him. "Should I stay?"

"No," Emma insisted. "You should go. I'm going to get changed. I'll be just a moment." She went back into her room and pulled out her skirt and top.

"What's up?" asked a sleepy Jeremy from the bed.

"Tim's sick, probably something he ate. He's staying here. I'll take Dora over to the bakery."

"Want me to go with you?" he asked and stated to sit up.

"No, you stay in bed. Someone should get some rest. I should be back soon."

"Okay." He didn't argue as he lay back and watched her pull her long hair into a ponytail.

"Don't forget your hat," he reminded her.

"Yes, I might need it." She checked it for her knife and, once she confirmed it was in place, she also attached her thigh scabbard. She grabbed her coin purse and her notebook and went to kiss Jeremy goodbye.

"Hey," he said, yanking her ponytail a bit, "stay safe, and don't take any unnecessary chances."

"Who, me? Would I do that?" she teased.

"Yeah, you would," he said. "Now promise me?"

"I promise," she said softly before she kissed him and headed to the living room. She closed the door softly and saw Dora waiting for her.

"Are we still okay on time?" Emma asked.

"Yes, but we should be going."

Dora saw the hat, "Are you expecting trouble?"

"Not expecting no, it's just a precaution," she said, placing the black hat on her head. Dora pulled on her coat and Emma her black coat, fashioned to look like a cape.

They walked to the door and out into the hallway. Once they were at the elevator, Emma pushed the call button. They heard it engage and, while they waited for it to arrive, Emma turned to Dora, "Did you get Tim back to bed?"

"Yes—it's probably something he ate. He seemed to get most of it out of his system."

"He should be better after some rest."

"I think so."

They got into the elevator and watched as the operator operated the lever that would take them to the lobby. Dora said, "I need to see if the doctor is available to go to our room."

"There should be one on call. Check with the desk manager in the lobby," Emma suggested as they exited the elevator.

Emma watched as her sister went to the desk; it was quiet and there was no line. It should only take her a moment. While she was doing that, Emma looked around the ornate lobby. The furniture, normally covered with people, could now be seen. It was a tasteful selection that went with the tile floors and painted walls.

She heard the elevator bell sound, then glanced toward it and saw the young girl from earlier in the night exit into the lobby. There was no companion with her this time, and she was obviously upset about something.

Emma hadn't noticed Dora was next to her and was startled when she heard her say, "We need to get going, Emma."

"Of course. On our way." As they turned to go out the doors, something hit them in the back, pushing them forward. Dora caught herself before hitting the ground and turned to check on Emma, who had fallen on her knees. Dora went to her and they both watched as the girl who ran into them didn't slow her pace as she sped out of the hotel. "Well, she certainly was in a hurry," said Emma wryly.

"Are you okay?"

"Yes, it was just unexpected," she said as she took Dora's hand. She straightened up and dusted herself off. "I hope she finds what she's looking for."

They stopped the bellman outside and asked for directions to the patisserie. He told them it was only a few blocks from the hotel. They put the event out of their minds and headed there. It was early morning and the chill made them sink into their coats as they walked arm and arm. Emma pulled out her portable gas light and used it to banish the shadows on the narrow roads. She paid attention to the path so she could make her way back to the hotel.

"Will you bring back some treats?" Emma asked, teasing.

"As many as I can carry," Dora promised.

"Wonderful. What time should I pick you up?"

"I should be on my way back about 8AM at the latest, but it'll be daylight. I'll be fine on my own."

"If, you're sure?" She wanted to be there if Dora wanted her, but sleep would be wonderful.

"I'm sure." They continued to walk and Dora asked, "Where will you and Jeremy be today?"

"The exposition. I want to spend a few more days exploring there and then I'd like to see the different arrondissements."

"Will Jeremy be spending some time with Abbey this trip?" asked Dora.

"I believe there are some people she'd like to introduce him to," Emma commented.

They got to the patisserie, and Dora noted, "Abbey said I'm to go to the back door." They went round the corner and found the door. Dora knocked, and it immediately opened. A tall man in white pants and a white baker's top with a bandana wrapped around his head.

"Bonjour," Dora said.

"Bonjour. You're Dora?" he asked in English.

"Je suis Dora et Emma," she said, indicating her sister.

"Will you be staying, Emma, to help us bake?"

"No, I'm here to make sure Dora arrives safety."

"I'll take care of her," he smiled.

She grinned, "Just be sure she brings some of the items you bake home!"

"She will," he said, grinning back.

"Bonsoir," Emma said.

He saw that Emma was alone and was concerned that she would be walking back by herself. "The area is more dangerous with so many people here for the exposition. Should you go by yourself?"

Dora knew her sister could take care of herself, "She'll be fine," she told the man.

Emma tipped her hat at them and made her way back down the alley. She pulled out her small gas light to help her find the way back. Some shadows seemed to move behind her, but she didn't think they were threatening. She kept going, listening intently to her surroundings. The shadow seemed to be keeping up with her. *Not a professional*, she thought. *The footsteps are loud.* They also started to speed up toward her. Rather than running from her pursuer, she let them get close and then she side-stepped and they ran past. Her pursuer noticed their mistake immediately and doubled back. She extinguished her light and stepped into the shadows. As she studied her pursuer from the shadows Emma noticed something over their face. *A mask* she thought. *Hmm.*

Her pursuer couldn't find her and looked to be increasingly frustrated. So much so that they pulled off the mask.

It's Michael! She stayed where she was until he left. *What was that about? Is he after me or Dora?*

She was thinking about the encounter as she entered the hotel lobby; the doorman opened the door for her. She nodded to him absently as she entered. Her eyes automatically searched for the girl who had knocked her down in such a rush earlier. The girl didn't seem to be around. *That's probably a good thing,* she thought.

She yawned and walked to the elevator, pushed the button, and waited for it to arrive.

Her time piece showed 4AM. *Still time to sleep,* she thought.

She was too tired to try to make any connections between Michael and her other clues.

Emma got to the hotel room and opened the door quietly. Her eyes moved ward Dora and Tim's door. *How is he?* The door was cracked open and she pushed it until she saw him on the bed. He was there and snoring loudly. *He must be better*, she thought.

She smiled and went to hers and Jeremy's room. He was lying on his back; she undressed quickly and crawled in, snuggling close to him.

"Hmm," he murmured. "Any concerns?"

"Dora got there okay. We can talk about my run-in in the morning," she murmured, going right to sleep.

That last comment shook him awake. "Wait! What run-in?" He started to sit up but realized she was out. It must not have been something that worried her too much or she'd have woken him to discuss it. He lay back down and went back to sleep.

Hours later, they heard a light knock on their bedroom door. Emma sat up, pushed her hair out of her face, and called out, "Yes?"

Tim stuck his head in, "I'm off to get Dora."

"Are you feeling better?" Jeremy asked.

"Much. Though now I feel hollow," the other man replied, rubbing his stomach.

Emma laughed. "I'd expect so. Make sure she brings home some of her work."

"I will," he promised. He closed the door and headed out, thinking of those pastries.

Emma fell back into Jeremy's arms, taking advantage of the time they had together.

"We need to talk," murmured Jeremy as Emma began running her hands over his body.

"I think there's something else that's much more fun that we could do instead," she said, raising her face to his for a long kiss.

"We still need to talk," he said, trying to be firm but not having any luck.

"Mmm, later."

Much later, as they were getting dressed Emma turned to him, "You'd better hurry. There'll be bread and croissants here soon."

Jeremy paused as he was buttoning his shirt, "You know we need to have that conversation now."

Emma wasn't ready to talk and walked over to Jeremy and started kissing him lightly to distract him.

He was enjoying the kissing but knew what Emma was doing. He backed away from her. "Emma, what did you mean this morning when you said 'run-in'?"

She opened her mouth to tell him, but there was another interruption—a knock on the door. "Tim must have forgotten his key," she said, relieved she didn't have to go into the details just yet.

"I'll get it," he said, finishing buttoning up his shirt. He pointed at her, "When I get back, you will talk to me. And no distractions. I'm on to you missy."

She smiled but didn't say anything.

Jeremy shook his head and headed into the living room to open the door. As he turned the knob, he said, "What, did you forget your key?"

Emma busied herself putting up her hair when she heard Jeremy call out, "Emma!"

"Is it breakfast?" she asked as she came out of the bedroom, pulling her hair into a ponytail.

"It's not breakfast." He stepped back and revealed who was at the door.

It was the girl from last night and she appeared to be about to fall!

"Jeremy!" Emma called. He caught her before the girl hit the floor.

He hefted the unconscious girl into his arms and looked at Emma. "Where do you want her?"

"For now, the couch." She indicated it with her hand. "Is she okay?" She didn't ask the question she wanted to. *Is she dead?*

"Looks like she's just unconscious," he said lying her on the couch, "What do you want to do?"

"Could you go downstairs and see if the doctor's available?"

"That's probably best. I'll go see if I can get him to come up." He walked to the door and opened it, but was surprised again. This time, it *was* Tim and Dora.

"Hi," he said as he hurried past them

"Where are you going?" Dora asked. "We have breakfast." She and Tim held large boxes.

He turned back to them at the elevator, "Save some for me. We have a guest, and I need to go for the doctor."

"The doctor! Why?" Tim called.

"Is Emma okay?" asked Dora worriedly.

He didn't wait to answer them and got on the elevator.

"Come in and I'll explain," Emma called out to them from their hotel doorway.

Dora and Tim moved toward the room slowly and entered, not sure what to expect. They saw Emma had moved back to the couch and was sitting beside a young girl. She didn't appear to be awake.

Dora handed her packages to Tim and ran over. She knelt next to her, "Is she okay?"

"I'm not sure," Emma admitted. "She just showed up at the door and then passed out."

"Let me get a wet cloth for her head," Dora said, standing to retrieve one. Emma continued to stroke the girl's long, dark curly hair off of her forehead.

Dora brought over the wet cloth and placed it on her forehead. She looked over at Emma, "Poor little lost lamb. What do you think made her come to our door?"

"I'm not sure."

Dora looked closer, "Isn't that the girl who ran into us this morning?"

"I think so. I had seen her earlier last night with a woman who might be her mother."

"Why come to us?" asked Tim.

"I don't know, but she was upset last night."

There was a knock on the door. "We stopped and asked for some tea and coffee to be delivered by room service." Tim said, "That should be them."

"I could use some tea," Emma admitted.

Tim got up and let room service in. They moved the tea and coffee to the dining table. He tipped them and they left. He and Dora busied themselves with coffee and tea. He also moved some of the pastries to a tray and brought them to the living area.

They started to eat when Jeremy came in a few moments later. He picked up a pastry before dropping into a chair. "They're sending the doctor up in a few minutes; the hotel's full and there's only one."

"It's probably the same one who came by here early this morning," said Tim, rubbing his stomach, remembering the pain from the night before.

They nodded and continued to eat their breakfast while they watched the girl sleep. A little while later, there was a knock on the door. Jeremy put down his coffee cup and stood, "I'll get it."

He came back into the room with a rather rotund man. The man's jacket was opened, showing his vest and shirt. He immediately headed over to Tim. "Bonjour, Tim. I thought we worked out your problem last night."

Tim held up his hand, "Oh no, doc, it isn't me this time." He motioned toward the couch.

That was when the doctor saw the unconscious girl. He walked over to her and knelt next to her. "What has happened here? Too much dessert, like our friend here?" he said as he referenced Tim.

Tim turned red as Emma answered, "We're not sure. She showed up in our doorway and passed out."

"Fainted, you say. Did she say anything before losing consciousness?"

"No," said Emma, wondering why he asked that question.

"She did say one word," Jeremy corrected.

"What was it?" asked Emma, not realizing she'd missed something.

"She said 'Emma,'" he commented.

"Well, I didn't expect that," Emma said in surprise.

"Do you know her?" asked Dora, looking at her sister.

Emma frowned, "No, not exactly. I've seen her in the lobby a few times. I've never spoken to her."

"I'll need to examine her," stated the doctor.

Dora turned to the group, "Let's give them some privacy." They agreed and moved to the dining room.

"You mentioned you saw her more than once?" Dora prompted.

"Yes, yesterday when I tried to catch Papa and Abbey, and again this morning when she ran into us."

"You've never talked to her?" Tim asked.

"No."

"How would she have known your name?" wondered Dora.

"No idea," Emma said honestly.

"Didn't you mention she was with someone?" asked Jeremy. *Normally, girls don't travel alone. There were exceptions,* he thought, looking at Emma.

"I did see someone. I had thought it was her mother, but I never had a clear view."

As they thought about that, the doctor called out, "You may come over."

"Will we disturb her?" asked Dora.

"No, she's in a deep sleep."

"Is there anything wrong with her?" Emma asked.

"No, I think it is just exhaustion. She'll need to sleep a long while before she can answer any questions. I'd put her somewhere comfortable, loosen her clothes, and let her rest."

"How long will she be out?" Emma asked.

"Probably a few hours," the doctor admitted. "I have to be going now. No rest for me."

"Will you come back after she's awake?" Dora inquired.

"Tell the front desk to send for me when she wakes," the doctor instructed as he walked to the door.

"Thank you, doctor, for a second visit," Tim said as he accompanied him out.

Dora, Tim, Emma, and Jeremy moved to the living room and stood over the girl. "Until we can find out who she is and why she wanted to see me, we should move her into the extra bedroom," Emma suggested.

"Agreed," Dora said.

Tim lifted the girl and moved her to the spare room. Dora and Emma pulled down the bedspread and sheets. Tim laid her down, and Emma and Dora slipped off her boots and loosened the top of her dress.

They looked at each other and Emma motioned to the door; they moved to the living room pulling the door closed so the girl could get some rest.

Emma saw Dora check the time, "You can rest if you need to. Jeremy and I'll keep watch," she said

"I could use a nap," her sister admitted.

Tim who was also looking a bit pale said, "I'll join you."

Jeremy and Emma settled on the vacated couch. He looked over at her teasingly and said, "I think there's more pastry."

She jumped up and he pulled her back; he wanted to get to the box first. He crossed the room to the box, she caught up quickly, laughing. He opened the box, "Wow, Dora brought more than bread and croissants." There was also decorative pastry; each had a label.

"I'm going try the eclairs," Emma said, reaching for the chocolate-covered pastry.

"I think I will, too," said Jeremy as he watched her take them from the box. He took the pastry Emma offered him, and they returned to the living room to sit down. As they bit into the pastry, the cream oozed out. "Yum!" she said.

"Definitely yum," he mumbled as he took another bite.

They ate slowly, enjoying the treat.

Jeremy finished his and wiped his mouth with a napkin. He looked at Emma, "What do you think about the girl? Why is she here?"

"Not much to think just now; though I do wonder where her companion is and where she was going in such a hurry last night."

"All questions that must wait until she awakens."

"Do we call the police?" she asked. They were in a foreign country and she didn't want to make any missteps.

"And report what? A girl shows up and collapses on our doorstep? No, no, I don't think so; at least not yet. Let's wait until she gets some rest and can talk to us."

"So, what do we do in the meantime?"

He reached past her and grabbed some books off the table. He tossed one to her and said, "Read."

She caught it and saluted him with it.

They relaxed and waited.

Several hours later, Tim and Dora woke and walked into the living room. "Has she stirred yet?" Dora asked with a wide yawn.

Emma glanced over to the door where the girl slept, "Not yet. We've checked on her, but there's been no movement. It may be hours yet."

Dora frowned. Emma noticed and said, "You don't have to

stay. We'll wait for her to wake up."

"Are you sure?" Dora looked worried; this was their vacation and she didn't want to say cooped up in the hotel.

"Yes. Do you have plans?"

"Well, yes," her sister answered hesitantly. She glanced at Tim and then back at Emma.

"With Lenora and Michael?" Emma guessed, squinting her eyes a bit. Jeremy glanced over sharply.

"Yes," Dora admitted.

Tim squirmed a bit but said, "There was a note waiting for us at the front desk this morning. We picked it up on our way in. They said they missed our company and would like to see us this afternoon."

"But what about what we saw?" Emma asked. There was also the added complication of Michael. *Why was he following me this morning? What did he want?* She still didn't know what it might mean. There was no reason to bring it up now and further antagonize Dora and Tim.

"We've been getting to know them. We know about their families. I know Michael is worried about Lenora's brother. I've told her about the loss of our mother. I want to ask them, to their faces. *What is going on?*" Dora wanted Emma to hear her out. She and Tim wanted to make the decision based on facts. Right now, they didn't have many.

"You're right. You know them better than we do," Emma conceded. She still had her concerns, thinking about Papa and Julian's conversation. "Where are you meeting them?"

"They want to meet at the Edison exhibit," Dora replied.

Again, thought Emma.

She saw Emma's look and said, "We'll be okay."

"I'd try to stay with other people. Don't be alone with them."

"We can do that," Tim said, thinking of the crowds at the exposition.

"Will you be leaving soon?" Emma asked.

"Yes, in a few minutes. Did you want us to get you some lunch before we go?" Dora asked, concerned that Emma and Jeremy wouldn't be able to leave the suite.

Emma moved her gaze to Jeremy's; he shook his head. She responded, "No I think we're okay. As long as one of us is here, we should be fine."

"As long as you're alright." started Dora.

"We are," she said firmly.

Dora and Tim got their jackets and hats and headed out to start their day at the exposition.

Jeremy and Emma watched as the door closed behind them. Jeremy turned a steady gaze to Emma, "Are you worried?"

"Yes, remember the run-in I mentioned?" she said.

Jeremy frowned, "You never did explain that."

"No, it was odd." She explained what had happened.

"What was he after?" Jeremy asked, confused.

"Who is what I'm wondering-me or Dora?"

"Why not tell them?" he asked.

"You heard them; they want the couple to tell them directly what they're involved in."

They sat in silence.

"We can't protect them from everything," Jeremy said finally.

"I know. I just don't normally have to worry about Dora. She's always so busy with the boarding house and family."

"Her only excitement is usually when we've included her in one of our cases. You know she has good instincts and Tim will always be with her," he reminded her.

"I know, you're right," she admitted.

They settled back down and waited, not only for the girl to wake up but also for Tim and Dora to return safely.

CHAPTER 10

*T*im and Dora walked down the hallway to the elevator. It was crowded with people heading to the same place they were. He inquired. "Stairs?"

"Yes, please." They found the door, descended quickly, and entered a crowded lobby.

"We should get lunch before we go over to the exposition," Tim suggested, anticipating the crowds.

They walked a few blocks, looking for an open café. They found one with outdoor seating.

"This is pretty," Dora commented, taking in the area around them.

He nodded and pulled her chair out for her. He sat and picked up the menu. "What would you like?" he asked. "Poulet?"

"Yes." She nodded. "Add carrots and a round bread."

The waiter came over and they ordered in broken French.

"Did we get the order right?" he asked as the waiter left.

"We'll see," she said with a smile. "I hate that Emma and Jeremy have to stay at the hotel,"

"Yes, who would have thought a girl would just show up at our door?"

Dora sent a side look to Tim. He laughed and said, "I know, I know. If a strange girl was going to show up anywhere, it would be at Emma and Jeremy's door. Those two are never short on adventure."

"I hope the girl will be okay," Dora said.

"Yeah, me too."

Their lunch was delivered; they viewed it happily and ate quickly.

Tim wiped his mouth and placed his napkin beside his empty plate. "That was good."

"It was," she said as she mimicked his movements.

He sat back, "I kind of missed seeing Michael and Lenora."

"Me, too," his wife admitted. "But Emma's right; we need to try not to be by ourselves, in case there *is* something to all of her observations."

"I'm hoping this is just a big misunderstanding. I like them," he said.

"Me, too."

Tim paid the bill, stood, and offered her his hand. She took it and stood. They walked outside and found a cab to take them to the exposition. "Where do we start?" he asked.

"They said the Edison exhibit."

"They really have an interest in the electricity exhibits. It seems we're always being pulled there."

"That's one of Jeremy and Emma's concerns," she murmured.

"That's true, but people have interests; maybe this is theirs," he commented.

"The exhibit is the talk of the exposition," she agreed.

They were quiet, listening to the rattle of the carriage as they made their way to their destination. She reached out and gripped his hand; he squeezed it back.

The carriage pulled up to the entrance, they got down, and headed to the science pavilion.

"Remind me of the location of the science pavilion?" he asked in exasperation.

"Just a moment," Dora said. They moved to the side to let other people pass and she pulled out the map. She pointed to the building to the right of them, "It's here."

"Okay, let's head that way," he said.

"Maybe we can get them to go to other areas. I heard there's a furniture area. I'd love to see it," Dora said hopefully.

"If not, we can break away from them and see it by ourselves." Tim asked, "Would you like that?"

"Yes, I would," she replied softly.

They headed toward the building.

As they entered, they looked around for the other couple. Dora saw that Tim was frowning and asked, "Is something wrong?"

"No, I just saw Lenora, she appeared to be upset."

"Where did you see her?" she asked, concerned for her friend.

"Over there." He motioned to the far wall with his hand. "Wait a minute. I see Michael. We can check with him."

"You do that. I'm going to see if I can find her."

"Okay."

He leaned down and gave her a brief kiss. She squeezed his hand and headed toward the wall where he had seen her. There was a door there, opened slightly. She reached her hand into it and opened it enough to go inside. "Lenora?" she called.

Dora heard a sound. She listened closely and called again, "Lenora!" When she got no response, she stepped into the dark room and headed toward the sound. Something caught her foot, and she fell to her knees. Picking herself up, she tried to find the lights. Before she could go too far, she felt something on her ankle again. She reached down and felt a hand.

"Oh my." The hand felt rough with calluses and seemed to

belong to a man. "Let me find a light." She tried to remember where the lights were during their tour. *The door*, she thought, and turned back, trying to avoid stepping on the man. She opened the door to bring in the outside light and found the switch. She flipped it and turned toward the person on the floor. It was Julian!

"*Julian!*" she called frantically and ran over to him. She knelt and realized he was bleeding from his chest. She put her hands on it to stop the flow of blood. "Hold on Julian, you'll be okay. I know you will."

She looked around desperately and said, "I need to get someone to help you."

His hand gripped hers and he said in a low voice, "Wait, Dora. I need to tell you something!"

She had to lean in to hear his low whisper.

"Bomb, Cervantes," With that, his eyes widened and he went limp.

"Julian! No! *No!*" Dora screamed, putting her bloodied hands on his face.

"You just had to leave him alive."

Dora went still as she heard a man's voice from the door. She removed her hands and sat back on her knees, stunned. It was Michael!

"He did die," Lenora said defensively, stepping from behind him. The look on her face was not one Dora had seen before. This was not the same woman she had gotten to know and called friend.

"But not soon enough," said Michael. "He was able to tell her something."

"Really? What did he tell you?" she asked Dora.

All that Dora could think was, *Bomb, he had said bomb and Cervantes.* Her eyes wide, she said nothing as she stared at them. The hand she absently raised to scratch her cheek left bloody streaks behind.

"She isn't going to answer. Instead of arguing with me, grab her!" Michael demanded.

Lenora did as she was told and took Dora by the arm, trying to haul her up.

Dora felt like she was swimming through the air.

At that moment, Tim walked in, "Dora, I couldn't find Michael..." He stopped when he saw Michael with a bloody Dora. "What happened? Are you okay?" He didn't notice Julian on the floor in his rush to Dora's side.

"Stop right there," Lenora demanded. She had a gun, and it was pointed at Tim.

He followed her direction and stopped just before he got to Dora. "I don't understand," Tim said, shaking his head as he tried to take in everything.

Tim's appearance helped pull Dora out of her fog. She spoke up and filled in some details. "Tim, they killed Julian. He's there on the floor."

His gaze followed her pointed hand and saw the body prone on the floor. "Julian?" he asked incredulously. Tim stared at the body, how had he missed that? He looked back at her. "Is that blood on you?"

"I'm not hurt," Dora said to him, knowing he was in the same fog she had just exited. "It's Julian's blood."

Tim had more questions and when he opened his mouth, Lenora snapped, "That's enough! We need to get out of here before he's found."

"A large part of this is your fault," Michael told her.

"My fault? How is this my fault?" Lenora demanded.

"Wasn't he supposed to be electrocuted?"

"It got complicated," she said. "I had no choice." She paused and studied Dora. "Clean her up. She's conspicuous."

Michael pulled out his handkerchief and roughly wiped Dora's face.

"Stop that!" Tim said. He stepped toward Dora, not wanting to see his wife get hurt.

"You can stop there," Lenora said pointing her gun at him. She said to Michael, without taking her gun off of the couple, "We need to go."

Michael looked helplessly at Dora's blood-soaked hands. Lenora got exasperated with him, "Dora, put your hands in your pockets." Dora did as she was told and continued to watch the two people who were their friends just hours ago.

"Let's go," Lenora said, waving her gun at them.

Tim didn't move, "Where's the guard? Why wasn't he at the door?"

"Oh, you don't have to worry about him," she said and glanced toward the wall. Tim's eyes followed hers and found the guard. He was slumped on the wall.

"Is he?" Tim asked.

"He is," she confirmed. She gazed at Michael and said smugly, "*He* was electrocuted."

Tim wanted to fight back and started to make a move. She grabbed his hand and shook her head, knowing what he was thinking.

Michael said to Tim, "I will kill her if you make any sudden moves."

Tim reluctantly nodded his head.

They left the area and took one of the many exits out of the exposition. The crowds made their movements harder, to control Tim they kept an arm around Dora, with a gun at her back. They had a carriage waiting for them. They climbed in and Tim sat next to Dora. "We're not heading toward the hotel," he muttered, watching the scenery go by.

"No," she said as they got further away from the exposition grounds.

When they arrived at their destination, they were told to get out.

They climbed down and entered what appeared to be a very large apartment building. Michael led them down the hall to an apartment on the first floor, with Lenora following closely behind. They entered a small room with a kitchen on the far wall. The furniture was older and was more patches than the original fabric. A small table and four chairs were in place near the kitchen.

"Wash up," she told Dora. Once her hands were clean, she ordered them, "Sit!" Lenora said, indicating the chairs around the table. They did as they were told, wondering how this was going to play out.

"Julian told me what you were planning to do," Dora told the duo boldly.

"You talked to him," Tim muttered.

"Just before he died," she muttered back.

"What did he say?" Lenora demanded.

"I know about the bomb."

Tim started at this statement. "Bomb? What bomb?"

"So, Julian got talkative, did he?" Lenora asked.

"Yes," said Dora, not sharing anything more.

"It's probably good that you know; that way, you don't accidentally share something you shouldn't."

"You don't think we're going to help you with this?" Tim asked incredulously.

"Yes, I do. At least until we have time to place the bomb," Lenora said.

"Why are you doing this? There must be a reason," said Dora.

Michael spoke up, "Electricity is dangerous and has no place in our society."

"You're one of those extremists against electricity?" Tim said. They didn't know these people at all. "Was it all fake? The family stories, the sharing?"

"We're not extremists!" Lenora shouted.

"Lenora," Michael cautioned.

She listened to him and said more calmly, "We're not extremists. Electricity kills; if a person touches it, they could die."

"Doesn't that make you a hypocrite?" Dora asked, "You killed two people in your effort to prove electricity is dangerous."

"I'll do what I have to. I'll prove that this technology cannot be utilized safely. And," she said, looking at them both, "you will both be active participants in our efforts."

"You can't make us do that," stated Dora.

"Really?" the other woman said, turning the gun on her.

"Do you want more deaths on your conscience?" Dora asked.

"Oh, I don't think I'll have to kill you, I have something else planned," Lenora pulled something out of her pocket. She held it up. It was a red ribbon and a lace hairpin.

Tim and Dora knew instantly what she was holding. "Lottie! You have Lottie!" Dora shouted. Tim wanted to respond in the same manner, but they had to hear more.

"I do and if you do not do what I want..." Lenora said, letting the words hang in the air.

"Where is she? Is she in Paris?" Tim asked in an oddly calm voice.

"She's in a safe location. That is all you need to know for now," stated Michael.

"Why us? Why involve us in this?" asked Dora desperately.

Lenora laughed a bit hysterically, "What better way than to have the great engineer's daughter help us take a closer look at how the security is set up around the electrical transformers?"

"Papa?" questioned Dora.

"Yes. Who else would have access to areas where regular people cannot go? You, as his daughter, can get access."

"We won't help you kill more people," Dora said, knowing she couldn't do what they asked.

"I think you will. In fact, I'm so sure you will that I'm letting you go back to the hotel," Lenore commented.

Michael said, "What!"

She explained, "They're going to find the bodies and we may need an alibi. You will provide that for us, in case there are any questions," Michael nodded, understanding her reasoning.

Emma, she thought. *We can get help with this.*

Lenora read her easily. "No, you won't tell Emma. You will follow our instructions to the letter or we'll have to do something we don't want to do," she said holding up the ribbon again, to remind her.

"Will you follow our direction?" asked Michael, ready to get them out of the apartment.

Tim knew the best thing for them was to agree. "We agree," he answered.

"But..." stuttered Dora, ready to speak up again.

"We agree," Tim commented again and looked her in the eyes.

Finally understanding, Dora said, "Yes, we agree."

"We'll transport you back to your hotel," Michael said.

"Don't bother," Tim said. "We'd rather walk."

Lenora reluctantly lowered the gun and didn't stop them from exiting the apartment. Once they were on the stoop, Dora looked at Tim, "Which way?" She hadn't paid attention on their way there.

"We need to head this way," he said, indicating the left. They walked for a while and stopped when they came to a park. "Would you like to go in?" he asked.

She nodded, keeping her head down, not saying anything. They went in and she started to cry uncontrollably. He guided her over to an empty bench near the fountains. As they sat, she continued to cry. With tears in his eyes. *Lottie*, he thought, hugging Dora tightly.

"Do they have her?" she asked.

"They showed us the ribbon and lace that Emma made her. Lottie kept it with her always," he said in a low voice.

That made her cry harder; his face was wet as he continued to hold her tightly. They sat there for a long time until, eventually, their tears dried up.

"We can't tell the family," Tim said wiping his eyes and pulling away from Dora.

"I know," she said miserably. "What are Lenora and Michael going to involve us in?"

"It appears to be murder. Maybe multiple murders."

"The bomb will kill more than a few people," she agreed. They both thought about how many people were attending the exposition.

"We can't just wait for them to tell us what to do," he said, thinking about how to move forward.

"No, no, you're right," she said and pulled out a tissue. She held it to her nose, "What are we going to do?"

That glimmer of determination reminded him of Emma when she had a new case. They were more alike than people realized. "I guess we ask what would Emma do?"

"Pull out her notebook and start making plans," Dora said, thinking of her sister.

"Well, we don't have one—let's think. What would be first on the list?"

"The hotel! They're staying at our hotel!"

"Yes, we can head there first."

"What do we do when we get there?"

"We need to get into their room and find some clues."

"What kind of things are we looking for?"

"I don't know," he admitted, moving his gaze from hers as he tried to hold his emotions together.

"Tim, we'll get through this," she said, taking his hand, tears filling her eyes again.

He didn't say anything but squeezed her hand. They couldn't just sit. Tim stood, "I think we need to head over now and get there before they can destroy anything that proves they're related to the murders in the transformer station."

"Could those be accidents and not on purpose?" She was grasping at straws. How could they have been so wrong about them? They were supposed to be their friends.

"Yesterday, if you'd asked me the same question, I'd have said no. But today, when I saw Lenora's face…" Tim said, his voice trailing off.

"I didn't recognize her at all," said Dora still dazed by it all.

"And even if the guard was an accident, Julian seemed very deliberate, they wanted to use him to prove a point."

"We still don't know what their relationship was with him and why he was the one they chose to show the dangers of electricity."

Tim nodded at her statement.

"You know," she said, thinking, "he might have been some type of investigator."

"He did remind me of Emma, the way he always had questions and turned up when least expected."

"We should go," she said finally.

Tim took Dora's hand in his and went to find a cab. They found one easily; there were many around to transport people to and from the exposition. They asked to go directly to the hotel. "Could you stop about a block away, please?" she asked the driver. "We should be carrying something. Some food, maybe flowers."

Tim nodded, "Props, to help with our story."

"Exactly," she said. "The patisserie I worked at this morning, let's run by there."

When they arrived, they climbed down, paid the driver, and went quickly to get croissants and baguettes. The florist was on their way back and they bought a bundle of flowers.

They carried their items, not saying anything, and headed

directly to the desk to try to get the room number. "Bonjour," the hotel clerk greeted.

"Bonjour," they responded.

Dora smiled, trying to put him at ease. "We're trying to locate our friends. They asked us to meet them at their room for a snack."

"Can you give me their names?" he asked and smiled back at her.

"Lenora and Michael Cervantes," she supplied.

"Yes, of course. Here it is," he said, pulling a card out of the file. "They're in room 412. It's up the elevator and to the right. I hope you enjoy your pastry."

"Thank you," she said, smiling at him again. They headed to the elevator and, once boarded, they stood quietly, not wanting to say anything in front of the elevator operator.

The doors opened and they headed to the right. Almost immediately, they saw the housekeepers in that area. They stepped back into the shadows to plan.

"What if they've already been to their room?" she asked worriedly.

Tim saw a maid enter the hallway from one of the rooms and he put his hand up to Dora's mouth. "Shh."

They watched quietly as the maids entered the next room to the right and left the cart in the hallway.

"Stay here," he said and slipped behind the cart to see what room they were working on. They appeared to have a few more still to clean before Lenora and Michael's.

He waved at her to walk to the room. He went back to the cart quickly and grabbed the keys, located on a hook. He took them and tossed them to her. She caught them deftly, opened the door, and tossed them back. She went inside and Tim immediately came in behind her. He put out the privacy sign and shut the door softly behind them.

"What would Emma look for..." Dora muttered to herself, taking in the room. "Trash," she said, spotting it.

Tim continued to study the room for letters and anything paper. "The desk," he said He went over to it and started opening the drawers.

Dora directed, "Okay, let's start there; I'll get the trash." She dumped the trash quickly on the floor. "Well, they've been eating a lot of chocolates," she said as she pushed the wrappers out of the way. "What is this? A brochure?" she murmured. She unfolded it. "Ah-ha!"

"What is it? Did you find something?" Tim asked. He dropped the papers he was holding and walked over to her.

"Remember the anti-electrical people Julian mentioned to Emma and Jeremy?" she asked, holding up the cartoon.

"Yes, I remember. We heard about them—are they part of that group?"

"This's why they wanted us here. You heard them earlier."

"You think they paid for this trip?" asked Tim.

"It makes sense. *IF* they took Lottie, she's the leverage to get us to do what they want. The papers on the desk—anything there?" Dora asked.

Tim went back and pulled out a letter he had found. He said, "Just this. It mentions... a woman named Janna who is holding something for them."

"Could it be?" she asked, excited to have found something.

"Let's not get our hopes up," he cautioned.

She walked over to him, "Does it give a location or a return address?"

"Yes, in the 3rd Arrondissement."

"So, we go there next and talk to this Janna."

"Just like that?" he asked, "You think it will be that easy?"

"No. I don't think it will be that easy, but it may help us figure out what her role is and if she has Lottie. Tim, what if she does?" she asked, reaching out a shaking hand toward him.

He took it, "I don't know. But if Lottie is there, we'll get her back."

"If not?" Tears welled in her eyes.

"Then we continue investigating. And in the meantime, we do as they ask."

"We can't allow anyone to get hurt because of us!"

"NO!" he lowered his voice and said, "No, of course not. We have some time to figure this out. If you'd like to go back to our room while I go over..."

She interrupted, her tone firm. "Tim, I'm coming with you."

He smiled, "I wouldn't have it any other way." He pulled Dora into his arms and gave her a long slow kiss. As they parted, he offered her his hand and she took it. They walked together to the door and picked up the flowers and pastries on the way. He held up his other hand, slowly opened the door, and stuck out his head. He pulled back in and said in a low voice, "The maids haven't finished the room next door yet."

She nodded and removed the privacy sign as they slipped out and locked the door behind them. They walked casually down the hall, back to the elevator, and pushed the call button.

It arrived and, when it opened, they were surprised to see Jeremy standing there.

As they boarded, he asked, "Hey, are you back from the exposition already? We weren't expecting you until much later."

They avoided his eyes and Tim replied, "No, we need to do a few more things today. We aren't coming back to the room just now."

Jeremy frowned, "Why were you on this floor? Did you get off in the wrong location?"

"No, no, we wanted to go to Lenora and Michael's room," Tim said truthfully. He just didn't mention they weren't there when they went in.

It was their turn to ask the questions. "Are you going downstairs?" Tim asked.

"Yes, I need to get a few things."

"How is the girl?" Dora asked, finding her voice. She wanted so badly to tell him what might be happening to Lottie. He and Emma could figure this out faster than them. Not thinking she took a step toward Jeremy. Tim intercepted her and pulled her to him.

"She woke briefly and told us her name and her room number. I'm going to get her clothes and things."

"Good idea. She'll want those when she fully wakes," Dora said softly.

The conversation stopped when the doors opened. They entered the lobby, and Jeremy turned to them both.

"Is everything okay?" he asked.

"Of course. Why wouldn't it be," Tim replied.

"I don't know. Something seems to be up with you two."

"We're fine," Dora said.

Jeremy wanted to push the issue but instead said, "You know if something's wrong, you can tell me and Emma."

"We know that," Dora assured him not looking into Jeremy's eyes. She felt that if he saw her eyes, he would know what was going on. If that happened, he would want to involve Emma and himself, go against the directions they were given.

Jeremy finally decided they weren't going to tell him what was going on. "Okay," he said. "We'll see you later." He headed to the desk.

They waved and headed outside. Tim pulled her to the side of the building. He took the flowers and food from her hands and threw them in a trash can. "You were going to tell him," he accused her.

"I wanted to," she admitted, staring down at her hands now empty hands. She clinched them tight.

He saw her anger had overridden her worry, but he had to make her see reason. He tilted her head up to him. "I'd like to tell them also, and I'd like to go to the police and let them handle this. But this is not something we can get help with. *WE* have to do this on our own, for Lottie," he stressed.

She was quiet for a long time, thinking about everything. She'd been thinking about herself and not Lottie. "You're right. I'm glad you stopped me. We need to do this on our own, for Lottie."

He pulled her to him in a tight hug. They slowly moved apart, knowing they must take the next steps. She asked, "What's the plan?"

"We don't go straight there. We investigate the area first."

She nodded and they walked to a nearby cab and asked to be taken to the address Tim had found. The carriage ride was tense and they huddled together. When they arrived, he helped her out after they paid the driver. They hadn't been in this arrondissement before. It had older buildings and stone roads. They walked around the building they were investigating. Dora commented, "It's a church."

"Or a school," said Tim, watching a group of children come down the stairs.

"Well, do we go in and ask for Janna?" inquired Dora. He nodded. She was apprehensive but followed his lead.

They made their way up the stairs, and Tim pulled the large, heavy double door open. They entered an area that had many closed doors. "Where do we start?"

As they were walking by, a young girl came out of one of the doors and Dora took a chance and asked, "Are you, Janna?"

"Yes, can I help you?" Suddenly, a baby crying could be heard from the room she had exited. "Tim!" Dora exclaimed.

He ran to the door and in the direction of the crying.

Janna looked wildly to the left and right and ran off. Dora ran after her. She chased her down small hallways and into a larger room. Dora stopped and realized the woman had just disappeared. *Where did she go?*

"Dora!" Tim called. "Where are you?"

"I'm here!" she called back. She ran back to him and asked, "Did you find her? Was it Lottie?"

He was angry and frustrated, "There were children, but Lottie wasn't one of them. Were you able to talk to Janna?"

"No, she just disappeared. This place is a maze," she said, observing the stone walls and many doors.

"We need to find an administrator; there must be someone in charge here," he insisted.

"Let's go to the sanctuary," she said. They went toward the large doors surrounded by glass. She peered in and said, "This must be it." The pews were still in place and the altar was set for services.

Tim pulled the door open and held it for her to enter. "That must be the man in charge," he said, indicating a man in a black suit with a white collar. The man raised his hand and walked toward them.

"Bonjour," they said as he neared.

He held out his hand toward them and said, "Bonjour, comment puis-je vous aider?" *Hello, how may I help you?*

Tim held out his hands to take hers and said, "Jes suis Dora et Tim Flannigan."

"I understand English, if it's easier for you. I am Pastor Franc," he said in a kindly manner as he released Tim's hand and took Dora's.

"Thank you. We have something important and private to discuss with you," said Tim in a firm voice.

"Let us go over to a quieter area." He indicated the alcove by the sanctuary. They nodded and followed him.

They entered a more enclosed space. He turned up the gas lights and asked them to sit on the low wooden benches. "Pastor, what is this place? A church, a school?" asked Dora, wanting to put him at ease.

"It's sometimes a church, a school, or whatever the community needs."

"You have employees working here?" asked Tim.

"Volunteers," he supplied. "We don't have a large operating budget; we make do with what we can."

Tim finally asked the one question they wanted answered. "Is a young woman named Janna one of your employees?"

That question seemed to give him pain. He stood and seemed to be saying a prayer before answering.

"You know her," stated Dora, her voice soft but accusing.

"I do. She's my daughter. What is she involved in?" They could hear the implied "now" at the end of the sentence. It was apparent this wasn't the first time he'd had this conversation.

"We believe she's part of an abduction of our small daughter," Tim said bluntly.

He frowned. "You're from America?" he asked.

"Yes," Dora answered.

"Did you bring your child here with you?" He seemed to be trying to put the pieces together.

"No, she was taken in Chicago."

The pastor shook his head, "Janna hasn't been out of Paris in a few months. Are you sure she's involved?"

"We think she's involved with a couple, Lenora and Michael Cervantes. They're American."

"I do not know those names. Can you describe them to me?" Janna's father asked, trying to help.

Dora started. "Michael's about this tall." She used Tim to measure, putting her hand on his shoulders. "He has lost most of his hair."

Tim interrupted. "There's still some in the back, dark brown," he supplied. "And I believe he's in his late thirties. He has some weight around his middle. She's about the same age."

Dora stated, "Lenora has reddish-blond hair."

That last part seemed to spark something in him. "Yes, they're familiar. I've seen them here, but they have not been introduced to me."

"When did you see them last?" asked Tim expectantly.

"Yesterday," the other man admitted. "They were speaking with Janna and they seemed upset with her."

"Do you know all of the children in school here?" Tim asked.

"We have so many," he said regretfully. "My daughter runs the program."

"Is there anyone who helps her, someone who might know the children brought here?" Dora asked, trying to be hopeful.

"Yes, Marcella. Would you like to meet her now?"

"Yes, please," Dora answered for them.

"What are you thinking?" Tim asked in a low voice as they followed the man.

"I'm thinking I can give them a sketch of Lottie and see if they've seen her. We need to know if she's in Paris."

They followed him to the room Janna had come out of. It was a long, narrow hallway with several doors to the left and right. The pastor pulled open the door and a young woman in the room screamed and pointed at Tim.

"Du calm. Leur enfant est porté disparu et Janna pourrait être impliquée," the pastor said with a raised voice.

"Non non, elle ne ferait jamais de mal à un enfant." She shook her head to prove the point.

The pastor turned back to Tim and Dora. "What is the child's name?"

"Lottie," they supplied together.

"Son nom est Lottie et elle a les cheveux blonds rougeâtres."

She started to wring her hands and said, in fast French, "Janna a mentionné son nom. monsieur je ne l'ai jamais vue, je vous le promets."

He told them, "She has heard the name from Janna, but there hasn't been a child brought here."

"I don't know whether to be relieved or more worried," Tim muttered to Dora.

"Do you have some paper? I'd like to give you a drawing of

Lottie. That way, if you may have seen her but they called her by another name," said Dora.

The pastor left them and returned with some paper and a pencil and handed them to her.

Tim looked around for a place for her to sketch. He saw a small table and chair and said, "Over here." She sat in the chair he pulled out and began sketching quickly on the paper. Within a few moments, she finished. She held it for a moment, fighting tears. *My baby.*

"Dora?" Tim prompted softly.

"Yes," she said, "here it is." She handed it to him.

He didn't look at it, he needed a clear head. He handed the drawing to Marcella. "Could you ask her if she's seen this child? It would mean so much to us."

She nodded, albeit reluctantly, and took the paper. She examined it. "Non! Je ne l'ai pas vue! Cet enfant n'est pas venu ici."

The pastor interpreted. "She has not seen her. This child has not been here."

Dora responded to this by taking Tim's hand in hers and asked the pastor, "Can you ask if she knows the couple?"

He looked at Marcella and asked, "Êtes-vous là où elle pourrait être?"

Her eyes were cast down and didn't respond.

The pastor eyed her sternly. "Vous devez me dire!"

"She'll have gone to a building, in the arrondissement—that is where they meet," she admitted in halting English.

"How do you know?" Tim asked.

"I was there once," Marcella said.

"Have you been back?" Janna's father asked.

"No, they are too revolutionary for me. I don't understand why they're so against new things."

"What types of new things?" asked Dora.

"Electricity."

Tim and Dora looked at one another. It was bigger than they'd thought. How many people were involved?

"Where do they meet?" Tim asked.

She answered, "In a basement at St. Thomas Place." She gave them the address.

They immediately turned, planning to go straight there. Janna's voice stopped them.

"They will not be there now," she said slowly.

"When will they be there?" Dora inquired rather desperately, her patience evaporating with every moment they believed Lottie was in danger.

"They meet tomorrow at 9PM."

Tim said to the Pastor, "We need to ask you not to say anything to them. It might jeopardize our daughter's life."

"We'll honor your request and I'll find Janna and question her."

Tim gave them their hotel to contact them with any further information.

"Thank you," Tim said.

They headed out and Dora said, "Oh, Tim, we still don't know anything."

"We have a lead, and we'll go to that meeting tomorrow," he promised.

"What if they see us?"

"I am not sure," he admitted. "It is our only lead."

CHAPTER 11

BACK AT THE HOTEL—PATRICE

a few hours had passed when Jeremy and Emma heard something coming from the room where the mysterious girl slept. Jeremy glanced at Emma, "Finally," he said. She stood and walked with him to the bedroom door. He knocked lightly and pushed it open.

They found the girl sitting up on the bed. Her eyes widened when she saw Emma and Jeremy enter the room. "It appears that she may stay awake this time," commented Jeremy wryly. The previous time she had awakened, she had only said Emma's name again before losing consciousness.

Before they realized what the girl was doing, she had thrown off the covers and ran toward Emma. Jeremy started to react, but Emma held up her hand to stop him. She caught the running girl in her arms and held her tight. "You wanted to see me?" she asked.

"You have to help me!" the girl said frantically.

Emma held her for a moment, then pushed her back, "Why don't we move into the living room, sit down, and you can tell me what you need help with."

That seemed to calm the girl, and she followed Emma into

the living room. She continued to hold Emma's hand in a tight grip.

The three sat. Emma held onto her hand, "What's your name?"

"Patrice Lanier, my mum is Catherine Lanier."

"You know my name," said Emma, "and this is Jeremy."

Jeremy leaned toward them and asked the first question, "Why did you come to our room?"

"For Emma," Patrice said, looking at Emma beseechingly. "I was told you were a brilliant detective, and I need someone to help me find my mother."

"Your mother? Was she the woman who accompanied you at check-in?" Emma asked.

"Yes." That confirmed Emma's guess.

"And you said she's missing? When did you see her last?" Jeremy asked.

"Last night. She got sick and I went down to the lobby to get a doctor."

"Was that where you were in such a rush too early this morning?" Emma asked.

"Yes, the man at the desk gave me an address to go get the doctor," she explained.

Emma frowned and moved her gaze back to Patrice. "The doctor should have been at the hotel. It's strange they asked you to go get him."

"Was he at the address you were given?" asked Jeremy.

"No, that was odd also. When I finally arrived at the address, there was no one there."

"What did you do then?" Emma asked, already caught up in the story.

"I came back, and I went to the desk to find out if I had the wrong address," Patrice explained.

"What happened then?" Emma asked.

"The man at the desk was different than the one who gave

me the information about the doctor. The question seemed to confuse him and he said the doctor could be available from his room at the hotel. He said there was no outside doctor."

"And?" Emma prompted when the girl went quiet.

Patrice pulled her hands out of Emma's and started to wring them. "They sent someone for him and we headed upstairs. When we got to mum's room, it was locked."

"Where was your key?" Jeremy asked. He already knew part of this story. When he went down to get the girl's clothes, the desk clerk said she did not have a room there. He had hoped it was because the room was under the mother's name.

"I had it with me; it didn't work. We tried it several times. We also knocked, but Mama didn't come to the door."

"Was it the right room?" Emma asked, thinking Patrice had been so tired that she went to the wrong room.

She frowned. "So much of last night ran together, I thought the same thing. We went back downstairs and told the clerk. He checked for our room and he said I didn't have one in that hotel."

"No room?" Emma murmured. *Is this girl just confused and lost or is there a mystery to be solved?* "Jeremy, could you go inquire at the desk?"

"I can do that," Jeremy said and stood. "Could I talk to you for a second?" he asked Emma.

"I'll be right back. Will you be okay?" Emma asked Patrice.

Patrice was uncertain but said in a shaking voice, "Yes."

Emma nodded and stood to follow him to the door.

"Is she at the right hotel?" he asked. "Her story sounds incredulous."

Emma commented, "She was in line for a room with her companion when I saw her last night."

"They're very crowded," he murmured. "I hope it's just a mix-up. I'll also notify the doctor she's awake."

"Good idea," she replied. She watched him leave and closed the door behind him.

She returned to the living room and stood in front of Patrice. "Would you like something to drink and a pastry?"

Patrice nodded.

"Stay here. I'll bring it to you."

She returned with the pastry and some water.

Patrice ate the offered pastry, and Emma was relieved to see her cheeks showing a rosy glow.

CHAPTER 12

$\mathcal{J}$eremy headed down the stairs and exited into the lobby. The check-in line was long, as usual, and he avoided it and went to the far side of the desk. A young man walked up and asked, "Bonjour, may I help you?"

"Bonjour. Yes, can I speak to the manager, please?"

The clerk studied him, "Yes, Monsieur. I'll get him for you." He waved for another clerk to take his spot at the desk. He spoke in a low voice to him and headed into the back room.

Moments later, another man accompanied him out of the back room and went directly to Jeremy. He was older and appeared to be a senior member of the staff. "Bonjour," he greeted.

"Bonjour," Jeremy responded.

"Monsieur?" The manager asked.

"Tilden."

"Monsieur Tilden, you wish to talk to me?"

"Yes, I wanted to ask you about a guest."

"My answer will depend on what information you're requesting," he explained.

Jeremy nodded, understanding his limitations. "Of course.

Her name is Patrice Lanier and her mother's name is Catherine Lanier."

The manager frowned and turned to the young man next to him, "Isn't that the young woman who said she has a room?"

The young man answered, "Yes, first she accused me of sending her to the wrong doctor then she demanded we take her to her mother."

"What was your response?" asked Jeremy.

He looked over at his manager, who nodded for him to answer. "I asked her for the room number and accompanied her there."

"What did you find?"

"An empty room and no mother," the clerk replied. "When it appeared that her mother wasn't in the room, I couldn't calm her down. She kept insisting that I had done something to her mother. I had planned to call the police if she didn't leave the hotel."

He asked, "Can I see your book from that night?"

The manager answered that question, "Of course, follow me."

He and Jeremy walked over to where people were checking in and the manager retrieved a large book. He placed it in front of Jeremy and flipped the pages until he found Monday night. He turned the book toward Jeremy and showed him. "She isn't listed. Neither of them is in the book."

The young clerk who had stood nearby spoke up, "That is what I told her."

"I understood Miss Lanier had two rooms. Both singles," Jeremy said.

"That is what she said."

"What about *her* room?"

"It was also empty," the young clerk confirmed.

Jeremy thought about that, "Could you check and see when the current people moved in?" he requested

"Yes." The manager turned the book back to himself and checked. "Those rooms were taken that next morning."

"Okay, thank you."

"Monsieur, will you make sure she doesn't cause concern in our lobby again? It was very disruptive."

Jeremy understood the man's dilemma; this was a very nice hotel. "I think we can manage that. Can we have the doctor sent to our room?" He confirmed his room number and headed back upstairs He opened the door and saw Patrice. "Feeling better?" he asked her.

"Somewhat," she commented quietly, afraid to ask what he had found out.

"I contacted the doctor to come up."

"For what reason?" Patrice asked, losing the color that had finally entered her face.

Emma reached over to her, "Your health must be considered. We can't find your mother if you're not able to participate. Do you understand?"

Patrice frowned; her experience with doctors at that facility had not been a pleasant one, but she understood their reasoning. "I'll see him."

A little while later, there was a knock on the door. Jeremy went to answer it and brought the same doctor who had attended her earlier into the room. His face was cheerful. "It's nice to see you awake, young lady," he said, looking at Patrice.

"Yes," Emma said, answering for the girl.

Patrice asked in a confused manner, "Who are you?"

"I'm the doctor," he explained kindly.

She frowned and shook her head vehemently. "You weren't there when I went to get you last night. I drove a long way to find you."

"Why would you have gone somewhere other than the hotel to get me?"

"No, that can't be right," Patrice muttered, sounding more confused.

The doctor commented, "I need to examine you."

"You won't leave me, will you?" Patrice said as she grabbed Emma's hand and held it tightly.

Emma patted it and reassured her. "I will stay with you. Why don't you let the doctor examine you?"

The girl nodded and quieted down. Emma looked around, "Why don't we move to your room?"

The doctor said, "Yes, of course. I'll follow you."

They moved to Patrice's room to begin the examination.

Jeremy remained in the living room and was reading when Emma and the doctor came out of Patrice's room.

"Is she doing all right?" he asked.

The doctor answered, his tone grim. "Yes. She needs rest and food and, hopefully, some of her confusion should be reduced."

Jeremy asked, "That is good right?"

The doctor answered him, his tone serious, "The confusion concerns me. What is this about her room not being hers and her mother being missing?"

"We're investigating," Emma answered "We don't know what's happened, though I did see someone with her that first day,"

"If your investigation does not turn up anything or if her confusion gets worse, you will need to notify me. We may need to have her hospitalized."

They both nodded, understanding what he meant.

"Thank you, doctor. Can I see you out?" Emma asked.

"No, thank you. I've been here enough, I think I can find my way out," he said and left their suite.

"Why don't we go check on Patrice? Then we can discuss what I found out," suggested Jeremy.

Emma nodded and accompanied him to Patrice's door. They

knocked lightly and pushed it open. They saw her taking something.

"Patrice! What are you taking!" Jeremy exclaimed.

"Pills," the girl said, swallowing the ones in her mouth.

"Where did you get those?" Emma asked, running over and taking the remainder from her.

Patrice frowned at them, "I got them here in my room."

"From the doctor?"

"No, it was the little ghost. He said I must take them."

Little ghost? Emma looked at Jeremy and he shook his head.

CHAPTER 13

*T*im and Dora returned to their hotel, feeling quite down at the events of the day. The loss of new friends, the suggestion of a bomb, threats on their lives, and finally Lottie.

They stood pensive outside their hotel door, not wanting to go in. The idea of hiding something from Emma and Jeremy was so foreign that it was making Dora physically ill.

Tim frowned, watching her lean against the wall, looking pale and unhappy. "We have to go in."

"Yes," she said softly. "Would Jeremy and Emma have seen something we didn't? Could they have figured out their attitude on the steamer and prevented the deaths that have occurred?"

"I was thinking about that, the way they avoided her and Jeremy. They seemed to know they couldn't let them get close or they'd be exposed." He started at the door and said again, "We need to go in. Can you manage?"

She straightened and said bitterly, "You mean lie." She thought of Lottie and took a deep, stabling breath.

"Ready?" he asked, not commenting on her statement.

"Ready."

They walked in, still so wrapped up in their own problems that they had forgotten about the girl who had shown up in their room that morning. Emma and Jeremy had been dealing with it on their own.

The girl they had only seen unconscious was walking around the room at a brisk pace and talking. "And then we came here," they heard her say.

Emma saw them in the doorway and called, "Come in, please."

They looked questioningly at the girl, who continued to talk and seemed manic. Emma ignored her and asked them, "How was the exposition?" She was eager to hear about what was happening outside the room.

"Emma, what's up with her?" asked Dora, watching the girl continue to pace and hold conversations no one was listening to.

"She took some pills someone gave her last night. I got her to purge them, but some managed to get into her system. We're just trying to keep her company until it wears off."

"She's talking. Is it important?"

Jeremy walked in with a glass of wine for Emma and sat down. He informed Dora and Tim, "This is all stuff we have heard a dozen or more times. She's stuck on a repeat of the scenario. We're hoping we can move forward again once she winds down."

Emma wanted to talk about the exposition, "Did you get to see the phonographic demonstration?"

"No, we didn't stay in the Gallery of Machines very long today," Dora said truthfully.

Emma's eyes widened in surprise. "Oh, did you go some-where else?" she asked, glancing over at Patrice. She pulled her attention away from the talkative girl, who continued to pace and focused on Dora. She noticed Dora didn't look right—her face was pale; her eyes had the appearance of crying. "Is something wrong?" she asked, walking over to her sister.

"No," Dora answered quickly, holding shaky hands to her pale cheeks. "It's just all the people and sites. I got overwhelmed."

Tim thought this would be the best time to leave and go to their room. He took Dora's hand and started leading her away, "She needs to rest," he said. He needed to get her away from Emma's prying eyes. He didn't know how long Dora would hold up to her questions. They had always been extremely close and their feelings could be read easily from one to the other.

"Can we talk later?" asked Dora as she was led away.

"Of course," Emma said, watching them disappear into their room. She glanced over at Jeremy, "What's happening there?"

He looked toward the door speculatively recalling the talk he had had with Dora and Tim earlier, "I don't know, but I think we need to watch them."

A knock on the door distracted them. Jeremy went to the door and was relieved when he saw who it was. "Doctor, thank you for returning." He had been unavailable when they tried to contact him earlier.

"Has anything changed?" he asked, entering the room.

"You could say that," said Jeremy in a lightly sarcastic voice, indicating the still agitated Patrice with his head.

The doctor followed his direction and saw the girl he had examined earlier was definitely more animated. He walked over to her and had to take her by the arm to stop her from moving about the room. "My dear, can we go back to your room?"

Emma walked over, "Yes, let's go let the doctor have a look at you."

"But," Patrice began rapidly, "my mum is still missing and I need your help."

"Yes," said Emma soothingly, "I know. And we'll find her, but we have to take care of you first."

Jeremy watched as Emma and the doctor accompanied Patrice back to her room and shut the door.

Emma watched as the doctor checked Patrice's eyes and heartbeat. He finished his examination. "Have you taken anything?" he asked her.

"No, I don't think so," she answered and started talking about her mother again.

Emma answered for her. "Yes, we found her taking these pills after you left. She said a small ghost gave them to her last night."

"Did this reaction start at that time?"

"What reaction? I'm fine," Patrice muttered and tried to stand up.

"No, you're different than the last time I saw you. Your hands and arms have tremors and your eyes are dilated," stated the doctor, holding her by the wrist.

"I don't know what you're talking about," she said defensively. "I took the pills, but first I took the drinking potion."

"What drinking potion?" the doctor and Emma asked at the same time.

"I was asleep, and I had a dream about a boy in my room, here."

"You're talking about the little ghost you mentioned earlier," Emma said, frowning. "What did he do?"

"He says I must drink this drink. He said he was a ghost," she said to Emma.

"Did you take the drink?"

"He said I had to. I didn't feel I had a choice."

"How did you feel after the dream?" asked the doctor.

"So sleepy," she said and started to get agitated again. "Then I woke."

"Was he still there?"

"No—he was a dream."

"Was he, though?" asked Emma, doubt clear in her voice.

"I'm not so sure." Wondering about this, she stood and directed, "You stay here with the doctor."

She made her way to the door and into the living room.

"Is she okay? Can he tell what happened to her?" Jeremy asked.

Emma continued to search the room. She finally located, what she needed – an umbrella.

He frowned at it and glanced toward the window. It was a clear day. "Uhm, are you planning on going somewhere?"

"Maybe," she admitted. "Can you join me in Patrice's room?"

He continued to frown at her statement, but he followed her into the room. "We haven't spent much time in here," he commented.

Emma motioned to the doctor and Patrice. "Can you go into the living room for a moment?"

The doctor was curious but he understood his job was to care for Patrice. She was animated again and was easily led out.

"You know we didn't pick our rooms; we didn't get an option," commented Emma, thinking of the day they arrived.

"That's true," Jeremy said and looked around. "They took us directly to the rooms—we didn't question that at the time. They didn't mention this room, except to say it was extra space. Do you think something was planned about Patrice being here?" he asked.

"I'm beginning to think so. This whole thing seems planned. Her showing up on our doorstep, this empty room."

He questioned the umbrella, "Are we looking for hollow spaces?" In a previous case, she had used one to find a hidden compartment in wood flooring. It guided them to a key piece of evidence that helped close a case they were working on.

"Yes, I was examining the room and saw that the size is smaller than ours." Jeremy left the bedroom and stepped out the distance between the rooms. He came back into the room. "I think it's on the left side," he said.

She walked over to the wall and used the base of the umbrella to tap across it. She listened for any changes in tone. About five feet in, she found what she was looking for—a hollow-sounding spot. "Here," she called to Jeremy.

They ran their fingers over the wall, feeling for the seam. "I know it's here," said Emma.

"Wait, I know what we can do," he said and left the room again. Emma waited and Jeremy came back in with a cigar.

"Is this the best time to be smoking?" Emma joked. Watching him light up, she had an idea of what he was thinking. If there was any air movement behind that wall, the smoke's movement would show it. He puffed and blew on the part of the wall they were suspicious of. Within moments and a few more draws on the cigar, they found the opening. "We need something to pry it open," Jeremy said, laying the cigar down on a plate.

"I have just the thing." Emma exited and returned with her long knife. It was something she kept with her always. She inserted it into the location where the smoke had been dissipated and pulled back. The knife was strong enough not to bend and created an opening where they could insert their fingers. They both pulled and the door opened, revealing a staircase.

"Ah-ha," said Emma.

"Hmm," murmured Jeremy, looking into it.

Emma started into the dark space. Jeremy halted her, "I know you love an adventure, but we need some preparation first. We don't know to where or to whom this will lead."

She paused, the temptation of the mystery pulling at her. "Do you think…"

"I think we should wait. We need to check with the doctor to confirm what those pills are."

"You're right," she said, absently staring at the space.

He decided to close it, removing the temptation for her.

She turned to him and smiled suddenly. He returned the smile, "Soon."

"I'll hold you to that." She gave him a quick kiss.

He took her hand and headed into the living room. "I know you will. Now, I need to get a book. We'll probably be here a while." He went directly to their room.

Emma looked around and noticed it was empty; the doctor and Patrice were missing.

"Dammit!"

"What is it?" he asked as he returned, reading his book as he walked.

"She left."

That caused him to look up, "But where could they have gone?"

"Check with Tim and Dora. I'll check the hallway. Maybe they're just walking."

She ran down the hallway, checked the elevator, and then used the stairs to run down to the lobby. Quickly, she glanced around the crowded room. There was no sign of Patrice. Pushing at people, she made her way through the crowds. *She isn't here,* she thought, turning in a circle. She saw the door and thought, *Outside!* She went to the door and spoke to the man working there. "Bonjour."

"Bonjour."

"Avez-vous vu une jeune fille? Cheveux bouclés foncés, le long de ses épaules et vêtue d'une robe rose?" *Have you seen a young girl? Dark curly hair, down around her shoulders, and wearing a pink dress?*

"Je suis désolé mais il y a eu trop de gens par moi pour identifier une fille. Si vous voulez bien m'excuser." *I'm sorry but there have been too many people by me to identify one girl. If you will excuse me.* He stepped away to get a carriage for a group of people.

She had disappeared. *What do I do?* Emma felt lost for a moment. *My team, I need my family.* She headed back upstairs.

She pulled the door open and saw Tim, Dora, Jeremy, and surprisingly, the doctor.

They looked at her expectantly. "I couldn't find her," She said, "I checked the stairs, the lobby, and questioned the doorman. She's gone." She turned her wrath and frustration on the doctor. "Where were you? Weren't you supposed to stay with her?"

"Emma!" Dora scolded her.

The doctor replied, not upset at the demand. "No, it's okay. I can explain. I got Patrice settled on the couch and she was resting. Tim came out and asked if I could take a look at Dora."

"Dora! Is something wrong with you?" Emma asked, immediately contrite at her attitude.

"It's just my nerves," said Dora honestly. "Too much has been going on today."

"Yes," Emma agreed, thinking Patrice was on all of their minds, not aware that Tim and Dora's were on Lottie.

"Doctor," said Emma in a calmer tone, "you said she was settled when you went to check on Dora?"

"Yes, and her anxiety was reduced. She had stopped talking and her eyes seemed less dilated."

"That's good," Emma said, somewhat relieved. At least she may have had a clearer mind when she left them.

"What's causing the mania and then the intense sleeping?" asked Jeremy, still wondering about their temporary guest's behavior.

"Could you show me the pills she took?" the doctor requested.

"I have some here," Emma said and unfolded the cloth she had put in her pocket. "Can you identify them?"

The doctor looked at them with a frown and picked up one. He pulled out his knife and scraped at it, putting the edge of it in his mouth for a small taste. Instead of answering her, he asked, "She mentioned someone was giving her a liquid that made her sleep?"

"Yes," Jeremy replied.

"The pills are cocaine," the doctor said.

"That's medication, isn't it?" asked Emma.

"I don't use it for my patients. I find there are features to the drug that can have terrible side effects. I saw those in Patrice's behavior."

"And the other? The liquid?" Jeremy asked.

"That sounds like laudanum," the doctor commented. "She had the normal symptoms for a too-high dosage."

"Does she look like a long-term user of cocaine? There are rumors the drug is addictive," said Emma.

"No, I didn't see any indication of that."

"Someone is trying to keep Patrice off-kilter, both high and low," Emma observed.

"Yes, I think so." He checked his watch and said, "I do need to go now."

"Doctor, I'll walk you out," Emma said. When they reached the door, she put a hand on his arm, and, when he turned toward her, she said, "I want to apologize for my rudeness. I should have waited for you to tell me."

"You were concerned and thought I had been negligent in my duties," he said, looking into her eyes.

She had the grace to blush red. "Again, I apologize."

"Call me if she returns. I'd like to monitor the behavior changes."

"Thank you," she said and closed the door behind him, then leaned on it. She pushed herself off the door and headed back in.

"Where could she have gone?" she asked, exasperated.

Jeremy sank down on the couch, "I don't know, and I'm not sure she wasn't just out of her head."

"Do we look for her?" she asked, sitting next to him and

putting her head on his shoulder.

"She knows where we are. If she decides she needs our help, she'll be back."

"Until then?"

"We're in Paris. I think we should go out and see it."

"I agree," she said, though she didn't move away from him.

Tim stepped out of the bedroom and shut the door softly behind him.

"Is Dora okay?" asked Emma.

"Just too much excitement. No sign of Patrice?" he asked as he looked around.

"No," said Emma shortly.

Tim frowned. "She just left?"

"We think so," Jeremy replied.

"What are the plans? Will you go after her?"

"Where would we start?" commented Jeremy. "We don't know her or Paris well enough to find her."

"Yeah," said Tim. "If you aren't going after her, what are your plans?"

"We're going out," said Emma definitively.

"And if she comes back? What do we do?" Tim asked, not wanting another worry. Dora was not handling the stress well.

"She isn't our prisoner. If she wants help, then she can stay," indicated Jeremy.

"All right," Tim said slowly.

"Tim," said Emma, "Patrice isn't your concern. Don't stay here on the chance she'll return."

He looked conflicted.

"Can you promise me?" she asked.

"Yes, I can," he said, somewhat relieved at being told he didn't need to help out.

They got up from the sofa and retrieved their coat and hats. Emma paused, taking Jeremy by the arm. She turned toward

Tim, "Tim, is there something you want to tell me?" Instinct made her ask.

Tim went as still as stone and stuttered out, "What makes you ask that?"

"Nothing," she said slowly. She wanted to push him further, but instead, she sent him a long look and turned back to leave.

"Emma," called Tim.

"Yes," she said, turning back to him.

"I'll let you know if we need anything. I promise," he said. He wanted to tell her more than anything. Dora was right; Emma and Jeremy could help. But he was too scared to take the chance that something they did could affect Lottie negatively.

She nodded and they headed out.

They pulled the door closed behind them and headed to the elevator. Jeremy pushed the call button and leaned on the wall as they waited, "What was that about?"

"I'm not sure. I just thought I'd put the question out there. Dora didn't seem like herself when she came back from the exposition today."

"She may have been tired," he suggested.

"Yes, but I thought it best to say something."

"Is it because they spent the afternoon with Michael and Lenora?"

"Yes," she admitted.

"You think it's something that may have happened today?" he asked.

"Yes."

"So, we have a case of a vanishing girl and..." he said.

"For now, the mysterious couple," she supplied.

"Looks like," he confirmed.

The elevator arrived and they headed downstairs. They got through the crowded lobby to the entrance and stepped outside. The man working the door hailed a cab for them. It pulled up in front and the driver asked, "Où ça?" *Where to?*

Jeremy looked at Emma, "I want to go to the exposition and see that Edison exhibit," she said. "Papa mentioned he'll be in town this weekend."

Jeremy turned to the driver, "Bonjour. La foire s'il vous plait."

The driver nodded and clicked his tongue to get the horses moving through the crowded street. They made good time and arrived at the Eiffel Tower in under twenty minutes. The carriage pulled to a stop and they got out. Emma stood, still awed by the design. *This will change the future design of buildings,* she thought.

She looked around as Jeremy paid the driver. "Au revoir," he said to them and drove away.

"What is that?" asked Jeremy, motioning toward the box-like structure under the tower. He hadn't noticed it previously.

"That's probably the elevator Papa mentioned," she said, studying it.

"Didn't I read something about that? That there was some talk of the safety of the device?" he asked.

"Papa mentioned it. They're Otis Elevators. It moves people up the legs to the first level of the tower," Emma said.

"What was the safety concern?"

"There wasn't one. Several journalists expressed concern. To prove it was safe, the Otis technicians filled one elevator with three thousand kilograms of lead, simulating passengers, and then cut the cable with an axe. The elevator's fall was halted ten feet above the ground by the Otis safety brakes," she explained.

"Do you want to get in line and go up now?" he asked, watching it move people up the tower.

"No, Papa mentioned the best view is at night."

"We haven't stayed for the light shows at night."

"I'd like to see it," she said wistfully. "Maybe tonight?"

"Ellis mentioned it's a combination of electric light around the water and gas lights on the tower, protected by opal glass cases. There's also a three-colored beacon housed in the campanile that sends out blue, white, and red light over Paris."

"That will be a sight to see," she said, her eyes shining.

"We'll come back tonight," he promised.

She turned to him and smiled. "I'd enjoy that."

"Train or walk?"

"Let's walk," she requested. When they didn't move forward, Emma asked curiously. Je. "What are you looking for?"

"Not a what. A who—Julian," he said warily. "Doesn't he normally turn up at this time? He has been our constant companion since we got to Paris."

"That's true." She frowned and followed his gaze. "It's rather odd that we haven't seen him today. I still haven't talked to Papa about their relationship. I think there's something there."

"And his connection to Michael and Lenora," Jeremy reminded her.

They started their walk, trying to avoid the larger crowds as they watched the flowing water and white statues. "I could stay here for months and not just weeks," Emma commented. Jeremy thought about that as they continued to admire the buildings leading to the main dome.

The crowds thickened as they made their way to it. She observed, "I thought the reason for the exposition was supposed to keep people away."

"Yes, that's true, it was supposed to." As they passed groups of people, the languages varied but the queen's English was prevalent. "Especially the English."

"I guess the spectacle was too hard to miss," observed Emma.

"That's true," said Jeremy.

They made it to the Gallery of Machines pavilion. Looking around, they saw signs for Edison's exhibit and realized that two-thirds of it were his works.

"What do you want to see first?" he asked.

"Edison's phonograph. I understand we will hear both the American and French national anthems playing it."

As they walked through the space, they marveled at the engines, dynamos, and transformers on display.

"Whoever put this together knows quite a lot about how much spacing and power is required for this design," Jeremy said.

"There is an easy explanation for that," said Emma. "The president of France Sadi Carnot, Jr and he had a part in planning the exposition. He had the advantage of being raised by Sadi Carnot, who gave us the second law of thermodynamics—the scientific law that limits how much power a machine will produce. He believes The modern world is being 'forged out of iron and smoke'."

"Iron and smoke?" commented Jeremy.

"The future is in the room," said Emma. "We'll see the future being built by the men who have created such amazing devices. Besides electricity and the phonograph, Papa mentioned we need to go to the moving pictures exhibit."

"Moving pictures?" he asked. "What's that?"

"Let's find out."

They looked around, trying to locate the area where the demonstration was set up.

"I think it's there," Emma commented, pointing to the huge crowd.

"You're probably right," Jeremy said as they headed toward it.

Large signs were suspended over the displays and, as they got closer, she could read them. "This is the phonograph demonstration. I understand you can buy these now."

Jeremy looked around, "Let's see what they're like."

They got to the long lines waiting to put earphones in their ears. There were multiple stations and the lines moved quickly. They reached the phonograph, and Emma was handed earphones. She eagerly lifted them to her ears and listened to the French and American national anthems. Her face lit up as she listened. She couldn't wait to hand the device to Jeremy.

He took it from her and put the device to his ear. "Wow," he mouthed. She nodded as she watched his reaction.

They passed on the earphones to the next eager person in the line. She said, "We should get one of these when we get back home."

"I agree. It's amazing."

They heard an announcer call out, "In 1888, American inventor and entrepreneur Thomas Alva Edison conceived of a device that would do 'for the Eye what the phonograph does for the Ear'."

They followed the crowds to the demonstration area; smaller groups were taken inside.

"Who's that on the stage?" asked Jeremy as they got closer.

Emma didn't know and was about to reply when a lady standing in front of them turned and said, "Bonjour, that is Étienne-Jules Marey. He invented the chronophotographic gun instrument capable of capturing images at a rate of twelve frames per second."

"Thank you," Emma said. The woman turned to look forward again. "What's being shown?" asked Emma.

"Monkey shines," Jeremy read on the sign.

They entered the darkened room and the demonstration started. "Tiny photos appear to be used," muttered Emma as the movie started. It was a woman who appeared to be exercising. Emma's head was humming as they left. Jeremy watched as she drummed her fingers on her lips; it told him she was planning something.

"What are you thinking about?" he asked.

"The future. If we had equipment like this, investigations could be improved. I was thinking Jake would love this development. We'll have to get as much information as we can for him." Jake Cooper was a team member and part of their family. He had lived in the boarding house since they met him in 1883. He was a forensic photographer with the Chicago police department and provided his expertise to the team as needed. Currently, he was home; he didn't take to traveling well.

They continued to wander around observing the displays for Telegraphone, General Electric, Westinghouse, and Tesla. They had been there for a few hours, going exhibit to exhibit, when she commented to Jeremy, "Still no Julian."

He looked up from his study of a large transformer in the Westinghouse display. "There's a lot to see here. Maybe he's just busy," he reasoned.

"You're probably right." Her voice drifted off. Julian's continued absences bothered her. The man had been with them almost constantly since coming over on the ship, always showing up when least expected and asking questions that she didn't want to answer. Emma had gotten used to his presence and was disappointed he hadn't shown up yet. *Maybe something happened to him* she thought. Before she could voice her concerns, an announcement was made—that the lights would be turned on at the Edison exhibit. "Would you like to go back and see it?" she asked.

"I would. I heard that the display is supposed to demonstrate color."

They headed to the crowded area, hoping to get close enough to see the lights. They held their breath, waiting for the demonstration. They watched as the lights flashed briefly but did not come on. Emma watched the men in charge of the exhibit. One of them flipped the switch next to him several times and whispered furiously to the man next to him. The man nodded and headed to the side of the exhibit.

"Something's wrong," she murmured to Jeremy pointing to the man moving to the side of the exhibit. They watched, expecting the lights to activate. Instead, that same man ran out and waved frantically, calling, "Police! Police!"

Emma frowned. "Something's happened. Let's go over and see if we can help."

Jeremy nodded and walked over with her. They got close but stayed back to observe. In a short time, the police had arrived and were setting up a boundary to keep the crowds back.

"Pardon, monsieur?" Emma asked the officer assigned to keep the crowds out.

"Oui, Madam?" he asked.

"Est-ce qu'il s'est passé quelque chose ici?" *Has something happened here?*

He looked down at her from his considerable height. "Je ne peux pas répondre à cette question." *I cannot answer that.*

She commented, "J'espérais offrir de l'aide." *I was hoping to offer some help.*

"Ce n'est pas necessaire, Madame," *That is not necessary, Madam*, he answered stiffly.

A voice spoke up in English just behind the officer. "Just a moment, officer. Are you Mademoiselle Emma Evans?"

"Yes," Emma said watching as the man stepped from behind the officer.

"You may let her and her companion..." He looked at Jeremy.

"Jeremy Tilden," he supplied.

"Mademoiselle Evans and Monsieur Tilden may step in," he said.

"Emma, please."

"And Jeremy, please."

"Thank you." He reached over to take her hands, "I'm Inspector Levan. I have heard you were in Paris." He looked over at the young officer and said, "She's a detective and her observation skills are well known."

"Jeremy is also a detective," Emma supplied, "he's with the Pinkerton Detective Agency."

Levan nodded; he was aware of the agency. "I'd appreciate your review of the scene."

"We'd like to help," Emma said for them.

"Wonderful, walk this way." The inspector motioned to the officer to lower the barricade so they could enter the controlled area.

They followed the inspector, not knowing what they were being taken to see. The door he opened led into a long utility corridor. The double doors at the end of the hallway stood open. As they entered, they saw a man lying on the floor, face down.

"Do you see anything?" Levan asked as they watched the man being turned over.

"Shot," she mentioned, examining the body first and not the face.

Jeremy touched her arm, "It's Julian."

Emma's eyes moved to the body's face and her eyes widened. She muttered, "Oh my."

"You know this man," the inspector stated as fact.

"Yes, yes we do. He's Julian Barnard," she commented shakily.

Jeremy supplied, "We met him on the steamship on our way from New York."

"Were you close friends?" Levan asked.

"No, just acquaintances," commented Emma.

"Do you know anyone he might have been close to?" he asked.

"I'm not sure close is the right word." She looked over at Jeremy.

He looked at the inspector, "Michael and Lenora Cervantes. We've seen them together a few times."

"Where was this?" the inspector asked.

"They were also on our steamship from New York."

"Were they friends?"

"No, I don't think so." Emma said, "When we saw them together, they were arguing."

"Do you know where they're located now?"

"I believe they have a room at our hotel, the Grand Palais."

"Have you spent time with them?"

"No, we haven't spent any time together. They have been spending time with my sister Dora and her husband Tim."

"Where are your sister and brother-in-law now?"

"They're back at the hotel, resting," she murmured.

"Where were they this morning?"

"I believe they were at the exposition this morning," Jeremy said.

"Do you know which exhibits?" the inspector asked.

"They mentioned the Gallery de Machines and that they were meeting Lenora and Michael," Emma said truthfully.

"We'll want to question them," Levan said.

"Of course, would you like to come by this evening?" Emma asked.

"Yes—I have to conclude things here. You will make sure your sister and her husband are available?"

"Yes, I can do that," Emma said. She looked around, "Isn't this room normally secure? I thought I noticed a guard earlier."

He started to talk and a voice called, "Inspector!"

He went in the direction indicated, then called back over his shoulder, "Emma and Jeremy, could you come here?"

They followed his direction and saw him with a lifeless body, this one in a uniform. He was slumped behind the transformer, against the wall.

"Careful," she called. "Don't touch him; he might be connected to the power. Check all around him and make sure he isn't touching anything."

They did as she asked and called back, "He isn't touching anything."

"Is he alive?" she asked.

"No, it does not appear so."

"Can you move him out?"

The inspector directed his men to carefully remove the man and place him in the middle of the room.

She knelt down and noticed his hands; they appeared to have a black mark.

"There doesn't appear to be an injury," commented the inspector.

"I think he's been in contact with the electricity," she said.

The inspector was not familiar with the new technology. "What makes you say that?" he asked, trying to see what she saw on the body.

"I've read that the circuit will try to be completed through the person if there's contact. Look at his hands and probably his feet also."

"Enlever ses chaussures," he directed his officers.

They removed his shoes and found another black mark. The inspector looked at her, "One electrical accident and one murder in the same area at the same time?"

Emma was frowning at the question. She didn't say anything but thought, *Julian mentioned there were radical people against electricity. He said they could be violent in their beliefs.*

The inspector stroked his beard and commented, "Michael and Lenora are our main lead. The questioning of your sister and her husband is a priority."

"I understand. We'll contact you as soon as we see them."

The manager of the Edison lighting exhibit walked over to them, "May we turn back on the transformer?"

The inspector knew Paris was relying on the exposition being a success, "Yes, we have it under control. You may turn it back on."

The manager looked relived, "Thank you so much." He nodded to the staff and a switch was flipped. They could hear the crowds respond to the lights as they came on.

The inspector watched as his men covered the victims with sheets.

"How will you move them?" Jeremy asked.

"We have several exits that will allow us to be discrete. Now, you must go on your way. We'll see you soon."

"Bonsoir," they called and walked out of the room, barely glancing at the now brightly lit exhibit, the excitement drained by Julian's murder.

Jeremy watched Emma drum her fingers on her lips, "What are you thinking?"

"That it's very coincidental that Julian and Michael and Lenora fight and then he's murdered."

"Do you think they had something to do with it?" he asked, thinking of the times they had seen them together.

"It's possible. I never liked how they avoided us."

"What about Tim and Dora? Do you think they knew about this?"

"I hope not. The injuries and blood lead me to believe this all happened this morning."

"You didn't mention that when you were evaluating the body earlier."

"No, I wanted to make sure I didn't accidentally lock Tim and Dora into a time where they don't have an alibi," she admitted.

"You think they're somehow involved?" he asked, startled.

"It's possible. Think of how Dora looked earlier today. She was as white as a ghost."

"Why don't we stop for some afternoon tea and gather our thoughts before beginning a long conversation with Dora and Tim?"

They headed out of the exposition grounds. The food there was good but the wait was too long. The further they got from the exposition, the more likely they'd be able to get a table.

They walked a few blocks and across the bridge before

finding a free carriage. They requested a restaurant for afternoon tea. The driver took them to the 5th Arrondissement, on the Left Bank of the Seine, the Latin Quarter.

He let them off at a small restaurant with outdoor seating.

"This is nice," Emma said as they sat down.

"You know," he said, "we never checked out that secret staircase in the middle room at the hotel."

"With so much going on, I forgot about it," she admitted as she looked at the menu.

"Secret passages have shown up in your cases before this," he said, referencing a previous case where one had been utilized to move about a murder house.

"It's true—they do seem a popular addition," she said quietly. "Though I think Julian's murder will take priority over that, especially if Tim and Dora are involved."

"It still might be worth checking out when we get back," he murmured.

"If there's time," she agreed. She laid down her menu and glanced at the area around them. "It's so beautiful here."

"Isn't this area named the Latin Quarter because of the Latin being spoken at the school?"

"Exactly, it's also one of the oldest areas."

The waiter came over and they ordered their tea and cakes. They sat enjoying their afternoon, not talking about their current cases. She stood up and went over to him, hugging him close.

"What's this for?" he asked, returning the hug, not that he minded getting free hugs.

"For this," she said, referencing the area around them. "It's wonderful to finally forget what's happening outside of here."

He didn't say it, but he knew as soon as they left the area that their reality would be back in full force. Julian, Michael, and Lenora; Dora and Tim's involvement, and Patrice.

"Why don't we head back to the hotel?" he suggested.

"Oaky. I assume Tim and Dora will be there." She checked her timepiece, "The police might be on their way, they didn't give us a time."

They passed a patisserie "Want to take some meat, cheese, bread, and wine back with us?" Jeremy asked.

"I think that would be wonderful."

They stepped into the shop and picked items for their dinner. On their way out, she looked around wistfully, "I'd like to stay here more full time."

"Yes, it's lovely. Maybe one day we'll live here."

"I'd like that," she murmured, looking around again.

They hailed a carriage and went back to the hotel. She continued to watch as the Latin Quarter got smaller behind them. As they entered the lobby, she paused to see if she could locate Patrice. When she didn't see her, she was two parts exasperated, and one part worried. "She's still not back."

"She might turn up. Maybe she's just playing hide and seek," suggested Jeremy with a twinkle in his eye.

"Hide and seek? Why would she do that?" she asked sharply.

"Hey, I was kidding." He held his hands up, "I surrender." He watched as she moved her fingers to her lips and began drumming them. "All right, what are you thinking?"

"I might know where she is," she said, mulling over the "hide and seek" comment.

"Where?"

"Follow me," she directed and headed toward the elevator.

They had a short wait for it. As they got off on their floor, Emma continue to think about everything they knew about Patrice. She increased her pace and almost ran to the door. Jeremy was close behind with the key. They went in and Emma called out, "Tim! Dora! Are you here?" She knew they had a responsibility to the police to question them.

Jeremy took the food to the small kitchen area as Emma ran quickly to Tim and Dora's room and knocked on their door.

When she received no answer, she went into the room. She came out quickly, "They're gone."

"They may have just gone out to dinner or went to see some sites," he suggested, knowing she was worried.

"You're probably right," she said looking at Patrice's door. "We have some time?"

"I think we do," he said and followed her to the middle room. She paused by the table to pick up her knife and her small portable kerosene lamp.

They immediately went to the wall they had opened earlier. She inserted the knife into the seam and pulled it back. As the door opened, she turned to Jeremy, "This time, I plan to go in."

He stopped her with a hand on his shoulder. "Why do you think she's in there?"

"I don't know, but I also didn't think she'd run from us."

"That was my thought. I wondered where she could be. She knows no one but us. And that little ghost."

"Exactly, he has been on my mind," she said as she entered the dark space, her heart beating so hard her chest hurt. She lit the lamp to illuminate the area. There was an opening the size of a closet. She called over her shoulder, "The stairs start right away and only go up."

"I'm behind you," he said. She felt his warm breath on her neck. She moved her skirt and held it so she could negotiate the narrow steps. They had walked for a few minutes when she said, "There's some sort of landing."

He was quiet as they continued up. When they reached the landing, she shined the light onto the floor. A huddled figure was there. She ran over and lifted her face, "Patrice," she said. Jeremy was silent as she checked her pulse. "Alive," she said.

"Good," he said. "Let me carry her back to her room." Emma backed out and allowed Jeremy to reach her. He lifted Patrice, and Emma led them back down and into the room. He moved her to the bed and placed her gently down.

He was frowning heavily as he looked down at the girl, "I'm sorry I said we should investigate the space later. We could have found her earlier."

"I don't think so," Emma said, watching Patrice closely. She used her hand to move Patrice's hair from her head.

"You don't?" he asked.

"She couldn't have been there yet. I don't know why she left the room, but I think she must have come in from where this finally lets out. We won't know until she wakes," she said, looking toward the passageway.

"We'll have to investigate that later," he cautioned when he saw where her eyes strayed.

"I know. I was thinking we should close it in case someone tries to come in again."

"Yeah—we don't want them to know we know it's there," he said.

"She mentioned a ghost before," she said, glancing at the now-closed secret passage.

"Do you think that's how it might have come in?"

"Yes. I should have taken the ghost talk more seriously," she murmured.

"You couldn't have known," he argued, keeping his voice low. "So, who is the ghost, and why are they haunting Patrice? Questions we'll have to ask Patrice."

"Oh, I think the ghost can also answer some questions," she said.

"What are you thinking?"

"We talk to Patrice," she said, thinking.

CHAPTER 14

*E*arlier in the day with Tim and Dora
Meanwhile, as Emma and Jeremy made their way to the exposition, Tim and Dora stared at the closed door. Dora was pensive. "I know they said not to wait for Patrice…"

Tim interrupted firmly, "Lottie's our priority. Jeremy and Emma decided they could leave without finding Patrice. So can we."

"You're right," she said, her thoughts turning to Lottie. They silently gathered their things.

"Should we leave a note?" he asked.

Dora shook her head. "No. They know if we aren't here then we're at the exposition for sightseeing."

"Are you ready?" Tim asked. They had looked at their clothes to determine what could be used to hide their identities at the meeting.

"Yes, I had some netting on my evening dress. I was able to remove it and whip-stitched it to my hat. What about you?"

"I will keep my hat pulled down and keep my scarf wrapped around my face. Do you think they'll be there?"

"I hope so," she said. "They haven't been in contact yet to tell us what our role is in this plot." They were just thinking of the next steps and not focusing on the possible outcomes.

They were quiet as they left the room to get to the elevator. They walked a few blocks and then hailed a cab. He donned his hat and scarf while she pulled the netting down to cover her face.

"If there's enough of a crowd, we should blend in," Tim said.

"If there's not?"

"It won't matter. We'll get some answers," he replied determinedly.

She nodded.

The trip did not take long; the neighborhood was removed from the tourist areas and not crowded. The driver looked over his shoulder, "Êtes-vous sûr de l'adresse?" Clearly, he thought his passengers were lost.

"Oui," Tim said. He paid the driver and they both exited the carriage.

As the carriage rolled away, they saw the location was an old building that appeared to be an apartment.

"She mentioned the basement," Tim said. Dora nodded and followed him. He stopped abruptly, "Wait a moment." He watched a couple walk up and head into the building.

He took her hand and they followed them in. They watched as the other couple took a door to the left of the stairs. They waited a few seconds and followed behind them. The stairs led down to what must have been the basement, gas lamps helping to guide the way. The closer they got to the bottom, they heard voices getting louder. The group seemed to be in the middle of an argument. They tried to get in without being seen and sat in the back.

"We need to come to order," called a young man from the front of the room. Everyone sat down and the two people they were looking for stood with the speaker. "We have to move forward at this time," said the apparent leader.

"What's happened that makes us have to move our plans up?" yelled a man from the audience.

"We had an investigator on our trail."

That caused the room to murmur loudly.

Tim muttered to Dora, "Julian was an investigator?" They didn't know that piece of the puzzle. It would explain the arguments with Michael and Lenora.

Another person from the group asked, "What are the final plans?"

"We're keeping that quiet, but we'll tell you that it will involve electricity and will show everyone that it's too dangerous."

"Are we sure no one will be hurt?" a voice shouted from the group.

"Yes, we'll make sure," they assured everyone.

Tim uncovered his mouth, deepened his voice, and yelled out in French, "What about the investigator and security guard killed today?"

Tim put his scarf back on and moved with Dora back into the shadows.

"What is he talking about?" several people in the group yelled. "You said we wouldn't hurt anyone!"

"How can you be sure, with your plan, and so many people at the exposition?" someone else yelled out.

Lenora and Michael came up from the first row and went to stand on either side of the gentleman running the meeting. They started all talking at once, trying to calm the crowd.

"We're sure. I want to remind everyone why we're doing this," said Michael.

Lenora tried to get them back to their cause. "Electricity is dangerous."

A woman with dark hair stood, "We must protect everyone from these devices. They're putting our families in danger."

"I'll not be part of murder," an older man with gray hair said, standing. Those around him agreed and departed the space.

"Are those of you left committed to our cause?" Lenora asked.

They took a moment to wait for the group to respond. The response was positive and they went on to discuss the main events where they would place the bombs. The meeting ended and the group stood and moved toward the exit. Tim and Dora watched each file out while they kept an eye on Michael and Lenora in the front of the room.

They stood and went over to them, Tim taking off his hat and Dora raising her veil.

"Ah, good. You're here. Now we don't have to find you," Lenora said, the satisfaction clear in her voice.

Michael looked over at Tim, "That was you," he accused. "Shouting out about Julian and the guard. Are you trying to destroy our cause?"

Tim didn't care for Michael or Lenora. "We want to see Lottie," he said forcefully. Dora gripped his hand, offering her support.

"Ah ah ah." Lenora stated, "You're in no place to make any demands; we're in charge here."

"That's where you're wrong. You need us. We're not doing anything until we see our daughter. How do we know you haven't hurt her?"

"You don't, but you will get her back after you help us."

Tim lowered his voice, "What do you expect us to do?" Dora was shocked at his response. She hadn't expected him to acquiesce to their demands. She tried to hide her reaction by lowering her head.

Lenora looked happy at the turnaround, "Well! We'll let you know our plans tomorrow."

"Tomorrow?" asked Tim. "Is something happening tomorrow?"

"Yes," they said noncommittally.

He nodded. "Then we'll head out and wait for you to contact us."

"No," said Michael. "I don't think so. I think it was a mistake to have you out of our grasp."

"You can't hold us here," Dora said.

"Oh, I think I can," Lenora said. Tim and Dora saw the woman had a gun pointed at them. "We'll be staying here tonight."

"In a damp basement?" asked Dora wrapping her arms around herself and shivering.

"No, we have an apartment upstairs," said Michael calmly. He seemed the more balanced member of their team.

"We thought you were staying at the hotel," Tim commented.

"Yes, that was more convenient, but someone searched our room today so we had to make a move."

Dora said loudly, "Emma will know something is wrong if we don't come back tonight."

"We can take care of that. You'll write her a note assuring that you're okay; that it got late and you're staying overnight with your new close friends," supplied Lenora.

Emma will never believe that, Dora thought but kept her mouth shut.

Michael led the way as Lenora kept the gun trained on their backs. They made their way up the stairs and into the first-floor hallway. The area was clean but had cracks in the walls and scratches on the floors. They took in all they could as they made their way upstairs to Michael and Lenora's apartment. It was located on the second floor. Michael opened the door and stood back to allow them entry. "It's not the Grand Palais hotel," muttered Tim. They were crowded into the small space that contained a living room and a kitchen. There were pads on the floor where they assumed they were going to be sleeping.

Dora's eyes darted around the room and landed on Lottie's

lace band on the table. "Can I have that please?" she asked, a note of pleading in her voice.

Michael looked at Lenora. She shrugged.

"Sure, why not?" He handed it to Tim.

Tim rubbed it with his fingers before giving it to Dora. Dora took it and squeezed her eyes shut, trying to stop the emotion from overwhelming her. Tim put his arm on her shoulder and pulled her to him.

"Is there any food?" asked Tim.

"There are some things in the icebox. Not as good as you've eaten since we got here, but it's food," Michael said. He walked over to the icebox to pull out ham, cheese, fruit, and a round loaf of bread.

When Dora didn't make a move to the table for the food, Michael said almost kindly, "It won't do any good to starve yourself."

They sat and ate. Each couple thought that, were this a day ago, the conversation would have flowed between them. Michael broke the silence, "We really did like you, you know." Lenora didn't say anything but kept her head down.

"Then why would you do this? Take our child?" Dora burst out.

"It's just part of the plan," Michael said, looking over at Lenora, who still had her head down.

"Was killing Julian and the guard part of the plan?" asked Tim.

Lenora lifted her head; her eyes glinted. "We'll do whatever it takes to prove electricity is wrong."

"What's so wrong with electricity?" Tim asked, not understanding such passion over a scientific advancement.

"We have our reasons," she commented, trying to shut down the conversation.

"Don't you think we deserve to know what those are?" Tim demanded.

"I think you should tell them," Michael commented. When she glared at him, he continued, "We have involved their family in our troubles. I think it's time."

"Fine. My brother... they're trying to kill him with electricity," Lenora said abruptly.

Tim glanced at Dora and she shrugged. "We don't understand."

Lenora stood and paced the small kitchen. She started to talk. "My brother made a mistake and he went to prison. It should have ended there, but now, the Edison invention has been experimented with and will be used to execute people."

"What did he do that he'd be executed over?"

"He didn't do anything that would warrant this!" she burst out.

"What's his name?" Tim asked.

Michael supplied, "William Kemmler."

Dora jumped. Emma had mentioned him and his case to their team when his case went to trial. William Kemmler had been convicted of murdering his lover Matilda Ziegler—with an axe!

Tim remembered also and reached out to squeeze her hand. "Why do you think this will stop the execution? Wouldn't it just stop the electrocution?" he asked.

"It's not humane; they do not know if it will kill him. It's an experiment. I don't want him to be hurt like that. He's my brother."

Lenora left the room. They looked at Michael.

"Do you think he did it?" Dora asked.

"Yes, I do. But he's her brother and she believes this plan is a just cause."

"Why would Edison be a part of something like this?" Dora asked.

"I don't believe this came from him. From what I have read, electrocution was suggested by Dr. Albert Southwick. He had witnessed an elderly drunkard 'painlessly' killed after touching the terminals of an electrical generator in Buffalo, New York," Michael said.

"If not electrocution, wouldn't he be hung?" Tim asked.

"Yes," he said quietly, staring at the door his wife had exited through.

"Why do you think he'll be first?" asked Dora quietly.

"Earlier this year, New York's Electrical Execution Law, the first of its kind in the world, went into effect, and Edwin R. Davis, the Auburn Prison electrician, was commissioned to design an electric chair. We have been notified he'd be first and that led us to put a plan together," Michael informed them.

"And you think by staging this event you can stop them from doing that?" Tim asked in amazement.

"We do. Once we show them how dangerous electricity is, it will make others question the use of the invention."

Once they had finished eating, Lenora returned and handed Dora a piece of paper and a pencil. "Write out what I tell you."

Dora took the paper and pencil and began writing.

Emma,

We're going to stay with friends tonight. They have an apartment in town. We'll join you at the exposition tomorrow.

Dora

"Will we?" Tim asked as Dora finished the note.

"Of course, you will. Just do as we say and we'll let you go," said Michael.

Lenora didn't comment but just stared at the note in Dora's hand.

"And we'll get Lottie back?" asked Dora softly.

"And, of course, you will have her back," Michael assured her.

Dora completed the note and handed it to Lenora.

Lenora checked it to see if she had added anything.

"When will you let us know our role in this 'event'?" asked Tim.

"Tomorrow," she said briskly, folding the note up not offering any information.

She left and Michael said, "I don't want to have to keep the gun on you, but you're too big for me to wrestle."

"You can lower it," Tim said. "I won't cause any problems."

Dora knew it wasn't the gun keeping Tim from attacking Michael; it was Lottie. They had to see this through.

CHAPTER 15

BACK AT THE HOTEL WITH PATRICE

*P*atrice was finally stirring again. She opened her eyes, and saw Emma, "You found me!"

"How did you end up in that space?" asked Jeremy as they watched her reaction closely.

She turned her eyes to him, "The little ghost. He was at the door. I opened it to confront him and he ran off. I chased after him."

"You followed him... Why?" Emma asked curiously.

"I don't know, to prove he was real. So much of what I told you seems like a dream."

"Where did he lead you?" Jeremy asked.

"He went into the stairway. We climbed so many stairs, they seemed to go forever. I got so tired that I sat down and closed my eyes."

"What happened then?"

"I opened my eyes and he was there. I asked him if he was real."

"What did he say?" asked Emma, fascinated by the story.

"He said 'drink this.' I was so tired that, when he held it to my lips, I drank it."

"Patrice! You really *have* to stop taking things from strangers," Emma said curtly.

"I know," the girl acknowledged unhappily. "I'll try."

"How did you end up back here in that space?" Emma asked, thinking about where they'd found her.

"I don't know. I dreamed that I was being lifted and then I woke here."

"That was probably the laudanum's effects," said Emma, thinking of what the doctor said.

Jeremy started to ask a question when they heard a knock on the hotel door.

Emma frowned, "It must be the police officers. Should we mention this?" The case was getting more involved by the minute. They could use some help.

"Please don't!" cried Patrice. "We haven't found Mama yet." The hotel staff had already threatened to lock her up, and she didn't know who to trust outside this room.

"No, you're right. We're in a location where we don't trust who we're working with," Jeremy said.

"And we need to know where that passage goes and just who that little ghost is," Emma said. The more she thought about it, the more she believed they needed more data before bringing the police into it.

Another knock sounded on the door, more demanding this time. "I'll stay here," said Jeremy, "if you want to answer the door."

Emma walked quickly out of the room, closing the door behind her. She took a deep breath and went to answer the loud knocks. As she opened it, she noticed not only the officers from earlier but also a bellhop from the hotel. "Come in, please," she told them.

Levan came in first, "We're here to interview Dora and Tim."

"Just a moment." Emma looked at the bellhop, "Bonjour, como talley vous?"

"A note," he said and handed it to her. She reached into her pocket and handed him several francs. "Merci."

She opened the note and saw it was Dora's handwriting. She looked directly at the police inspector, "Well, I'm sorry to say they're staying with friends tonight."

"Where are they?" asked Levan. This was their second dead end today.

"She doesn't say," she replied lightly, tapping the note on her hand.

"Do you know these friends?" Levan asked, opening up his notebook.

"I'm not sure. She doesn't mention their names." She didn't want to answer questions that might get Tim and Dora in trouble.

"Did they have any other friends here?"

"No, I don't think so." She decided to ask her own questions. "Did you look into Michael and Lenora?"

One officer glanced at the other. The inspector responded to her question. "We did and they're no longer at the hotel."

"They're not?" Jeremy asked as he walked into the room.

"They checked out," he said simply.

"Did they say when?" she asked pulling out her own notebook. Jeremy's mouth quirked as he looked at both of them comparing notebooks.

The inspector glanced down at his notes, "It looks like last night."

"Can we see their room?" she asked.

"No, the hotel has already booked another family."

"That was fast," she muttered.

"The exposition," Levan explained. "Would you mind if we go through Dora and Tim's room here?"

"I don't see why not. It is that far one."

He waved the other officers to the room. A few minutes

later, they returned, and the officer stated, "We're finished. Thank you."

"Did you find anything?" Jeremy asked.

Levan looked over, "One thing." He pulled a folded paper out of his pocket and showed them.

It was a cartoon showing the hazards of electricity. Emma frowned, reaching for it. "I haven't seen this before."

"We have trouble in the city with these people. They're meeting and making threats. Have Dora and Tim been talking about these groups?"

"No, they haven't." Not that she was aware of.

"What about Michael and Lenora? Could they be part of this group?" the inspector asked.

"I haven't heard them say anything," she said truthfully. She thought about Julian's warnings but didn't mention them.

"We'll want to see them as soon as they arrive here. Do you understand?" Levan said with a frown.

"Yes, I understand." She'd find them and see what was happening.

The police took the pamphlet back and left the hotel room. She closed the door behind them and leaned on it.

Jeremy stood, "Coming back?"

"Yes," she responded and went to Patrice's doorway. "How is she?"

"Better," he said. "What about Tim and Dora?"

Emma handed him the note, "I'm worried about them, but we have no way of knowing where to look."

"Are they wrapped up in Julian's death?" he asked after reading the note.

"I think they're somehow involved," she said, thinking of Dora's response earlier that day.

She looked over at Patrice and could see the girl was feeling better. She was sitting up and had some color on her face. Her hair was a tumble and she was still in her gown, but her eyes were clear. "It's time for a hard conversation," Emma said.

"Do you think it would be all right to move her into our room?" Jeremy asked, eyeing the secret passageway door.

"Yes, I think so."

They put the question to Patrice. "What do you think?"

"I'd love that. Can I change?" The clothes she was wearing were dirty from the passageway.

Emma had sent out her clothes to be cleaned. "They should have been delivered. Let me check."

"No, please, could you stay with me? I don't want to be here alone," Patrice requested. Things happened when she was alone.

"I'll stay," she promised. "Jeremy, can you check to see if the clothes have arrived?"

"Of course." He went to check and called from the living room. "They're back." He carried them into the room and laid them on the bed. "I'll be out here."

He closed the door and Emma smiled. "He's such a good guy."

Patrice moved to the edge of the bed, "The last few days have been a blur."

"Yes, hopefully, we can hear everything and see how to move forward."

She nodded and stood.

"Careful," Emma said, walking over to the girl with a pitcher of water and a rag. Once she was refreshed, Emma retrieved her skirt and top and helped her dress.

She saw Patrice grimace and asked, "What is it?" Was something else wrong with her?

"My hair is so tangled. Can I borrow a brush?"

Her response represented her age so much that it made Emma laugh out loud. "Yes, I can help with that." She handed her the brush and she pulled it through. When she finished, Emma said, "Let's move to the living room."

She took Patrice's arm and helped her walk to the couch in the living room. Once settled, Emma and Jeremy sat across from her, "Would you like to tell us the whole story now?" Emma asked.

At that moment, Patrice's stomach rumbled. She put a hand on it, "I'm so hungry. Can I eat first?"

"Yes," Emma and Jeremy said together and laughed.

"We haven't eaten either," Emma admitted.

"But," Jeremy said, getting up and walking to the dining area, "we did bring food back with us." He pulled out the rotisserie chicken and containers of vegetables and some round bread. "What would you like to drink?" he asked them.

"A little wine, please," Emma requested.

Emma and Jeremy set up their plates and moved them back to the living room. They ate, letting the silence settle around them. Once they finished, Patrice said, "Okay, I'm ready for your questions."

"Where are you from?" Emma asked. She knew from the accent that Patrice had spent some time in the United Kingdom.

"London," she confirmed. "My mum and I lived there, up until this week."

"Why are you in Paris?" Jeremy asked.

"That is a long story."

"I think we need to hear the whole thing to make sense of this," Emma told her.

"Of course. Then I'll start with how my papa met my mum. She was educated by her father. She was part of his household and, after her mum died, he let her stay on and manage his home. When he died and she wanted to find a life for herself. She applied at a hotel for a personnel management position."

Emma was impressed. Women were just entering the workforce and management positions were difficult. She had seen a woman in her own life move into a management position within an engineering company. Hopefully, this would continue to be true.

"Is that where she met your father?" asked Emma.

"Yes, Papa was there to oversee the restructuring of the staff. There had been some theft and he wanted to make sure he had people in positions he could trust. It was on the day Mum went for her interview that she met him."

He stood outside the hiring manager's door, concerned about the quality of personnel being hired for his new hotel in England. What he had not expected to hear was an argument. He could hear the woman quite clearly as she stated her case. Her voice was clear and concise regarding how she expected to be treated.

"You have applied for the wrong position," stated Mr. Horace Brooks. "You may apply for the positions listed." He indicated the sheet in her hand.

She looked down at it, "These are for maids. I do not want to apply for a maid position. As you can see from my education, I'd like to work for your management staff."

"I don't see how that would be possible. We do not hire people like you for those types of positions."

"And why not? I'm qualified," the woman said with quiet dignity.

He gave her a long look, "You know why. Why not just take one of the maid positions?"

The office door opened. Mr. Brooks was surprised to see Charles, the owner of the hotel. Horace stood immediately, "Mr. Lanier, we did not expect you this morning."

"I know. I wanted to check in on our hiring process." It was then he got his first look at the applicant. He stood still, taking in her visage; she was a lovely light negroid woman.

She sent him a cool steady gaze, expecting the same response that she had gotten from Mr. Brooks.

Surprising her, he stuck out his hand to her and said, "I'm Charles Lanier, the owner of this hotel. What position are you here for?"

"Personnel manager," Catherine said, feeling like it would be her way to make positive changes in the workforce.

"Mr. Brooks, let me take over the interview from here," Charles said.

"Yes, sir," Brooks said and stood to leave the room. He looked back and realized he had no say in if she'd be hired that day.

Charles sat at the desk and picked up the paper listing her credentials. "Miss Catherine Belle."

"Yes?" she asked, wondering where this was going.

"I want you to have a fair interview. Can you tell me about your background and why you think you're the right person for this job?"

"I have been educated by tutors at my residence and I'm well-read. I have also managed my father's household since I was sixteen."

"How large was this residence?" he asked, thinking about how many people she'd be responsible for at the hotel.

"We had over twenty-five servants and multiple locations."

He continued to ask detailed questions about the budgets, payments, schedules, hiring, and firing. Each one was followed up with a professional response.

"May I ask, what made you leave your father's home? It sounds like you were happy where you were."

Catherine looked down for a moment and back up to him, directly in the eye. "My father died and the bulk of the estate went to his white family."

He asked gently, "Do you have papers that allow you to work?"

Catherine knew what he was asking; he wanted to know if she was a free woman.

"Yes, I have my papers. My papa made sure I was a free woman as part of his will."

"I'm glad," Charles said, not wishing any hardship on her. He sat back, "I'd like to allow you to run the personnel department, but you must be aware you have chosen the area where the staff may not want a woman directing them. Can you handle that?"

"I can if I have the approval to replace whomever I might need to," she said firmly.

"You do, but you must not leave us understaffed," he warned.

"I understand." She knew if he took a chance on her there would be little room for mistakes.

"There will be pushback, not just the fact that you're a woman but also because you're black. But this is my hotel. You will come to me if things become too much for you."

"I will," she said, hoping she hadn't picked too big of a challenge.

"I'll need to meet with my central management, but plan on starting tomorrow," he said, standing and extending his hand to her. At their touch, her face grew red and his smile broadened.

The next day, Catherine did as Charles asked and entered the hotel, ready to start work. She was dressed in a dark blue skirt, a dark blue jacket, and a white shirt. She kept her hat to a small size. Entering, she felt the employee's eyes on her, but when she looked toward the main desk, she saw Charles waiting for her.

"Welcome to your first day. Let me walk you to your office."

They made their way there; she was so excited, her hands were shaking. She clasped her hands and told herself to calm down. The office was at the end of a long hallway. When it opened, she saw she had windows, a desk, and a table to work at.

"Will this do?" he asked.

"It will," she murmured, running her hand across the desk.

"The position you have taken on will require long hours, especially in the beginning. We're restructuring and you're a big part of that process."

～

"Was she a success?" Emma asked, fascinated by another woman not wanting to take the traditional path in life.

"It wasn't easy," Patrice admitted. "Some people would not change. There were several violent confrontations. Papa had to make sure she had an armed guard with her."

"How long until it was okay for her to go without them?" Jeremy asked.

"Almost two years."

People don't change easily, Emma thought. "When did your parents marry?" she asked.

"That was about the two-year mark. When she started feeling safe."

"You mentioned your mum and you live in the United Kingdom? Does your father live there with you?" asked Jeremy.

"He lived with us when he wasn't in France checking on his other hotels. Like this one," she said, looking around.

"Why isn't he here with you and your mum?" Emma asked.

"He said it was time for us to meet and start acting like a family. He arranged everything and went ahead of us. He was supposed to meet us here."

"Have you never been here before?" asked Emma.

"No, Papa's family didn't approve of his marriage."

"But I thought Parisians were more open about..."

"Interracial marriages?" she supplied. "They are, but some of the older families would prefer it didn't happen to them."

"So, you just didn't meet?"

"Papa said it was easier this way, that his family could be vicious."

"Were you happy?"

"Yes, we were very happy," she said simply.

"Okay, let's go back over when you arrived at the hotel here," said Emma, thinking methodically.

"We arrived three nights ago. Mum and I were standing in a long line; we got in late and there were delays in getting the rooms."

"Yes, I saw you," Emma said.

"Did you see Mum with me?" Patrice asked excitedly. No one had believed that she and her mother had checked in together.

Emma cautioned, "I saw someone but it was from the back. What was she wearing when you checked in?"

"She had this plumb-colored suit she loves and a matching hat. I've tried to get her to change it for ages."

Emma nodded, "About how tall is she?"

"She's about 5'3, coming to here," Patrice said, holding up her hand to her shoulder.

"That sounds like who I saw, but I didn't see a face."

"Oh," the girl said, looking down, her disappointment apparent.

"What happened next?" Jeremy prodded.

"We got to our rooms and Mum wasn't feeling well, so she didn't leave her room."

"Had she seen anyone or taken anything that day?" Emma asked, thinking of the cocaine and laudanum that kept being fed to Patrice.

"Not that I..." She trailed off. "There was the clerk at the desk; he offered her some water. I had forgotten about that."

"Did she drink all of it?" Emma asked.

"No, I don't think so," Patrice answered, frowning.

"How was she when you got to your rooms?"

"Tired but able to walk."

"She didn't finish the water, so the effects would have been less than the ones you experienced," Jeremy said.

"Did you get the doctor at that time?" asked Emma.

"No, we thought it was the traveling that did it to her. She just wanted to rest."

"What about your father? You were there to meet him. Was he aware you were at the hotel?" Jeremy asked, thinking if it was him, he'd have been waiting at the ship for them.

"Mum had told the desk manager to let him know we had arrived. We waited for him all through the next day," she said forlornly. "That evening, after dinner, she seemed to get worse, so I went downstairs to get a doctor."

"Did you order that dinner?" Emma asked.

"Mum thought the hotel sent it, because of Papa."

"Did you eat any of it?"

"No, I'm not a good traveler; my stomach was still upset."

"Did your mum eat it?"

"Yes, she was hungry."

"How soon after she ate did she get sick?" asked Emma.

"Soon," she confirmed.

"There was another opportunity to feed her laudanum," commented Jeremy. They knew the rest.

"I also demanded to see my papa."

"Did they call for him?"

"They said he was unavailable. I don't think they believed I was his daughter," she said unhappily.

"We need to follow up on that," Emma said to Jeremy. He nodded.

"And there's still been no word from your papa since you have been here?" questioned Emma.

"No," Patrice said miserably.

Emma glanced over at Jeremy, "I think we have a lot to investigate, but we'll have to do it so that no one can get to Patrice."

"Agreed, but we also need for Patrice," he turned and talked directed to the girl, "to stay here and not be led away. And, not to eat or drink anything that comes from someone you don't know."

"What to do," Emma said and looked at Patrice.

Patrice immediately responded "I can lock myself in your room until you get back. I want to find Mum."

"That's an idea. We don't need to be worrying if you will be here if we go," Jeremy said. "Okay, let's get her organized in our room."

"Yes, we should confirm the walls are all solid in there," Emma replied. They both went and tested all of the walls. "Solid," she said.

They moved Patrice back into their room and gave her several books and some desserts. "I won't budge from here or open the door," she promised.

"Oh, just a second," Emma said and opened a drawer, pulling out pants and a shirt.

Jeremy saw what she was holding, "Were you expecting something to happen on the trip?"

"You never know," she said philosophically.

They closed the door and Jeremy called, "Lock the door!" They waited for the click. Once they heard it, they moved back to Patrice's room.

"First, I'd like to go into the passage," commented Emma, studying the wall.

"Somehow, I knew you'd want to do that first," teased Jeremy.

She dropped her voice, "Should we do this and leave her alone?"

"I don't think we have a lot of options. Whoever is sneaking into her room will have to be caught. We can't do that if we don't know where they're coming from."

She changed quickly and laid her skirt and top on the couch. She pulled on a cloth hat and stuffed her hair into her collar.

"Ready?" he asked.

"Yes," she said as she pulled out her portable kerosene lamp. They headed back into Patrice's room and opened the passage. It was narrow, requiring them to go single file. Emma led the way. She could see footprints on the dusty floor and commented over her shoulder to Jeremy about it.

"I don't guess there has been housekeeping in here," he said reasonably.

They continued up and noticed there were no other openings on the ascending floors. She called back, "Keep going?"

"Why not?"

They continued to ascend and found what must be the final door. She put her ear to it, trying to listen.

Jeremy leaned in, "Anything?"

"I don't think so," she said, shaking her head.

"Want to try it?" he asked as he felt for a way to open the door.

"Yes," she said. She extinguished her lamp and moved to help him push the door open.

They both paused as it eased open. The room wasn't what they had expected. Dazzled by the décor they moved slowly into the room. It was done in a grand manner and it was full of furniture, rugs, and art. Hints of gold were found around the room and walls that seemed to have no end. "This must take up the entire top floor," Emma said, moving further into the space.

Jeremy followed her and muttered, "I don't want to be arrested for breaking and entering." He listened intently for any steps that might be coming their way.

"You have a point. Let's head back." They passed a gallery wall. "The family that lives here?" she murmured. She studied them closely. Emma paused when one caught her eye. "Well, well," she said.

"What is it?" Jeremy asked, he had moved back to the door they entered.

"Paul!" a voice called from another room. Emma rushed over to the door where he was waiting. "I'll explain downstairs." They hurried back into the passage, down their stairs, and back into Patrice's room.

"Another question to add to our list. Who lives on the top floor of the building?" he asked.

Emma nodded, mulling over who that might be, based on that painting she'd seen. She looked at Jeremy, "We'll need confirmation, but I think it's a relative of Patrice."

He asked curiously, "What did you see that makes you believe Patrice's story about her father?"

"Patrice has very distinctive blue eyes. The painting I saw could have been Patrice in fifty years."

"The likeness was that close?"

"Yes," she said. "Definitely."

"Let's check with Patrice and let her know she can come out." They knocked softly and called to her.

Patrice answered the door quickly, "Did you find anything?"

"Why don't we move back into the living room?" Emma suggested.

They sat and discussed what they'd seen. "Where do we go from here?" Patrice asked.

"The goal would be to have more answers to our many questions," Jeremy said. "I'd like to find out who lives on the top floor of the building."

"Do you think it's my papa's family behind all of this?" she asked, hoping it wasn't true.

"We'll reserve judgment, but they're somehow involved," Emma told her.

Jeremy said, "We'll have to have one person with Patrice."

"I'll stay with her," Emma said, "while you try to get those questions answered."

"I'll do that. You might want to get cleaned up," he suggested.

She looked down and grimaced at the dirt. "Yes, that would be a good idea. You might do that also."

"I'll get my clothes changed and head downstairs." He got organized and headed out, locking the door behind him.

Emma looked over at Patrice, who got the message, "I'll stay here and not answer the door."

She glanced at the middle room and back over at Patrice. "Come help me with this." They went into Patrice's room and Emma stood to one side of the dresser. She motioned Patrice to the other side and they moved it in front of the wall and blocked the door into the passageway. "There, that should keep it closed until I get cleaned up."

Emma washed up quickly, changed, and stepped back out of her room. When she didn't see Patrice right away, she called for her. "Patrice, where are you!" When she still didn't see her, she ran around the large room. She heard a door open and was relieved when she saw Patrice come out.

"I'm sorry." The girl apologized, "I went to get a book from the bedroom."

"That's okay," Emma said relieved. "Why don't you come sit with me and tell me more about your mum and papa? When did they marry? Did they come to Paris for the ceremony?" She was curious if her mum had been here before this.

"No, they married but Mum never came to Paris."

"Why not? Wasn't his business based in Paris?"

"Yes, but his family didn't approve of mum. They didn't want anyone they hadn't picked out. And my mum, they felt she was too common. She works, you see."

CHAPTER 16

*J*eremy took the stairs, contemplating the questions he would ask. The most important of these was trying to locate Patrice's father. *The exposition happening at the same time is complicating things,* he thought, looking at the crowded lobby. *Whose idea was the timing of this move?*

He mulled those questions as he waited in the long line at the desk. He resigned himself to a long wait. When he finally reached the front, the clerk inquired, "Bonjour, vous avez une reservation?"

"Bonjour," Jeremy responded and asked for the manager.

The clerk gave him a long look and then called another clerk over. "If you will step over here," the clerk said, "I'll go get him."

Jeremy stepped out of the line and waited for the manager. The clerk returned with the manager. He stopped when he saw it was Jeremy.

"Bonjour," the manager said, with no welcoming smile this time. "Please follow me." He turned and exited the desk area. Jeremy followed behind into what must be his office.

The room was large and had a desk on the far wall. He sat in his chair and asked, his voice weary, "I thought we had settled this matter. We do not know the girl and she has never been registered at this hotel."

"I have new information that might be of interest to you," Jeremy commented laconically.

"And that is?"

"She's the daughter of Charles Lanier and granddaughter of Sasha Lanier."

The manager looked down at his desk before he asked, "The name is fairly common. How can you be sure?"

"I'm fairly certain," Jeremy said, thinking of that painting Emma had seen.

The manager sat back and looked contemplative. "Monsieur Lanier has not been around for a while now."

"I understand the family owns the hotel."

"Yes, this one and many others," the manager confirmed, wondering where the other man was going with this line of questions.

"Does the family live on the top floor?" Jeremy asked.

The manager's eyes dropped, "Part of the family does occupy that space."

"Can I get a message to them?"

"They will not see you," he said in a firm voice.

Jeremy frowned, "But if I have Monsieur Lanier's daughter, wouldn't they want to know?"

The manager stood and went over to his decanter. He inquired, "Would you like a drink? Scotch?"

Jeremy nodded and walked to where the manager stood. Drinks were poured. Jeremy drank some and enjoyed the smooth Scotch.

The manager pulled at his tie, "You know, I have worked for this family for most of my life. I started out moving luggage and then working the desk, and now I'm the manager."

"You must like them if you have stayed this long," Jeremy commented.

"Hmm. I'm not sure about that. I was hired by Charles Lanier's grandfather. I worked with him, the father, and then finally Charles."

"You don't like Charles?"

"I do, but he's not in France as much as I'd like."

"Who do you report to when he's not here?"

"His sister," he said simply.

"Have you seen Charles in the past few weeks?"

"No, he hasn't been here. His sister says he's in England."

"Do you know why he spends so much time there?" Jeremy asked, wondering if this man knew more than he let on.

He looked like he didn't want to answer.

"You know about his wife and daughter!" accused Jeremy.

"I only know of them; they have never been here," the other man said defensively. "I wouldn't be able to identify her."

"But you know she'd be mixed race."

"I do know that," the manager acknowledged, "but there has to be more proof, or Charles' sister will not accept it. There are many mixed-race people living here. This girl could have been anyone."

"Tell me about her. Would she have welcomed her brother's daughter? Or helped her if she were in trouble?"

The other man let out a strangled sound, "Her? No, I think not. The sister runs things. Their father died two months ago and Charles was notified to come home and take over the business."

"What about the other family members? Grandparents? Other siblings?"

"Gone," he said. "The father died and left everything to Charles."

"All of it? Then why is his sister running things now?" Jeremy asked, trying to remember everything.

"Once Charles came back, it was assumed he'd take over and replace his sister."

"But he hasn't returned?"

"No, not that I know of. There are other hotels he could be working at, but I have no information."

"I need to speak with the sister," Jeremy commented.

"Her name is Abella, but you may have a better time speaking to the Madam."

"The Madam?"

"Their mother."

"Then we need to see her. Where is she?"

"That might be a problem. She's in mourning for her husband and has not left her rooms."

"Is she in this hotel?"

"She has her home in one of the older ones in the arrondissement."

"Also owned by the family?"

"One of our finest," he confirmed.

The manager watched as Jeremy set his glass down and asked, "What will you do now?" Before Jeremy could answer, the manager's eyes widened as he said, "Oh no, the girl's mother is actually missing!"

"Well yeah. That's what we've been trying to tell you," Jeremy said, "We still have to find her and we may also have to look for her father. We'll take care of Patrice and make sure nothing else happens to her."

"Is that her name?" the manager asked. He hadn't taken the time before this to find out.

"Yes," Jeremy said, watching the manager's face show regret.

"You might mention that to the Madam," he suggested.

Jeremy raised his eyes brows and asked, "Why?"

"Her name is also Patrice," he explained.

"I'll keep that in mind," he said as he held out his hand for the other man to shake. "I'll be on my way."

"You might try Madam early tomorrow," the manager said as Jeremy walked to the door.

"Why is that?"

"Mademoiselle Abella sleeps in," the manager said helpfully.

Mulling all of the information over, Jeremy headed back upstairs to share what he'd learned. He exited the elevator and saw a boy of about nine in the hallway. Jeremy stopped and said, "Bonjour."

The boy stared at the door and didn't appear to hear. "Are you all right?" Jeremy asked.

The boy looked startled at his appearance and violently shook his head before running off in the opposite direction.

"That was strange," Jeremy muttered. He put the boy out of his mind and used his key to open the door. When he entered, he saw Patrice and Emma were still talking.

Emma called out, "Did you find out anything?"

"Always impatient," he called back. "Let me sit down first." He went in, sat down, and deliberately took his time starting.

"Jeremy!" Emma said loudly.

"Okay, okay, a few things," he said and looked at Patrice. "Your grandmother is in residence at another hotel in the city."

"Then who's on the top floor?" Emma asked, thinking of the painting she'd seen.

"Abella, Patrice's aunt," Jeremy supplied.

That made Patrice frown. Emma was watching her, "What's the matter? That news seemed to bother you."

"Papa mentioned we were to live in this hotel," Patrice said, remembering her papa's description of their new life here.

Hmm, thought Emma, *something to think about. What if Abella didn't want to move?* "Does anyone else lives with her?" Emma asked Jeremy.

"I didn't ask," he admitted.

"We'll have to find out. I expect the 'ghost' lives there," said

Emma. "You mentioned a grandmother. What are you thinking?"

"I think we need to go see her. Also, I found out her name is Patrice."

"It is?" she asked, as she glanced over at Patrice.

"I was named after her," the other girl said helpfully.

Emma smiled, "Then we'll have to see her. I think, once she takes a look at you, there'll be a large number of questions answered."

"When will we go?" asked Patrice, ready for this to be over.

"Tomorrow morning?" Jeremy suggested.

"Why not now?" Emma asked.

"Well, I learned that Abella likes to sleep in. So, I'm thinking that'll make it easier to leave without her being notified."

"I like it," Emma confirmed. "We'll need to be refreshed and ready for the meeting."

Patrice was hopeful for the first time, "Do you think she knows where my mum and papa are?"

"I think that'll be a good start," Jeremy said.

"We should try to get some rest," suggested Emma.

"What about that?" Jeremy used his head to indicate Patrice's room.

"I think we've had enough drama tonight. Patrice can sleep with me in our room," said Emma. "You can sleep in Dora and Tim's room."

"What about Patrice's room? What if someone comes into the suite?" asked Jeremy.

"Patrice and I moved the dresser in front of the door. We can also move something heavy in front of the hallway door. If the 'ghost' tries to come in, he shouldn't be able to move it," said Emma. After they closed the door to the room and moved a bookcase in front of it.

"That's done," said Emma. "Bedtime." She took Patrice's hand and headed toward their room.

Jeremy stopped them, "I learned one more thing. We may have a difficult time getting to Patrice's grandmother."

"Why's that?" asked Emma.

"Her husband," he looked at Patrice with a serious expression, "your grandfather, has passed away. I was told she's in mourning and may not be seeing anyone."

"Grandfather? I never even got to meet him." The small happiness Patrice felt drained out of her.

"We're sorry," Emma said in sympathy.

They headed to get their things to prepare for bed. Jeremy exited their room and Emma followed him. "Hey, I'll miss you," she said softly as she kissed him.

"It's only for the night," he reminded her, tucking her hair that had become loose behind her ear.

"I hope this goes well tomorrow."

"Me, too," he said. He noticed she was staring toward Tim and Dora's room.

"We'll find them tomorrow," he promised.

"Yes, once we get Patrice settled, we can find them," she said determinedly.

CHAPTER 17

The next morning, Emma, Jeremy, and Patrice entered the Assond Hotel. They paused and Jeremy observed, "I don't think we're going to get anywhere with the desk. Their main job is to keep people from bothering her, especially now."

"I agree," Emma said and they headed to the elevator. It opened as they approached and they stepped in. Emma studied the board and noted the highest floor just under the penthouse. Jeremy frowned and she mouthed, *Later*. She didn't want the elevator operator to know where they were going.

"Floor?" the elevator operator asked in French.

"Nine please." The three were quiet as the elevator made its way to the requested floor. When the elevator stopped, they disembarked and waited until the elevator doors closes before moving.

"Why didn't we go to the top?" asked Jeremy.

"I think we wouldn't have been allowed up there. I bet the elevator opens into the residence," she said.

Emma started down the hallway to an unmarked door. Patrice and Jeremy followed. She reached out and tried the knob. It was locked.

"We'll have the same issue; this time a locked door," Patrice said, looking at it.

"Oh, that's okay, locked doors are not an issue," Emma said as she pulled out her lockpick kit. Jeremy watched with a smile.

After a few minutes, the lock clicked, and the three made their way inside and up the stairs. "I'm hoping this is the service entrance."

They climbed the stairs, each person lost in their own thoughts, not wanting to voice their nerves. The stairs stopped at another locked door.

"Will you open this one?" asked Patrice.

Emma looked thoughtful, "Hmmm. I think I'll just knock on this one." Jeremy grinned at her. "Ready?" she asked her small group.

"Yes," Jeremy and Patrice answered together.

Emma raised her hand and knocked. It was only a few moments before the door swung open, revealing a tall man dressed in a black suit and tie. *Butler,* thought Emma.

"Oui, vous avez une livraison?" he asked, looking at their hands. *Yes, you have a delivery?* He frowned and continued in French, "How did you get up here if you were not accompanied? This is a private residence. I'll have to contact security and report you."

They heard a woman's voice ask in French, "What is happening here?"

"Nothing, madam, these people have made a mistake. I'll have it corrected."

Emma raised her voice to make sure she was heard. "Patrice we can come back later."

"Patrice?" the woman questioned, her voice faint.

Emma answered for her. "Elle s'appelle Patrice Lanier."

"Move aside, William," they heard the other woman say in English. The man moved and, for the first time, they saw the woman they had been speaking with. She was in all-black lace.

It was an intricate dress with a high neck and long sleeves. Her dark hair, streaked with grey, was done elaborately on her head. "Patrice, come to me," she said in a commanding voice.

Patrice kept her eyes downward and gripped Emma's hand tightly. Emma looked at the Madam, then back at Patrice, "It's okay, go on," she encouraged

Patrice removed her hand from Emma's and went to where the Madam stood.

"Let me see your eyes," the Madam commanded, using her right hand to lift Patrice's chin gently.

When brilliant blue eyes met an identical set, they both gasped.

"You're Charles' Patrice," the woman said and pulled her into a fierce hug. The Madam looked over Patrice's shoulder at Emma, "You're not Catherine."

"No, I'm Emma Evans and this is Jeremy Tilden," Emma answered.

"Let us move into the sitting room. I think we're offending William's sensibilities."

They observed William and saw he was indeed uncomfortable. Emma answered, "Of course." They moved to follow the Madam.

William rushed ahead of her and held the door open for them. The room they entered was large and similar to the penthouse at their hotel. It was decorated in dark browns and burgundy, with large couches and rugs that covered the space. The dining room was located at the far end of the room.

Patrice wasn't interested in the room; she was staring at her grandmother.

The Madam sat, "Now, sit." She kept Patrice next to her and asked, "Where is your mother? I have wanted to meet her for such a long time."

"You have?" Patrice asked, astonished at her grandmother's statement.

"Yes, *I* have," said the Madam. Her emphasis was noted by Emma.

"Mum is missing," Patrice said loudly. She lowered her voice and continued, "She disappeared from the hotel."

The Madam seemed shocked and looked over at Emma and Jeremy for confirmation. "And what do you know about this?" the Madam asked Emma. It came out as a demand, but Emma could see the worry in her eyes.

"I can tell you what we know," Emma commented. She and Jeremy went into the description of how they met Patrice. They hadn't yet mentioned the ghost or the secret panel.

"You say the hotel claimed you didn't have a room?" Her voice raised at this outrage, that someone from her family would have been treated this way.

"Yes," commented Patrice.

"Why isn't my son with you?"

"Papa told us to meet him at the hotel. Mum thought we'd be seeing him and then visiting you. Did you know we were coming to Paris?" Patrice asked.

"No, I haven't been myself as of late," her grandmother replied, touching the broach at her throat.

"We heard that Grandfather passed. I'm sorry," commented Patrice.

The Madam pulled herself back from her memories, "Yes, thank you." Her gaze moved back to Emma and Jeremy, "Did you speak to the manager of the hotel? Or just a clerk?"

"I did speak to both," commented Jeremy. "I was shown the register and was told neither Patrice nor Catherine ever had a room there. They also mentioned that no one accompanied Patrice."

"Who would have set up the room for them?" Emma asked.

"My son would have done that. You say Catherine was sick?"

"She seemed to be," Patrice said and looked at Emma and Jeremy for support.

"There's another part of the story you're not aware of," commented Emma.

"Well, tell me," the Madam said impatiently.

Instead of answering, Emma said, "We're staying in a suite on the third floor."

The Madam was a little shocked, "How would you have gotten that room?"

"What do you mean?" Jeremy asked.

"That room is normally only for guests we need to have private meetings with."

"So, you do know about the secret panel that leads to the penthouse?" he asked.

"I do, but I don't know who would have assigned it to you." She frowned at them, trying to understand their part in her family drama. "What does this have to do with Patrice's mum being sick?"

"Someone has been drugging Patrice to keep her off balance," Emma answered, "We believe her mum was also drugged before her disappearance."

The Madam looked at her without expression. Instead of responding to that, she asked, "What was your purpose for coming to Paris?"

Emma decided to let the Madam guide the conversation. She responded, "We were invited by The Art Curator's Society. They said it was because of my work on a case a few years back, that saved art within their community."

Madam studied Emma with renewed interest, "Yes, I read about that, but that name you mentioned, The Art Curator's Society, I have never heard of it."

"Neither had the local gallery owners," Emma informed her. They had received confirmation from the museum manager that the society wasn't real.

"You were brought here under false circumstances," stated the Madam.

"Yes, we believe so."

The Madam asked, "Do you think someone at the hotel might be involved in this?"

"We're not sure," Emma admitted and looked over at Jeremy.

He started, "The manager that Patrice dealt with was not the same one that's there now."

"Did you inquire about the man?" the Madam asked.

"I was told he left and isn't expected to return."

She frowned but didn't say anything.

Patrice asked, "Grandmeir, you own the hotel, can you inquire about this man?"

"That is rather complicated," the Madam said and glanced away.

"Why is that?" Emma asked.

The older woman sighed, stood, and walked to the mantle. She picked up a small painting and looked at it for a long time. Finally, she turned back to them still clutching the picture tightly. "Abella is running the hotel. I'm not involved in the day-to-day business there. She would not like my interference."

"I thought Papa was running the hotels here in Paris," commented Patrice.

"He does. But that one... I agreed to let my daughter run it."

"What is the concern?" Emma asked.

"It was a trial having her run it, and she wasn't working out. Charles was going to come back and take over. Which is why I was finally going to meet my family. Charles needed to relocate here." The Madam looked thoughtful and asked, "The passageway you mentioned, did you see anyone come through into that room?"

"Yes, a small boy of about nine. He's blond with blue eyes and a slim build." Emma saw Jeremy's surprise at the description and explained, "Patrice remembered more when you were with the manager."

"I saw a boy that met that description in the hallway near our hotel room," Jeremy responded.

"What was he doing?" the Madam asked.

"Watching the door," he commented, wishing he had stopped him and asked who he was.

"You didn't think that odd?" the Madam asked.

"No, not at that time. We've seen kids all over the hotel. I just thought it was another one running around."

"Is this him?" asked the Madam as she held out the portrait to them.

Jeremy took it first and studied it. "Yes, I believe so." He passed it on to Patrice, "Do you recognize him?"

Patrice's face went white, "It's him."

"He's my grandson, Paul," the Madam said tightly.

"Do you think his mother did something to Mum?" Patrice asked tremulously.

"I hope not," her grandmother said as she walked over to take Patrice's hand. She was resolved and asked, "Where do we go from here?"

"I was thinking about that," said Emma. "Patrice, how did you find us? How did you know to come to our suite?"

"The bellman told me," Patrice said.

"The bellman?"

"Yes, I was giving up hope and the hotel had threatened to have me removed, then this man in a uniform came up and whispered to me that Emma could help me."

"What happened next?" Jeremy asked.

"He helped me to your room and left me outside your door."

"Why didn't he stay and how did he know about Emma?"

"I don't know," Patrice answered simply.

"We need to talk to this bellman. Did you know his name? Can you give us a description?" asked Emma.

"I don't think there was a name, but he had a mark on his hand. A black circle."

"Thank you, Patrice, that'll give us something to go on," Emma told the girl, "We'll need to go there next." She glanced over at the Madam, "We need a safe place for Patrice to stay."

"She will stay here," she said firmly. She placed a hand on her hair and asked, "Would you like that?"

"I would!"

"Good, we have a lot to talk about," The Madam said and smiled at her granddaughter warmly.

Patrice smiled back. "I'd like that."

"We'll leave now and investigate this," Emma said softly. "Please, keep her presence here quiet."

"I will," promised the Madam.

"Your staff…" started Emma.

"They can be trusted," the Madam said, her tone brooking no argument.

"Patrice, we'll be back," Emma assured the girl.

"I'll be okay here," she said, her hand still in the Madam's hands.

They stood and turned back toward the kitchen. The Madam called to them, a laugh in her voice. "You may use the front entrance to leave."

"I'll take them, Madam," William said quietly. He had entered the room and heard her last comment.

Emma grinned back and Jeremy laughed as they adjusted their path and followed William to the elevator. "Thank you," Jeremy said.

William nodded and pushed the call button for them. When it appeared, the operator looked surprised at the persons waiting to board. How they had gotten to the penthouse without him seeing. His frown spoke volumes and William spoke up, "You need not concern yourself."

The operator opened and closed his mouth several times but didn't say anything. He finally nodded and waved them into the elevator. He didn't say anything as they rode down and exited into the lobby.

Emma pulled Jeremy to a halt as they strode through the lobby. "This is a beautiful hotel," she observed.

"Expensive," he murmured, taking in his surroundings.

"There's a lot of money at stake here, and only one sibling left to take it all," she said contemplatively.

He nodded. "Let's find that bellboy."

They were able to get a carriage to take them back to their hotel. Once there they found the lobby was full of people. Emma asked, "How do we find him?"

"Let's ask them," Jeremy said, indicating the bellmen grouped across the room.

"Casually, we need to look for that mark," she suggested.

They headed over to them. Jeremy asked in French, "Can I get directions to a local patisserie?"

Two of the men pointed. Emma shook her head; she didn't see the mark. They needed to talk to one of the men alone. She continued her observations and saw a man standing away from the other bellman on the opposite side of the desk. Emma cleared her throat and nodded toward him.

Jeremy and Emma walked over to him, "Sir, can I speak to you for a moment?" she asked.

The bellman had straightened as they approached. "Do you need some help with your bags?"

"No, we have a question about another bellman. He has a circle mark on the back of his hand," Emma said, keeping her voice low.

He glanced around quickly, "Not here." He nodded to the corner and they followed him to a closet where bags were stored when rooms were unavailable.

"His name is Etienne and you won't find him here," he said.

"Where is he?" asked Emma.

"He's gone," he said simply.

"Do you know if he left of his own accord?"

"Definitely not. He supports his family and he's worried about his job. He's in hiding."

"Why?"

"For helping that girl and getting her to you," the bellman said.

"You know about that?"

"Etienne and I are friends," he said simply.

"Do you know his address?" Jeremy asked.

"I do, but he isn't there."

Emma's mouth twisted; her patience was waning. "Do you know where he is?"

"Yes," he answered simply.

"And," Jeremy prompted.

"He's at my place," the man admitted. "It's in the 18 Arrondissement." He wrote it down quickly and handed it to Emma.

A voice called the bellman's name. He was distracted by the call and said, "I have to go. I have to keep this job."

"Go on," Emma said. "We'll be getting back with you."

"Don't let anything happen to Etienne," he pressed.

"We won't," she promised.

They studied the address. Jeremy said, "Should we head over there now?"

She looked conflicted. "Jeremy, I know this is important but I am worried. What if Dora and Tim are with Michael and Lenora?"

"Isn't that what we suspected all along?"

"Yes, but what if they're there against their will? Inspector Levan mentioned they had checked out," she speculated.

"Before we head to the bellboy's apartment, we should probably go check their hotel room," Jeremy suggested. He glanced over at the desk, "I see the manager who talked to me earlier. Let me see if I can get their room number."

She nodded and stayed where she was as he went to the desk.

"Let's go up to the room," he said coming back.

They went two floors up and stood in front of room 2958. Jeremy knocked and they waited, not expecting anyone to answer. However, they were surprised to come face to face with someone they didn't recognize.

"Yes?" the man asked.

"I'm sorry to bother you. We're looking for information about the couple who stayed here. Could you tell me when you checked in?" inquired Jeremy.

"Well," the man admitted. "I was lucky. I showed up without a reservation and the hotel was full. I was told that the room had come available at just that moment."

"When was this?" asked Emma.

"Yesterday evening."

"Thank you," said Jeremy.

The door closed and Emma observed, "That was when we received the note about yesterday. They must have come by to the hotel to leave the note and check out."

The worry about Dora and Tim made its way to the surface. "Two cases," she said, "both involving vanishing people."

"Do you think they're connected?" Jeremy asked.

"I don't think so; these appear to be two separate cases."

"Where to next? Bellman?"

"It's our best bet for finding Patrice's mum," she confirmed.

"And Tim and Dora?" he asked, knowing she was worried. Should that case take precedence over this one?

She shook her head and said, "We should move forward on Patrice's case. We have a definite location for the bellboy. We can re-evaluate after that."

They exited the hotel and walked a few blocks to get a cab. "This would be easier," she muttered, "if it wasn't so crowded."

Jeremy just smiled in response.

The cab took them to an older apartment building. They paid the driver and went into the older building. There they found the door and knocked. A scurrying could be heard inside but the sounds did not approach the door. "Etienne, we're here to ask you questions about Patrice," she called in French.

"You might mention your name," Jeremy suggested.

"Etienne, Etienne, I'm Emma you told Patrice to come to me for help."

After she made that statement, the lock on the door could be heard unlatching.

A young man appeared. "Etienne?" she asked.

"Oui." This was confirmed when he rubbed his hand across his face and they saw the round mark on his hand.

His eyes went to Jeremy. "He's with me," she said firmly. She saw his hesitance and said, "We want to help Patrice."

He stepped back, "Come in, and you can speak English."

They entered the apartment and he locked the door quickly behind them.

When he noticed the security measures, Jeremy asked, "Is someone threatening you?"

Etienne didn't answer. Instead, he waved them to the small sitting area, "Please, sit." He waited for them to take their seats and took the one across from them. He started to explain his role in Patrice's adventure. "It all started when Monsieur Lanier told me to keep an eye out for his wife and daughter."

"When was this?" asked Emma, pulling out her notebook.

"It was the morning before Patrice and her mother arrived. He said he was being called out of the country on critical business. His father had died and there were concerns he needed to deal with immediately."

"Did it seem like it was planned?" Jeremy asked.

"No, he found out after his family was already traveling. He said he'd leave them a letter."

Emma made note of that; there had been no mention of a letter. "What did he ask you to do?"

"To watch out for them," he said simply.

"Watch out?" Jeremy questioned. "Why?"

"At the time, I thought it was just the request from a worried husband and father."

"And now?" Emma asked.

"I think he knew something might happen while he was gone," Etienne admitted.

"What were his exact instructions?" Emma asked. She had to know the connection between Patrice and herself.

"He said if Patrice or her mother needed help for any reason, I should tell them to find you," he explained.

"How would you know where we were located?" asked Jeremy. *What was the tie-in to their suite?*

"Mister Lanier saw your name on the reservation books. He moved you to that suite you're in now. He wanted to make sure his wife and daughter could find you if they needed help."

"So, our being located in that room *is* related to the Vanishing lady case," Emma murmured to Jeremy.

"Did you see Patrice's mother arrive at the hotel?" asked Jeremy

"They arrived late, and I was off duty at that time."

"Did you follow up the next day?" asked Emma.

"No," he said miserably. "My directions were that they'd come to me if they needed anything. I should have checked them that day. I told myself they were resting."

"How did you know they'd checked in?" Jeremy asked as he thought of his conversation with the manager.

"I checked the reservation book," Etienne admitted. It was normally off-limits to personnel other than the clerks assigned to that area.

"Are you sure?" asked Jeremy. "I saw the reservation book; it didn't list either of them."

Etienne nodded his head, "Oh, I'm sure. Their names were both listed."

"There must be a second book. We need to find it," Emma told Jeremy.

And what else did the manager hide from me? Jeremy thought.

"Why are you hiding?" Emma asked.

"I had to. After Patrice's mum disappeared, the managers were making plans to have Patrice taken away. I heard them discussing how troublesome she was becoming. I knew I had to act and get her to you. Then I left."

"Who knew that you did this?"

"Just my friend Howard. He let me stay here. We can trust him."

"No one else?" Emma asked as she took notes on his statements.

"No, no one," he confirmed.

"Why not take her to her family, her aunt lives in the hotel," asked Emma

"Mr. Lanier," Etienne supplied. "When I asked him why I just didn't take her to them, he was clear I was not to do that."

Emma frowned, "Why would he say that?"

He turned red, "I don't like to gossip, but his sister never liked Mister Lanier. They do not get along. I believe she has also said some terrible things about Patrice and her mum."

"How do you know that?"

"That one, she can be loud and doesn't care who's listening."

"We took Patrice to her grandmother. Will she be safe there?"

"If she is with the Madam, then yes. Listen, I'm planning to leave town until I have heard from my friend that it's safe to come back."

"We understand. How do we get in touch with you?"

"Let Howard know; he'll find me."

"Thank you. You probably saved Patrice's life," Emma said.

"I wish I'd done more, but I was so scared," he said, looking down at his hands.

"Maybe next time something like this comes up, you will," she suggested quietly.

He nodded.

They stood and Jeremy said, "Etienne, we wish you well and will try to get word to you soon."

"I hope so, thank you," the other man said gratefully.

Jeremy and Emma stood in the hallway after the door was closed and locked. Jeremy leaned against the wall, "It looks like Abella is behind all of this."

"Yes, and everyone seems to know," Emma said wonderingly. "How could she do this to her family?"

"Do you think Patrice's mum is still alive?" asked Jeremy, wondering if they were chasing a ghost.

"I do. It makes the most sense. It would be hard to get rid of a body, especially with all of those crowds."

"But then they'd have to house and feed her," he reasoned.

"That's true," she said contemplatively. He noticed she raised her fingers to her lips to drum them.

"What are you thinking?"

"*If* she's alive and Abella is involved, I'd say she's in the penthouse of our hotel."

"Sounds reasonable," he said, always up for an adventure. "When do we go in?"

"Tonight, late. Agreed?"

"Agreed." He could see her face becoming more serious. "What are you thinking of?"

"The same thing that's been on my mind for the last day."

"Tim and Dora," he guessed.

"Yes," she said.

"We can work on their case. Where do you want to start?"

"Michael, Lenora, and Julian seem connected to the Galerie des Machines."

"That's true. Since we've been in Paris, that's where we have seen them together."

"And that's where Julian died," she reminded him. "I'd also like to talk to Papa and find out about the meeting he had with Julian. We need to know if he's aware of what Julian was involved in."

"So, we go to the Galerie des Machines?"

"Yes. We can stop for something to eat on the way and then head to the exposition."

He offered his elbow to her; she took it and they walked downstairs. "I think I saw a small café nearby."

"Lead the way."

They found it and had a light lunch with a round loaf of bread, cheese, and wine.

They finished quickly and found a cab to the exposition. "This has been an active vacation," Jeremy commented.

"Aren't they all?" Emma teased as she leaned on him.

"It does make things interesting."

"Yes, it does," she murmured, tilting her head back to kiss him. After their kiss, she settled with her head on his shoulder. Emma didn't mind that the ride took some time.

As they arrive, they stepped off the carriage. "It seems more people are here than in the morning," she said. Jeremy nodded, took her hand, and started walking with her through the crowds.

"Want to try the train?" she called.

"If we can get on it," he called back, continuing to go through the crowd that seemed to flow to the long train line. "We haven't made our way to the country exhibits yet," he said, looking toward that area.

"Funny thing about that. Julian wasn't sure we should. He didn't believe it adequately represented the different cultures. Though I'd still like to see them," said Emma.

"We'll get over there before we head home," he promised.

She continued to look around as they made their way to the front of the line. They boarded and took their seats. As it started to move, she glanced to her right and frowned. "Is that? It has to be... Jeremy," she said in a low whisper. "It's them, isn't it?"

"It's them, Lenora and Michael," Jeremy muttered, watching the duo.

Before he could stop her, Emma jumped up and yelled out the window, "Lenora! Michael! Stop!" Her voice must have carried because the two stopped in the crowd and turned toward the moving train. When they saw her, they took off at a run. The train was moving smoothly, but they were faster.

"We need to get off," she muttered as she dropped back into her seat.

Jeremy wanted to as well, but the train was very crowded and would likely not stop for them. She sat back reluctantly in her chair.

"They're headed toward the gallery," he commented, continuing to monitor their movements from the window.

Emma's enjoyment was gone for the train ride; she strained, trying to catch a glimpse of Lenora and Michael. The train came to a stop and they filed out. Emma and Jeremy were seated in the middle and had to wait until the people in front of them moved.

Once they were off, they moved through the crowd quickly, breaking into a run as they got closer to the Gallery de Machines' outer entrance. They pulled open the large glass doors and entered quickly, running through the exhibits. They were no longer fascinating, they were in the way. They continued to run through the maze of machines. Jeremy was a little ahead of her and said over his shoulder, "They've split up. You go after her and I'll go after him."

She nodded and headed in the direction he indicated. She slipped her hand into her skirt pocket and pulled out her knife, palming it as she ran. Lenora was just ahead on a parallel walkway. Emma jumped on a table, crossing quickly, and leaped onto Lenora's back. Emma pulled her hair back and placed the knife under her chin. "Go along with what I say," she growled in a low voice, "and you might live. Do you understand?"

Lenora nodded and they stood up. Instead of going docilely forward, she pivoted and, to Emma's surprise, was wielding her own knife.

Emma had just a moment to respond. She bent backward to escape the slicing motion of the knife. The corset limited her movement, but when she felt the knife go across her ribs, there was a quick burn but not a deep cut. *Corsets? Who knew?*

She pulled herself back up and kicked the other woman in the stomach. It knocked the breath out of Lenora and the knife flew out of her hand. Emma deftly caught it.

"Are you ready to accompany me now?" Emma asked, rubbing the blades together.

"Yes," Lenora mumbled.

A group of people had formed a circle around them.

Emma palmed the knives, "All part of the show folks, we were just having fun, weren't we?" She nudged the other woman to respond.

"Yes, we're friends," Lenora said, standing close to Emma.

"Was that you running across the displays?" asked the owner of the area she had run across.

"I'm sorry. I got carried away with our game," Emma apologized.

"Take it outside," he demanded.

She nodded and turned to Lenora, "Come with me."

The group parted as they left the area. Lenora started to struggle against the firm hold Emma had on her as she was pulled along through the crowd. Lenora continued to slow their progress by dragging her feet, which caused Emma to stop short.

Emma turned back towards her, "Come on. Stop stalling."

Lenora's eyes widened and she opened her mouth. The expected sound didn't come out; instead, blood flowed out and she fell forward into Emma's arms. "What?" Emma stopped when she saw the knife sticking out of Lenora's back. What she heard next was a scream.

Damn. Should I stay or make a run for it? she thought for a brief moment. *Stay,* she decided and lay Lenora's body down. Emma took off her jacket to staunch the flow of blood. Voices penetrated her intense concentration and she realized another crowd had formed around them.

"Get help!" she yelled at them.

Her order seemed to unfreeze them. "Police! Police!" several voices called out.

A policeman ran up and told the crowd to clear. He knelt, feeling for a pulse. "I do not believe that is necessary any longer," he said to Emma, causing her to stop pressing down on the wound.

She nodded and thought, *Who killed Lenora?*

The officer pulled her up and away. More officers arrived and quickly removed the body to a nearby room. The people who had organized the exposition would want to minimize any publicity of the event.

"You will need to come with me to the station," the policeman said brusquely. He was still unsure what her role in the murder had been. "Wait here. Do not leave, I need to tell the detectives I am taking you to the station."

"Of course," Emma said. She knew the procedure would require questioning her. *Though,* she thought, *I don't know how much information she could provide.*

There was a noise coming toward her; a man pushed through the crowd. Jeremy's face came into view. He took in the scene, "Are you okay?" he asked.

Emma looked down and felt where Lenora's knife had made contact with her. "You know, there's something positive about corsets. The whalebone in the garment helped protect me. It was just a glancing blow."

Jeremy put his hand on the torn fabric and said, "Good. Maybe you should wear those back home."

"I'm thinking the same thing."

"So, what happened? Who killed Lenora?"

"I don't know. I was trying to get her out of here to question her and then this happened," she said, waving her hand towards the policemen taking away Lenora's body.

They continued to watch the policemen discuss the scene. Two bodies in two days; there would be questions. An officer walked over to her, "You know this woman? You were with her?"

"I was," Emma answered.

"We understand that you jumped on her and effectively dragged her away." It was a statement, not a question

"I just wanted to speak with her."

"Do you speak to everyone in that manner?" the officer asked as he watched her carefully.

She kept her face blank, "Sometimes."

A familiar voice spoke. "Two scenes in two days," Inspector Levan said in an almost jovial manner.

"Inspector Levan," she said, relieved to see a familiar face.

Jeremy stepped up, "Can we go somewhere to talk?" He didn't want Emma taken into the station.

Levan looked at them and back at the scene. He dismissed the two officers by saying, "Get pictures before you move her." He looked back at them and said, "Come with me."

He seemed to realize where they were. "There is nowhere in the city to be alone anymore," he said, shaking his head. "Over here." He waved them into a workroom that seemed to be for cleaning supplies. He closed the door and turned toward Emma, "Did you kill her?"

"No," she answered without hesitation.

"The weapon used to kill her was a knife," he said with little emotion in his voice. "I understand that the knife is your weapon of choice."

"It is," she commented. A knock on the door interrupted their questioning.

He frowned heavily toward it and said loudly, "Come in." The officer came in and handed him something wrapped in a cloth. "You may leave now." The officer glared at him and stomped out of the room.

Levan revealed what the cloth covered. It was a lethal-looking knife. It was hard for her not to reach for it. She studied it and thought, *It was well-balanced and the artistry is there.* He watched her, "Is this yours?"

"No, it's not."

"I don't think you'd admit to it, even if it was," he said, examining the knife, then back at her.

"I wouldn't," she admitted.

Jeremy stayed silent, letting the scene play out. He didn't think she was in trouble, but the inspector knew there was more to the story.

"You told me that you didn't have a relationship with Lenora and her husband Michael," Levan accused.

"We didn't. They're friends of Dora and Tim."

"The ones we cannot seem to find to interview," he murmured.

"Yes, they're missing and we think Michael and Lenora know where they are," she said boldly.

"That is what I thought. Why not tell us right away so we could help out?"

"I thought we could handle it ourselves."

He let that go, "Tell me what you know."

Jeremy stepped up, "We don't have a lot of information so far."

"Have Tim or Dora shown back up?" asked Levan.

"Not yet," Emma admitted.

"How did you know to come here? How does the Galerie des Machines factor into this? How did you know Lenora would be here?"

"Michael was here also," commented Jeremy. "I chased him but he got away."

Emma answered the inspector's question. "Since arriving in Paris, besides the hotel, this was the only location we've seen them. It seemed like the most likely spot."

Levan looked around, "What is it about this particular exhibit that would be of such interest or a location for intrigue?"

"We think there's going to be some kind of planned event by the anti-electrical people," Emma admitted.

"Oui," Levan murmured, "it all seems to be going that way. But if they are behind this, why would they go after one of their leaders?"

Emma's gaze first went to Jeremy and then back at Levan, "We'd hoped to get information on their plans from Lenora. Someone must have decided she was a weak point." At that moment, the door opened. They saw the body being taken away.

They were silent as they watched it go by. "Our main goal is to find Tim and Dora and make sure they're okay," Jeremy said.

"If that is true, why wait until today to investigate their disappearance?" Levan asked.

Emma said, "We've had another case that needed us."

"Another case?" he murmured. "Maybe it's something I can help with?"

"Possibly. It's stable right now, but we may need your help soon."

"Are things normally this interesting around you?" he asked.

Jeremy answered that with a hearty laugh. "Yeah, this is pretty normal for us."

"I think I can help with Dora and Tim's disappearance," the inspector said thoughtfully.

"How so?" Emma asked eagerly. She was desperate to have something to help move the case forward and get her family home.

"We have a lead on Lenora and Michael," he stated.

"You started to look into them?"

"Yes, there were just too many coincidences, and now this."

"What did you find?" asked Jeremy.

Levan checked his notes, "They're actually from the United States."

"That isn't much of a lead," she commented. "They came over with us."

"Yes, you're right, but we did find out they rent several apartments in the city. We also had several anti-electricity demonstrators picked up who were able to identify them."

"What type of demonstration were they involved in?" asked Jeremy. He wondered about their level of violence. They knew Lenora and Michael would do what they had to, but what about their other demonstrators? Were they as committed?

"Up until now, they've been just a nuisance. They hate the tower, they hate the changes for the exposition, and they hate anything to do with electricity."

"Electricity," Emma murmured. *It keeps coming up. Could that be it?* she thought, looking at the exhibits showing through the door. But why involve Tim and Dora?

"What are you thinking?" Levan asked.

"Tim and Dora. Why would someone involved with the anti-electricity movement want them?" she asked. "They're no one special. They don't have any connections to any of this. Unless...."

Levan didn't interrupt, waiting for her to explain her thoughts. Jeremy watched Emma formulate ideas and possibilities in her mind, discarding some, and accepting others. He saw her eyes widen.

"Jeremy!" she said, turning to him, "It must be Papa!"

"Ellis? How so?" he asked, trying to keep up with her.

"Come on, I'll show you." Before Jeremy and Levan knew it, she had exited the room. They had to run to keep pace. She stopped abruptly in front of the Edison exhibit. "This is it," she said and whirled around.

When they didn't respond, she held her arms open wide, taking in her surroundings, "Don't you see? They hate electricity; they're here on the world's biggest stage to prove something."

"Prove what and how?" asked Levan.

"That, I'm not sure of," she admitted, "but I think Papa, Tim, Dora, and Mr. Edison are all connected to this. "

"Why?" Jeremy asked.

"Papa's note," she said. "There's something very special happening this evening and I believe it involves Mr. Edison."

"And they want to interfere in that, to prove a point about electricity?" Levan asked.

"Yes, but I think it's more than interference," she said.

Levan protested. "These people are normally not violent; they demonstrate and loudly discuss their concerns and then leave."

"I think Lenora and Michael were pushing for a dramatic demonstration. You know we were sent tickets and brought over by people who haven't revealed themselves yet."

"You think it was them," the inspector asked.

Jeremy spoke up, "I think we were brought here for a reason and this, along with Tim and Dora disappearing, seems to confirm it."

"Where do we go from here?" muttered Emma, looking at the brilliant lighting exhibit.

"Find Tim and Dora," suggested Jeremy.

"I wonder," Emma said, "what about the security for tonight, in case something is planned."

The Inspector was surprised, "Yes, we'll have extra security but we do not expect the crowds to be unruly."

Emma looked around, "Oh, the crowds will be involved, but not in the way you think. I think they want a large group of people here to prove their point..."

"That electricity can be dangerous," Jeremy finished her statement.

The inspector's face went white and he put a hand to his heart. "We can't call off the event." He walked closer to them and lowered his voice. "Edison and Tesla will be here tonight."

"Both of them? Here?" asked Emma, astonished. "I thought they didn't get along."

"That is just a rumor," said Levan. "They're meeting at the Eiffel Tower."

"That must be it," Jeremy said, "That would be quite a splash. Go after the men at the head of the technology."

"No, I don't think so." Emma said slowly. "I read about this. The tower was supposed to be electrically lit, but there were problems and they had to use gas lamps."

"Then where?" Jeremy asked.

"It could be anywhere," she admitted.

"But that installation is very big. We don't have time to find it," Levan said. He was right; the sun was starting to set.

Emma said, "Inspector, can you round up your people and start inspecting the lines?"

"Even if we could, there's no way we'd be able to walk all the lines," the inspector insisted.

"Can we stop the program?" Jeremy asked.

The inspector said, "France's national pride was tied up in this exposition. Anything but that."

"What time is it expected to start?" Emma asked, thinking about what they could do.

"At 10PM."

"We have four hours then."

Levan was resigned, "I can have my men walk the lines, but what are we looking for?"

"A bomb," Emma said with certainty.

"A bomb?" questioned Jeremy. "What makes you think it must be that?"

"It's the electricity. A bomb could be used to complete the circuit. It could be anywhere." She glanced at the inspector, "Do you need a drawing of what types of things to look for?" She could draw out the basics for them.

He shook his head and assured her, "No, we have studied the 1884 and 85 London bombings. We have drawings of the devices, so we're good with the identification."

"Are there drawings of the light exhibit?" she asked, wanting to narrow down the options.

"I'm not sure," Levan admitted.

"Papa said something special was happening tonight; he must have meant Edison and the installation," she murmured.

Jeremy looked at the inspector, "You start the search, and we'll find Ellis."

"I think he's probably at the Eiffel Tower," said Emma.

The trio separated, their tasks clear.

The inspector called to his men and headed toward the outdoor lighting installation.

Emma and Jeremy headed toward the Eiffel Tower. They were jogging, but the crowds prevented them from moving too quickly. She wanted to push. The people seemed to be deliberately getting in their way. Jeremy had her hand and was pulling her through the crowd. They were feeling desperate and she told him, "Keep going. I'll keep up."

He looked at her, "Grab my coat and hang on."

She got a grip and called, "Go!" They forced their way through with complaints all around.

They pushed past a very large man. "Hey!" the man called loudly. He was obviously American. "Where are you going in such a hurry?" he said, grabbing Jeremy by the collar and lifting him off of his feet.

We don't have time for this, thought Emma. The man holding Jeremy didn't seem to notice her. The crowd naturally gave the large man space, not wanting trouble. He had a firm hold on Jeremy but swayed from the alcohol he had imbibed. She glanced around quickly and saw he had a bottle of wine next to him on the fountain basin's edge.

Jeremy hammered his fist at the hands holding his collar, but the man had a stranglehold on his neck. Emma took the opportunity to kick him in the back of the legs. It had a dual effect; he dropped Jeremy and fell to his knees. The man was still on his knees when he turned toward her and yelled out, "You, girl, come here!"

Before the large man could get to his feet, Jeremy grabbed her hand and pulled her into the crowds. They saw a police officer and Jeremy thought fast. "Officer, officer! There's a man back there, he's waving a gun...at a woman." He waved toward the man still barreling in their direction.

The man yelled at them, "There you are. I need to talk with you!"

The officer saw the man pushing people out of his path. When he shoved a child to the ground, the policeman quickly turned away from Jeremy and called on his men. They could not stop him with one person, so several jumped on his back.

Emma and Jeremy sank back into the crowd and looked toward the elevator. "We don't have time for the line," Jeremy commented.

"No, we don't," Emma said, reviewing the area. "It will have to be the stairs." There was also a line there, but it seemed to be progressing more smoothly.

They headed over, trying to find a way to skip the line. They didn't have to work out a plan as the people moved out of the way to watch the large man fighting with the policeman. She and Jeremy moved quickly up the stairs. He looked back and saw the police had wrestled the man to the ground. Jeremy smiled; the big guy had actually helped them.

They made it to the first level, both breathing heavily, but they didn't delay as they headed to the next set of stairs. They were almost vacant; most people stopped on the first floor for the restaurants and the view. The second level was steeper and harder. Once they exited and headed to the final stairs, Emma doubled over trying to catch her breath. "Ready?" she asked gasping.

"The things I do for you," he muttered, following her up another set of stairs.

"Oh, you love it," she said cheekily as they ran.

They headed to the last stairs, which were a spiral, and realized there were guards. *This part should be easy*, she thought. "Bonjour, Monsieur et Monsieur," she addressed them.

"Personne n'est autorisé à monter."

"What now?" Jeremy muttered.

"I have this," said Emma as she leaned toward him. She looked at the guards and said in French, "Please tell Ellis Evans his daughter is here."

The guard watched her closely and finally observed her nod to the other guard, "Tell him to come down and see her."

"Where's the trust," muttered Jeremy.

She smiled slightly as they waited.

They heard a shout from up above. They looked up and saw Ellis and Abbey waving down at them.

"Papa! Abbey!" she called.

He called down to the guards, "I'll claim her. She's my daughter; she can come up."

The guards separated to let her pass but stepped together again when Jeremy tried to go through.

"Uhm, Ellis!?" Jeremy said.

Abbey whispered into Ellis' ear.

Ellis laughed, "Oh, all right, him also,"

The guards begrudgingly separated to let Jeremy pass.

Emma had gone ahead up the final stairs. When she reached the top, she hugged him. "Papa!"

"Emma, what made you come up here tonight? Jeremy, my boy. It's good to see you," he said, reaching around her to shake Jeremy's hand.

"Ellis," Jeremy commented as he shook the other man's hand. "Had me worried there for a minute."

"Papa, can we talk in private?"

"Well, that will be difficult here," Papa said laconically.

She frowned, "Why is that?"

"Come on up and I'll show you," he directed. They followed him up into a room.

The apartment he had told her about, she thought.

It wasn't the office that Jeremy noticed; it was the people in the room. "Emma." He nudged her.

"What?" she asked, finally looking at the people in the room. She felt faint as she identified Thomas Edison, Nikola Tesla, and Gustave Eiffel all in the same room.

"Tesla and Edison," commented Emma faintly. "I thought …"

"That we didn't get along? Yeah, well, that's sometimes true," Edison said and laughed. Tesla started laughing as well.

"They're here for the initial unveiling of my tower," Eiffel said. "Emma, we have heard much about you. Jeremy, it's nice to meet you."

"Thank you," Emma said, forgetting for a moment why she was there. She shook herself out of the daze and said bluntly, "We have a concern. There's a possibility of a bomb being placed by the anti-electrical groups."

Edison was contemplative. "Using the circuitry to set it off.

Yes. That would work and, to their minds, prove electricity is indeed dangerous."

"It's something we fight continually. We want to normalize it so that it's in every household," Tesla added.

"We've had a few demonstrations by these anti-electrical people when they found out about the lighting displays. We didn't publicize Thomas' trip to prevent a similar demonstration," Eiffel said.

"Sir," Emma asked Edison, "did anyone know you were coming to Paris, especially to the tower?"

"Well, yes, we did keep it a secret, but household staff, family members, and the people who work with me were aware I was coming over. Also, we have employees here working at the Galerie des Machines to maintain the exhibits."

"That's a large number of people and word could have gotten out."

Jeremy nodded.

"What are you thinking, little girl?" Papa asked.

"I think the two people who traveled over with us are involved with the anti-electric people and are trying to create a big event here. We also think they're behind the tickets that got us here. And then," she said, studying her papa, "then there is Julian."

Papa sat suddenly and Abbey went over to him to hold his hand.

"Who was he, Papa?" she asked, giving him a long steady look.

"Was?" That shook Ellis, "What has happened?" he asked.

She sent Jeremy a wide eye look and then shifted back to her papa. "I thought you knew. Papa, he was murdered, in the Galerie des Machines."

Edison stood up and paced. He turned to her, "Where? What display?"

"It was in one of the rooms that supplied the electricity, with the large cabinets and cables," she responded.

"How did he die?" asked Papa.

"He was shot, but we believe he was meant to be electrocuted. They did electrocute a guard."

Edison paled and sat down. "This isn't good. They are serious this time."

"That's what we believe," Jeremy confirmed.

"Papa, who was he? Who was Julian?" she asked again.

Papa pulled his hands down his face and then turned a pale face toward Emma. "He is—*was*—an old friend. Someone I knew a long time ago."

"Is he some type of police officer or detective?" she guessed.

"I shouldn't be surprised that you worked that out," he said dryly. "Yes, he was with Interpol. I met him while working on a special project in London. He approached me and asked me to work for him as a specialist when needed."

Emma smiled suddenly, "Oh, is that why you thought of using specialists for me?" Papa had introduced Emma to different people with skills to teach her and that she used in her adventures.

"It is. If you wanted a life like Julian's, I wanted to make sure you were ready for that."

"Oh, Papa," she said and went to him. "Now, why was he here?"

"He was trailing Lenora and Michael, investigating them. There were suspicions that they were up to something nefarious at the exposition. He wasn't sure what the actual plan was."

"Did he think Tim and Dora were targeted?"

He looked at her appraisingly. "Yes, we had words about that."

"Was that when you and Julian were arguing at the hotel?"

Papa laughed suddenly, "You don't miss much, little girl." He sobered suddenly and said, "Yes, he wanted to let it play out to determine what their plan was."

"And you?"

"I didn't want my children to be in an unsafe condition. I told him we needed to remove them from this observation. He pushed for a few more days; he felt he was close."

"Then he died."

"Yes," he said, wiping his eyes. The emotion of losing an old friend was overwhelming him. Abbey clasped his hand and pulled it to her.

Emma studied Edison and Tesla, "Where do you think would be the worst place to put something that would interfere and cause a large explosion?"

"That would cause the biggest problem?" Edison asked.

"Yes,"

"The transformer room," Tesla and Edison answered at the same time.

"Tim and Dora took Michael and Lenora there during their tour," said Emma.

"When?" Edison asked. "It's a secure room; no one should have been allowed."

"They used my name, didn't they?" Ellis asked.

"Yes," confirmed Emma.

"When was this?" Edison asked.

"Earlier in the week."

Edison said, "Ellis, we need to get to the transformers."

Emma held up her hands to stop him, "Sir, the last thing I think we should do is put their enemy in the area."

Ellis said, "Tom, she's right. You need to stay here."

"Mr. Edison, what should we be looking for?" Emma asked the scientist

"My engineer will be in the area. He should be able to help. If not, there should be a main panel that completes the circuit. If there is something, it should be there."

"Got it." Emma and Jeremy stood and started to head to the door. Ellis started to join them,

"Ellis, dear, I'd like you to stay with me," Abby told him.

He was conflicted, but knowing he'd slow them down, he agreed, "I'll stay here."

The group watched Emma and Jeremy leave and when the door closed, Ellis followed Edison to the windows.

"What do you think it could be now that we know the location?" Ellis asked him.

"I'm thinking they're correct; it's a bomb. It makes the most sense for a large-scale demonstration and maximizes the death count," Edison commented.

"It'll be hard to watch and not be involved. Will they need help?" Ellis asked, gripping Abbey's hand tightly.

"Jeremy and Emma indicated the policemen were searching the lines. We can have our security tell them to meet them at the transformer," suggested Edison.

Ellis nodded. Edison walked out to call one of the guards up. He walked back over, "Do you think they will stop it?"

"I do. If anyone can, those two can," Ellis said as he pulled out his pipe and tobacco.

Edison looked over the crowd and back at Ellis, "So, this Julian. Is there more to the story?"

"Yes."

"Well, go ahead," Edison prompted.

Ellis told his story.

CHAPTER 18

*E*mma and Jeremy got through the crowds, trying not to create a scene this time. They could see the building in the distance and made their way to the entrance. When they got there, they started to approach the guards, Emma grabbed his arm and suggested, "Let's look around first."

Jeremy hesitated and looked around. "Okay." They waited for the two guards standing at the door to walk away before they made their way around to find an alternate entrance.

"Over there," said Emma pointing to the door.

Jeremy looked around and said, "It's clear," Emma pulled out her lockpicks and knelt quickly by the door.

It took her moments to get the door opened. She pushed it wide and saw it led to a hallway. Emma held up a finger to her lips; he nodded and reached down to slip off his shoes. She did the same and they crept down the hallway. There were several locked doors. She knelt and used her picks to open it up.

"Just a closet," she muttered and they continued to the next door. Once it was opened, they saw it was an office. "Should we go in?" she asked.

"Why not?"

They went in and closed the door behind them. The room wasn't big; there was a desk and chair on the far wall and what looked to be a small storage area. Jeremy gestured toward it, "I'll check the closet if you check the desk."

She nodded and headed to the chair. She turned it to face her and let out a strangled scream. A man was in the chair, dead, shot in the head.

Jeremy turned toward her in reaction to her scream. "Same thing over here." She hurried over and saw another person lying against the wall, looking like he was asleep except for the bullet hole in his head.

"Where are their clothes?" Emma asked. "It's odd they're undressed. Why do that?"

"I believe these two are the guards."

"The people guarding the building are the anti-electrical people," she deduced.

"It appears that way," he agreed in a low voice.

"Too many people have died already. We have to get to the main room and find the device."

They left the room, taking time to lock it behind them. As they continued down the hall, they heard a buzzing as they moved closer got louder. Jeremy nodded toward it, "That should be it. Do you think anyone is in the room?"

She thought about that, "They may feel safe enough not to worry about that. Though someone will need to come in to connect the circuit."

"Do you think they're aware that the person flipping the switch will probably be blown up with the room?"

"I don't know how committed these people are," she responded. "Would it be a suicide or another sacrifice to the cause?"

With that, they made their way to the door. Emma turned the knob; she pushed, expecting the door to open. When it didn't, she looked around.

"Should you pick the lock?" Jeremy asked.

"No, I think we need an element of surprise." *There had to be another way.*

The other buildings in the exhibit were built out in extreme detail. This being a utility building, it was more basic. There were utility panels in the ceiling. Emma pointed up and Jeremy got the message. He knelt, and she climbed on his shoulders. He stood carefully, and she was able to reach the panel. She pushed on it and dislodged it. "I got it."

"Can you climb up?"

"I can," she said. She put her hands up into the structure and found it was supported with iron and was structurally sound.

Once she was up in the space, he asked, "Can you see into the electrical room?"

"No," she called. She stuck her head out. "I need to move further in. It appears to have a similarly structured ceiling to that of the main Galerie des Machines."

"Okay, be careful," he cautioned.

"I will." She smiled and blew him a kiss.

Emma inched her way forward and searched for an opening into the electrical room. She found the opening and raised it by an inch and looked into the room. It appeared to be empty, as she started to remove the panel so she could jump down. With her legs dangling in the opening, a young man eating an apple walked under her. She didn't hesitate and dropped down on him. Taking him by surprise, and he fell on his hands and knees. She twisted his arm behind him and when he yelped, she put her clutch knife to his neck to silence him.

She said, "No. You will stay silent. You be very quiet or you'll find out how sharp my knife is. Can you do that?"

He nodded, taking her threat seriously.

"Okay. I want you to remove that block from the door there."

He frowned, "Why should I?" She tightened her hold on his arm. "I'll do it."

"I'll let you go, but remember, I have a very sharp knife," she reminded him.

He walked to the door to do her bidding, but before he got there, he reached for something in his pocket. He turned suddenly and slashed at her with a knife. Emma reacted instantly, kicking it out of his hands. Next, she kicked him in the stomach to make him move back. She gathered up his knife watching him cough and stay bent over on the floor. "Well, that was stupid," she said as she walked to the door and quickly removed the block to let Jeremy into the room. As Jeremy entered, the boy looked surprised. He wasn't aware there was someone besides her.

Once they tied him up, Jeremy asked "Any problems?"

"Him?" she laughed.

Jeremy pulled the boy to his knees, "Okay, what do you know?"

"About what?" he asked belligerently.

"About the switch, you're supposed to flip," Jeremy said.

He responded without thinking. "How did you know about that?"

"We didn't know for sure," Emma said, "but you just confirmed it. Answer now, what's your part in this? Are you a member of the anti-electrical group?"

"Non, I was given some money and told to flip that switch," the boy said, indicating the panel behind him.

"When?" she asked.

"What time is it?" the boy asked.

Emma checked her timepiece, "It's 9:40."

"About twenty minutes," he answered "They said it needed to be dark."

"What's your name?" Emma asked the boy.

"Jacques."

"Look, Jacques. What do you think will happen when you flip that switch?"

"The lights will come on," Jacques said with a rather blank expression.

"Why would they have YOU do this? Where are the people who run this place?" She knew the answer but wanted to know what part he played.

"I don't know. I was just told to be here."

"Who let you into the building?"

"Monsieur Alaire and Monsieur Garnier."

"Are those the men outside?" Jeremy asked. *They probably killed the men they found.*

"Yes."

"How do you know them?" asked Emma, wondering how this kid got picked to die for their cause.

"My mama goes to the meetings."

"We have some news for you; you weren't meant to make it out of here tonight."

"What are you talking about? I was told to leave as soon as I flipped the switch."

While he was talking, Emma traced the line from the box through the room. "Found it," she called.

Jeremy walked over, dragging the boy with him. They looked at the rather unassuming device, which consisted of a package of dynamite. Connected to it was a rubber tube filled with gunpowder and some detonators. The circuit connection would like off the gunpowder and set off the dynamite. "What is it?" Jacques asked.

"A bomb," said Emma bluntly. "Had you flipped the switch, it would have set it off and the building would have gone with it."

"But what about me?" the boy asked, finally realizing what would have happened to him.

"You'd have been gone with the building."

He turned pasty white at that comment and held a hand to his mouth.

"Hey, don't throw up here," said Emma. "Take deep breaths." She looked at Jeremy. "We need to remove it."

He was studying it, "I think, as long as there's no power, we can remove it."

He started working on the connections and Emma took the device from him once the dynamite was removed. It was a fascinating device.

"I think I can hook everything back up to the main line," said Jeremy, examining the line. It was simply a matter of hooking the disconnected lines back up.

She looked at it consideringly. "Wouldn't it be shocking to them if the lights came on and there was no explosion?" she smiled "Yes, let's hook it back up."

She continued to examine the device. "Are we sure this is the only one?" Jeremy asked as he worked.

"I walked down the entire line here, and this is the only one."

"What if there are different bombs outside the building?"

"I don't think so. They wanted Dora and Tim primarily to access this building. I think anywhere else would have been too obvious."

"I can't believe they were going to leave me here to die. Did my mama know?" Tears were starting to make their way down Jacques' face.

"I don't know," she said quietly.

At that moment, the police rushed into the room. Emma showed them the device was disabled, "Were you able to check the cables?"

"We walked them all down; no extra devices were attached," Levan reassured her

She checked her timepiece," I think it's time to light up the exposition." She walked over to the panel, "Everyone ready?"

Everyone responded in the affirmative. Even with the assurances of safety, they held their breath as Emma flipped the switch. The lights in the room blinked, and then an officer ran in.

"The lights! They're on! Come see!"

They followed him out and saw that the lights had come on and highlighted the fountains and area around them. The area glowed lending a magical air to the night.

Emma pulled on Jeremy's sleeve. "We need to tell them about the guards."

"Yes."

They turned and faced the police, Emma and Jeremy were resolved to the grim task of showing the police the two bodies that had been found earlier. They had already taken the fake guards into custody.

They waited in the hallway as the police. At that moment the outside door opened and Levan walked in with Tim and Dora.

"We were able to locate them at one of their two apartments."

"Are you okay?" Emma asked as she ran over and took Dora's hands swiftly.

"Yes."

She noticed that, even though Dora had been released, she didn't look happy. Her face was red and her nose was running. "What's wrong?"

"Emma, they have Lottie," Dora said and burst into tears.

"What are you talking about?" Emma asked, confused.

Tim answered, wiping tears from his eyes. "They have Lottie and were forcing us to help them get access to this building."

"We used Papa's name and told the guards that we were interested in the exhibit. They let us come in whenever we liked," Dora admitted.

Jeremy and Emma stared at Tim and Dora. "How could they get Lottie?" Emma asked trying to make sense of the conversation, "She's home with Amy. You know she'd never let her out of her sight."

"I thought that, but Lenora gave me this," her sister said as she placed her hand in her pocket and pulled out the lace hairband she had been holding onto for days.

Emma frowned when she saw it, "Yes this is Lottie's—or *was.*"

"*Was?*" Dora asked through her tears, feeling hopeful for the first time in days.

"Yes," she said taking it from her and tossing it in the air. The group watched it go up and then come back down to Emma's hand. "Funny thing about this, Lottie gave it to me when I kissed her goodnight. She said she wanted her Aunt Emma to take it to Paris with her."

"Then why did they have it?" Tim asked.

"I left it on the table in the foyer. I didn't realize until we were on the train."

Dora felt faint. "You think she's home and never part of this?"

"I do," Emma confirmed. "I can't imagine that they'd want to care for a baby all of this time. I also think we'd have heard about it."

Dora and Tim embraced, praying Emma was right and Lottie was safe.

Emma watched them, understanding their concerns. She loved that little girl so much. "I know she is home."

Tim felt relief wash over him and took Dora in his arms.

Emma gave them privacy and walked over to where Jeremy stood. "Want to go see the lights?" He nodded.

"Dora, Tim do you want to see the lights."

"There are some unhappy people out there," he said, looking at the crowd. *How many were the anti-electrical people?*

"Yes, do you think they will be apprehended?" she asked Levan.

"We have a good chance with this young man here," the inspector said, referencing Jacques. "He says he's willing to give us names of people who attended those meetings. We'll send word to you to come to the station once we have them in custody."

"I guess them sacrificing him for the cause didn't sit well with him."

They didn't leave the area until adequate security was in place. They started toward the tower, but this time they moved at a slower pace now that they were four instead of two. Jeremy was leading the group and accidentally bumped into someone.

Emma saw who it was, "Oh, no."

Jeremy was resigned, and put up his fists.

The big guy who had inadvertently helped them earlier saw who it was and raised his fists. A friend next to him said, "It's not worth it. Enjoy the lights."

"You're right," the man said. With one last glare, he turned back to them.

The tower was still extremely crowded, but this time Eiffel had left word the foursome was able to come up at any time. They were allowed to bypass the crowds. They ascended at a slower pace than before and stopped at the main deck and strolled to the outer boundary.

The four stood together and, for the first time in days, enjoyed the sites in front of them. "It's so magical," said Dora, watching the shining lights. "Imagine one day having this in our homes."

"Yes, we'll probably always have people fighting against changes like these."

"Why was Lenora so passionate about this? Why this topic and why now? And to make the process so involved with so many people?" asked Emma.

"It was her brother," Dora explained and told Emma and Jeremy all the details of the electric chair.

They went upward, hesitating at each level to see the different vantage points. At the final floor, the guards let them up without question. As they entered the room, introductions were made.

Mr. Edison walked over to Emma and Jeremy, "It appears you were able to remove the device."

"We were, sir," Emma said. They explained what they had found.

"Hmm, they were serious about this. It wasn't just a demonstration this time," Edison observed.

"Yes, a large number of people would have been killed to prove their point."

They watched the lights continue to sparkle below.

"What will happen next?"

Jeremy answered that. "The police are gathering up the demonstrators and will find out more about the movement."

"Let me know the outcome."

"We will," they promised.

They stayed and enjoyed the company. A knock was heard at the door. Eiffel got up to answer it.

"Emma and Jeremy, it's for you."

Emma jumped up and accompanied Jeremy to the door, "I hope this is what I think it is."

It was an officer and he said formally, "Mademoiselle, we have been sent to bring you, Jeremy, Tim, and Dora to the department." Dora and Tim were already up and ready to leave. They wanted to hear from Michael that Emma was right, that their baby was safe at home.

They followed the officer down the many flights of stairs. Reaching the bottom, he said, "We have a carriage, but we'll need to walk a few blocks to reach it. The crowds are making the roads impassable."

They walked briskly. Most people were still arriving to witness the light display. Everyone was quiet during the carriage ride to the station. They arrived and ran up the front steps. As they entered, they saw the police force was being kept busy by the people from the exposition.

Inspector Levan came out of the back, "We're back here." They met him and followed him down to the interview room. He stopped them, "Michael's in this room and he knows his plan has come to naught." He looked at Emma and Jeremy, "Would you like to interview him?"

"What are you charging him with?" she asked.

"We'll start with kidnapping." He nodded to Tim and Dora. "Then conspiracy and terrorism."

"And the two dead men at the station?" she inquired.

"Yes, that will also be included."

She took a deep breath "I'm ready." She held out her hand to Jeremy.

Before they could go, Dora stopped her, "Please ask about Lottie."

"We will," she promised, knowing what her sister was asking her to do. Lottie was on all of their minds.

Tim and Dora stepped back and sat on the nearby benches. The officer opened the door and entered; Emma and Jeremy followed close behind. She had known Michael but didn't expect to see him look so much older than on the steamship. The stress of this had changed him. *Was it the failure of the plan or Lenora's death?*

She sat down and looked at him.

He spoke first. "You never did like us, did you?"

"That's not true," she corrected. "I never got to know you. You and your wife avoided any interaction with us."

"Yeah, well, we couldn't take the chance you'd catch on," he muttered.

There were questions she wanted answered. "Why were Dora and Tim involved?" She didn't mention Lottie.

She didn't have to; he brought her up first. "They were perfect. We could get access to anywhere Ellis Evans could go.

We just had to get close to Dora and Tim."

Emma had been thinking about this for a while, "Did you pay for our trip and send us the invitations?"

"We did," he conceded. "Having you along was a chance we had to take. Your investigative skills were a challenge, and we knew we had to stay away as much as possible."

"Did you take Lottie?" Emma asked bluntly.

He knew the child abduction charge could lead to his death. "No, we just needed something from the house we could say was hers so that we could persuade Tim and Dora to help us. Lenora saw the hairband as soon as she entered your house."

"When was this?" Emma asked, trying to put the timeline together.

"The morning you headed to the train."

"You were in Chicago?" she asked, surprised.

"Yes, we needed to make sure you got on that train. We all needed to arrive at the same time."

She frowned. "Why was there a timing element here; what's driving that?"

He looked down, then suddenly back up and into Emma's eyes. "Lenora's brother."

"Yes, we heard about that. All of your posturing about the general public being harmed by electricity was a lie. You were just trying to keep Lenora's brother from being electrocuted."

"He was her only family," he said simply.

"She had you!" she protested.

"She didn't see it that way, and I'd do anything for her," he said quietly.

"Do you know who killed her?"

He put his head in his hands and mumbled, "Yes. We had a contingent at the Gallery, mapping things out. One of our more fanatic members saw you take Lenora into custody and took it upon herself to remove her."

"Who was this person?" Jeremy asked.

Taking his hands down slowly he said, "Analise Fontaine."

"Well, well," said the inspector from the wall. "That is Jacques' mother."

"Wow," said Jeremy.

Emma continued. "Why did you continue after Lenora died?"

"I wanted to make sure her dream was fulfilled and that her brother was not electrocuted."

"And the people involved in the taking of the station?"

"People I stirred up with my rhetoric. They wanted something to fight for, and I provided the cause."

Emma watched him, "If it had worked, do you think it would have stopped electricity from moving forward? Sir, nothing is going to stop this. Nothing."

"I know that now."

Jeremy asked suddenly, "Who killed the men in the station?"

His eyes dropped to his hands and he mumbled. "I told them to just capture them and tie them up so they wouldn't interfere."

"That sounds good, but the number of explosives would have killed anyone in that building and a fair radius around it. They'd have died anyway," Emma observed.

He had no answer for that and went quiet.

"You know you'll be in a Paris prison for the rest of your life?"

"Yes," he acknowledged.

With that, she sat back and said, "That's all the questions I have."

"You may leave. We have a few details to take care of. This matter is far from over." Inspector Levan stated.

"We'll be outside," Jeremy said.

They exited. Tim and Dora stared but didn't say anything.

"They don't have her," Emma said.

"You're sure?" they asked, not believing what they were hearing.

"Yes," she said firmly. "He knew exactly where the hairband was located. He also has nothing to gain by lying."

"Tim, I want to go home," Dora said into his chest.

"I do as well," he said, hugging her close.

"We can check on tickets back for you both, but I don't think there are any available." The exposition had strained resources and there wouldn't be any available on ships to return home early. "Why not stay?" Emma reasoned. "We're only here about a week longer and we can head home together." She didn't mention the other case was still in the works and needed to be resolved.

Tim said quietly, "Why not stay a little longer? We have parts of Paris we've yet to see."

"Yes, I'd like that. I wish telegraphs could make it across the ocean," Dora said. The transatlantic cables had been laid but were not available yet in France.

Their group moved into the hotel. The clerk at the desk called to Dora. "Mademoiselle, You have mail."

"Mail?" Dora asked, puzzled. They walked over to the desk to see what had arrived. It was a letter from Amy. Dora tore it open and out came a ribbon. *Lottie wanted to send this to you. She and Patrick are doing wonderful and can't wait to hear about Paris.*

"She's home," she said, crushing the letter to her. Tim asked to see it. He grinned ear-to-ear.

Emma understood she needed the reassurance that her baby was safe and back home. "Why don't we go upstairs? I'll order some tea and a tray of sweets to be brought up."

The three went on upstairs and Emma stayed to place the food order. Just as she walked to the elevator and pushed the button, the doors opened unexpectedly. A very stylish woman in a large, somewhat overdone hat walked out, pushing past her. *I must be invisible*, she thought.

Emma watched her and noticed she was trailed by a little

boy who looked about nine. *Could it be...* She turned and found a bellboy to ask, "Who is that?"

His mouth twisted and he responded, "That is the owner of the hotel. Madam Lanier."

"And the boy?"

"Her son."

"Oh," she said, watching the other woman carefully. Her appearance was impeccable; the tailoring and detail on her clothes were flawless. She was also a striking woman. The similarities to Patrice were visible. *Did this woman go to extremes to not only get rid of Patrice's mom but also try to get her locked up in an asylum?*

Emma tapped her fingers on her lips, planning. She glanced at the elevator and then back at the bellboy. "Could you also see this note is delivered to my room?" She pulled out her notebook and wrote that she needed to go out for a little while and would be back. *"Don't worry,"* she penned.

She knew her family. They trusted her to take care of herself. Emma hurriedly gave the bellboy the note and a tip. She ran outside quickly when she saw the woman and boy walking out the front door.

Abella Lanier's carriage was waiting for her. She and the boy climbed in. Emma looked and saw a bike parked outside. She ran over quickly and picked the lock. *I'll return it before they need it.* The carriage headed out and Emma followed. They had gone a few blocks when Emma realized where they were. They were at Patrice's grandmother's hotel, exactly where Patrice was. *Oh no! Did we leave her with the wrong person?* She slowed the bike and parked it by the wall of the hotel. The woman and child walked into the hotel with Emma right behind them.

"Please tell my mother I'm in the lobby and would like to come up," Abella said in a demanding voice.

"Yes, Madam." The clerk pulled out a piece of paper. After he finished writing, instead of giving it to a bellboy to transport, he took out a container and slipped it inside. He opened a slot in the wall behind him and put the container in. With the door closed, he flipped a switch. A whooshing sound could be heard as it started its journey.

Pneumatic tubes, thought Emma. She had heard about them but had never seen them in practice. It reduced the number of personnel needed to transport messages. London was said to have twenty-one miles of tubing in place.

Within seconds, the whooshing sound could be heard again, this time with a plopping sound. The manager turned and opened the door. He took out the capsule and removed the paper. He read it silently, "You may go up," he told Abella. She and the boy headed to the elevator.

Emma walked slowly over and waited next to the elevator nonchalantly. The woman looked Emma over and then moved herself and her son some distance away. When the elevator arrived the three boarded. Emma got off on the floor she and Jeremy had used during their last visit and made her way to the kitchen door. She knocked and, when it opened, the same butler answered. He didn't look surprised at the intrusion.

"I saw the Madam's daughter come over to the hotel. I wanted to make sure Patrice is okay."

"Who, me?" asked Patrice. The butler stepped back and revealed Patrice. She appeared to be snacking on chocolate; and from the multiple empty dessert glasses in front of her, she was enjoying it.

The butler waved her in. Emma immediately went to Patrice," Are you okay?"

"Oh, yes, Grandmeir and I are getting along famously," she said with a grin.

"Do you know who's coming in the elevator?" Emma asked.

"Yes—Grandmeir said I'm to stay in here and not make a sound," she replied.

"Good," Emma said, mulling over what to do next.

"Mademoiselle, would you like to hear what is being said?" William asked.

She glanced over and said, "I most definitely would."

The butler moved to the vent; they had a boiler hooked up and the vent would carry steam as well as voices. "The sound can go both ways," he said as he put his fingers to his lips.

Emma and Patrice understood and were quiet as he opened it. Immediately, she could hear the conversation between the Madam and her daughter

"Abella, you've come to see me. Paul, how are you?" The elder Patrice's tone was less warm than Emma had heard in her conversations with her.

Emma leaned in to hear more.

"How is the hotel getting on? The rooms are full?" she asked, her tone brisk.

"Yes, Mama, I have it under control," Abella said, her voice bored.

"Hmm," the Madam murmured. "Shouldn't he be in school?"

"I pulled him out," Abella said defensively. "I need him."

"For what? I'd assume you have enough servants at your beck and call." Her mother's tone was derisive.

"Yes, but I missed him."

"Humph. That would have been the first time," the Madam muttered, her tone not changing.

"How dare you?" Abella said, her voice going shrill.

"Abella, you'd think I don't know you. That boy needs to be in school." There was silence for a few moments and then, "Have you heard from Charles?"

"No. Have you?" she asked.

"No," her mother responded. "Abella, it's time to get to the point."

"What point, Maman?" Abella asked, sounding board again.

"Charles' wife and daughter are in town to meet me."

"Are they? You'd think they'd stay at one of our hotels," Abella said dismissively.

"They were."

"Were?"

"Yes, I have reason to believe Catherine is missing."

"No loss there," her daughter responded.

"Abella, I'll not dignify that with a response!"

"Why should I care about them? Are we even sure he married her?"

Emma glanced over at Patrice; tears streamed down the girl's face. She turned to William and asked him in a low voice, "Can you take Patrice to another room while I listen?"

"I can. Mademoiselle Patrice, would you like to see our small dogs?" William tempted in a low voice.

She was torn she wanted to stay but wanted to escape more. "Yes, please. You'll let me know what happens, Emma?"

Emma nodded and continued to listen as she watched them exit to another part of the house.

The Madam's patience appeared to have waned, "Have you seen them at Charles' hotel?"

"You mean my hotel," her daughter said, the shrill tone returning.

"You know the hotel is only yours until Charles returns," her mother reminded the other woman.

"And if he doesn't?"

"If you have done something to my son..." the Madam started to warn her.

"My son," Abella mocked. "Yes, you're always so protective of him, the golden boy. The heir apparent."

"You know this is what his father wanted."

"Yes, HIS father. Why is it you always say it that way?"

"I don't know what you're talking about," said the Madam. She was sounding defensive now.

"You don't know! Why am I treated differently from

Charles? Why is it that? I have a talent for management, yet I'm discarded and my hotel is given to my 'brother'."

"I don't want to talk about this," the Madam said stiffly.

"You will talk about this." There was a sound of breaking glass.

"Do not speak to her that way!" Emma jumped at the new voice.

That voice was the butler! What's going on here? Emma asked herself.

"Why should I listen to you?" Abella asked belligerently.

"You know why," William said with authority in his voice.

The room became quiet and the Madam finally broke the silence, saying in a faint voice, "You know."

Know what? thought Emma.

There was a second sound of glass breaking.

"Just stop this," William's voice sounded again. "You've known for a while."

"When did you find out that he's your father?" asked the Madam.

Wow! thought Emma.

"I was sixteen," Abella said nonchalantly.

"Who told you?"

"That was 'Papa'," she said lightly.

"François told you? But why? Why would he do that?"

"He was writing out his will and said he refused to leave any part of the business to the butler's daughter. At first, I didn't understand," Abella's voice sounded bitter.

"What happened then?"

"He explained in quite a lot of detail about you and your 'relationship' and that he had allowed you to stay after he found out."

"He forgave me," the Madam said, "and I was allowed to keep you. For years after you were born, he seemed to have a genuine affection for you."

"I know what made that change," her daughter said, her voice bitter.

"Charles was born," William said. "I could see it in him. The affection he usually displayed for Abella was now reserved for Charles."

"I didn't notice," the Madam commented faintly.

"No, you didn't, but it was also when I was sent away to school," she snapped.

"All proper young ladies go to boarding school," the Madam said defensively.

"I wasn't allowed to come home for vacations," Abella reminded her mother.

"Your father told me you didn't want to come home, that you were having a good time with friends," the Madam said weakly.

"And you believed him! You never asked me!"

"You never wrote me."

"I did. You never wrote back."

"But I never received them,"

"I intercepted them," William admitted.

"You did?" Abella asked her father.

"Yes. And I came to see you," he commented.

"Yes, you did," she said faintly. "It was the only thing that got me through those terrible days."

"I'm glad I was there."

The room went quiet.

Emma heard the kitchen door opening into the back staircase and glanced toward it. She saw Patrice. Emma reached up and closed the vent before she asked, "Where are you going?"

"Away from these people. They did something to Mum and Papa." With that, she left through the door and down the stairs.

Emma followed and grabbed her arm to stop her. "Patrice, wait. We need more information before we make accusations like that."

"You heard the same thing I did."

"Yes, but what I also heard were people having a hard time with their circumstances."

Patrice stopped struggling, "So, we should give them a chance?"

"Yes."

Patrice stood still a moment longer and said, "Okay, I'll give them a chance." They headed back upstairs.

"What now?" Patrice asked.

"We go in," Emma said determinedly.

Patrice squared her shoulders, "I'm ready."

They headed in and walked to the door that led to the main room. She moved her gaze toward Patrice, who nodded. Emma pushed the door open and they both entered. Paul's eyes opened wide and he moved to hide behind his mother's chair. Of the three, the surprise was most evident in Abella.

Abella sat up from her slumped position in her chair and stared at Patrice. "That settles it. She could be my twin," she said, her voice resolved. Her eyes moved to Emma for the first time, "And you, weren't you in the elevator with me?"

"Yes, that was me," Emma answered.

"What do you have to do with this? This is a private family issue," Abella said in French.

The Madam said, "Use English."

"Why should I? For them? Bah! This is France. They should speak French!"

"If not for them, for me, please," her mother requested.

Abella's mouth tightened but nodded in agreement.

"Emma is here for me," Patrice said.

Emma took Patrice's hand and asked Abella the hard question. "Did you do something to Patrice's mum or papa?"

She watched Abella for any tells. The first thing she noticed was hesitation.

Patrice pulled on Emma's hand and leaned in to whisper, "The little ghost is here."

"Where?" she whispered back.

"There, behind her chair," the girl said, indicating the chair Abella sat in.

"Is someone behind your chair?" Emma asked.

Again, it appeared that Abella wasn't going to answer.

"Abella answer," the Madam commanded. When she continued to stay silent, the Madam said, "Paul! Come out from behind there."

A small figure came slowly from the back of the chair. "It's him," whispered Patrice furiously.

"You're sure?" Emma asked.

She nodded frantically. Emma didn't confront the child but chose at that point to say to the Madam, "He was in our suite."

The Madam studied her daughter, "Did you place Emma in the suite?"

"No," Abella said. "I didn't know who she was."

"But you knew when Patrice was with us," Emma said.

"How would she have known that?" William asked defensively, wanting to protect his daughter.

"I know because that little guy there," Emma motioned to Paul, "was entering Patrice's room through a secret passage."

The Madam took a long moment to observe them, and frowned, "Why was he there, Abella?"

Abella hugged her son close but didn't say anything.

"They were giving her drugs," Emma said, "one to make her feel out of control and another that put her to sleep. We believe they were cocaine and laudanum."

The Madam jumped up and glared at Abella accusingly. "Is this true?"

Abella wouldn't talk, but Paul spoke up, "I took the medicine to her through the door."

"Why?" asked the Madam. She didn't want to believe her daughter could be behind this.

"Maman said we had to. She said that girl could take our home from us," the boy explained.

Patrice had heard enough and asked Abella directly, "Did you take my mum?"

The answer was immediate, with no hesitation. "No, I did not."

"Do you know where she is?" Patrice asked, wanting answers from these people.

"I was informed when you and your mother arrived," Abella started.

"By whom?" asked Emma, taking over the questioning.

"The night manager."

The one they have not been able to locate. "So, there was a record of Catherine and Patrice at the hotel?" asked Emma.

"Yes, the managers keep two books in case an important guest needed privacy. That way, the log can't be accessed easily."

"I'll ask Patrice's question again: do you know where her mum is and who might have taken her?"

"I think so," muttered Abella. The desperation was clear in her voice when she said, "I didn't take her."

"But you took advantage of the circumstances and did nothing to help," Emma said.

"I did," she admitted. "I was desperate."

"Tell us everything!" shouted Patrice.

Emma thought about what she had been told "It's the night manager, isn't it? He's behind the abduction?"

Abella was surprised at the observation and agreed, "That's my suspicion."

"Who's the night manager?" asked the Madam. She hadn't been involved in the daily operation of that hotel for a while.

"It's Alfred Remy," Abella said, lowering her head.

The Madam's face went white and she said faintly. "I know that name." She explained to Emma and Patrice, "He was around, always following Abella like a lost puppy."

"He wanted more than I could give, and then I met Paul's father," she explained to Patrice and Emma.

"Were you still friends?" Emma asked.

"Yes, and he's an excellent manager," she said.

"Well, he's gone," stated Emma.

"Gone?" Her face turned white with the news. "I didn't realize."

"Yes, and he was the only person who could confirm that Patrice's mother was actually at the hotel. He disappeared the same night she did."

"Where do you think he has her?" asked William.

"Them," Abella murmured.

"Them?" Emma asked. "A second person was taken?"

"I believe so. I received word a few days ago that Charles never arrived at the hotel in Germany," Abella admitted.

"Charles is missing?" asked the Madam, going white.

William grabbed her hand in his and patted it.

"Where are they? Where are my mum and papa?" asked Patrice.

"I'm not sure, but Alfred has an apartment in the city," said Abella.

"Don't his parents live just outside the city?" asked the Madam.

"Yes. We should also check there," Abella said.

Emma was thinking ahead. "It's time to call in the police. Can we get access to that private sign-in book?" she asked Abella.

"Yes, it's in the safe of the manager's office."

"Can we go there now? I'd also like to notify the police to meet us there," commented Emma.

William stood and said, "I can have them meet you at the hotel."

They confirmed their plans and stood. Abella went over to Patrice and took her hands in hers. "I took advantage of something I shouldn't have. I hope you will forgive my part in this."

Patrice slowly pulled her hands away, "Once we find my parents, we can talk again."

Abella stepped back and gave her some space. "I understand." She stepped away to take her son's hand. They moved to the elevator and Abella, "Maman, you should stay here."

"No, this involves my family. I want to be there."

Abella understood and didn't try to stop her mother. They stood together and waited for the elevator. The doors opened, they went in and rode to the lobby. Once there, they separated; William went to the police and the rest got in a carriage headed to the other hotel. Once they arrived, they made their way to the desk. The crowd recognized the Madam and whispers followed them.

It was only a matter of moments before the manager on duty came up swiftly to them. "Madam, welcome. We were not expecting you this evening."

"Yes, we're here about something important," she said.

Abella spoke up, "We need to talk to you in the office."

He saw Patrice and his eyes widened. It was time for him to face how he had treated this girl.

They headed that way and Emma heard Jeremy call her. She turned toward him and saw him exiting the stairway. She waved him over.

"What is going on?" he asked

"We have some movement on The Vanishing Lady case."

He didn't respond but followed the group into the office.

Abella stopped at the door and turned. She noticed Jeremy, "Can I help you?"

"He's with me," Emma said, her tone firm.

Abella nodded and allowed them into the room. The manager stopped midway, "What is this about?"

Abella answered, "I need to review the registration book from two nights ago."

"The book. I'll need to go back out to the lobby," he said and started that way.

Abella stopped him, "I need the one we keep for special visitors."

He halted suddenly and looked around. His glance landed on Emma and Jeremy. "With them here?"

"Yes. Please retrieve it," Abella said firmly.

He nodded slowly and went over to the picture hanging behind his desk. He took it down and a safe was revealed. He twirled the dial and turned the lever to reveal the inside. The logbook was on top. It was black and red and large. He slid it out and started to hand it to Abella.

"Hand it to me," the Madam said. It wasn't a request.

He didn't hesitate. She had spent her life working in the hotel business, from the smallest beginnings of four rooms to their empire now. She had worked every job and could read the book. She quickly flipped to the page she needed and found Patrice's mom's signature. "That firms it up."

"What are you talking about?" asked the manager.

"This." She showed him.

He felt faint when he saw the name. He focused his gaze on Patrice. "Miss, I'm so sorry I didn't believe you."

Patrice nodded but didn't say anything. The apologies would have to wait until her parents were found.

"Where is Alfred, the night manager?" asked Abella.

"He's out on vacation," the manager responded, wondering why that question was being asked.

"Was it planned?" Emma asked.

"No, we had canceled all vacations because of the exposition."

"Why was it allowed?" asked the Madam.

"Alfred came to me and said that it was personal. I approved it."

A knock sounded on the door. The manager went over to open it and found the police standing there; Inspector Levan was with them. "What is happening here? We understand there's been a kidnapping?"

"Yes, it's my mum and possibly my papa," said Patrice.

The officer with him frowned, "Now, miss, I talked to you a few days ago and the management here assured me you were not accompanied and you did not have a room at this hotel."

He moved his gaze to the manager, who said, "I was wrong when I reported that. You need to listen to them."

Emma filled them in on what had occurred. She left the drugs and the small boy's role out. The family would need to work that out.

"I can send men out to Alfred's apartment and his parents' house. It will take a few hours to check both," Levan said.

As they were separating to investigate, Paul boy walked over to Emma and Jeremy, "There is another hiding place."

"There is?" she asked, bending down to hear him. "Where might that be?"

"The basement is full of rooms," he explained.

Jeremy and Emma said to the group, "Wait, we should check the basement first. Abella, how do we access the basement?"

"This way," she said. They followed a long hallway that led to the staff's quarters. She took out her key and inserted it into a door lock. "We'll need to take the stairs." They followed her down and found another locked door. This time, her keys wouldn't work. "The locks have been changed," Abella muttered. "We'll have to get someone down here to open it."

"No, I can take care of it," Emma said as she knelt and pulled out her tools. She chose two to turn the tumblers and unlock the door.

"You will have to tell me more about yourself when this is over," Abella said in admiration.

Inspector Levan spoke up, "Please, step back." They did so while he rushed in to investigate. He came back out, "This place is a maze. Does anyone know how to navigate it?"

"I do," Paul said.

"Can he help?" asked Abella.

"Yes, he can." He looked down at Paul and said, "I'm going to carry you and, if there's any danger, we'll move you quickly."

Paul nodded and the inspector lifted him onto his shoulder. The boy directed them through the maze of long hallways. "There's a far room at the other end that has running water," he said.

Levan placed Paul to the side and rushed to the far room. It had a lock; this time they didn't need a key. An officer rammed it, shattering the door and entering the room.

Their group followed closely behind. Patrice didn't hesitate, she pushed past the officers and entered the room. The two people that meant the world to her were there and chained to a bed. "Mum, Papa!" She rushed to embrace them. The officers moved quickly to cut their chains off. When they were free, they both put their arms around her and held her tight. "I told them you were with me. Nobody believed me!" she said.

"Where's Alfred?" asked Abella.

"He comes in the evenings, but I think he stays elsewhere," Charles stated.

"We have men at his apartment," Levan said. "If he's there, he'll be found. Let's get you both upstairs." They nodded gratefully, ready to get out of there.

"Maman, Abella, did you help with finding us?" Charles asked.

"That is something we need to discuss privately," said the Madam.

Before they climbed up the stairs, the Madam turned to Charles, "I'd like to formally meet my daughter-in-law, please."

"Of course, Maman," he said and took his wife's hand in his. "Maman, this is Catherine."

"I have waited for so long to meet you. We need to talk soon, but I think we all need some rest tonight," the Madam said warmly.

"Thank you," said Catherine.

They started to walk away, and Charles stopped Emma and Jeremy. "I can only thank you. I'd like to speak to you later."

"We're glad you and your wife are well. We also have some questions, when you're ready," said Emma.

Patrice said something low to her mum and ran over to Emma and Jeremy. She hugged them both quickly and then returned to her parents.

"Tired?" Jeremy asked Emma.

"Not at all." She smiled, "I'm so glad William got the officers here so quickly."

Jeremy shook his head, "He didn't. I called them when I got your note. I figured the final confrontation was happening."

She drummed her fingers on her lips. "If William didn't get the police officers, then where did he go? I'll have to think about that."

He pulled her to him, "Would you like to walk with me while you think?"

"That would be nice," she said. They walked around and enjoyed the night air, then slowly made their way to their room.

CHAPTER 19

They returned to their room to retire for the evening. A knock sounded at the door. Emma frowned, drew her knife, and accompanied Jeremy to it. "Yes?" she called. Too much had already happened that evening.

"I have a note for you," a voice called.

"Slide it under the door," Jeremy requested.

"Under the door?" the voice questioned.

"Yes, just slide it under," he said again.

There was a moment of hesitation and then the note appeared.

Jeremy reached for it and opened it.

Emma reached into her pocket and pulled out a few francs and pushed them under the door.

"Merci!" he called. They could hear him walking away from the door.

"Who is it from?" Emma asked.

"It's from Abella. She wants us to come upstairs."

"This late? I thought we were going to meet in the morning. Hopefully, after they catch the night manager."

"Yes," he said as he continued to study it.

"Can I see it?"

He handed it to her.

She stared at it for a long moment.

"What do you see?" he asked, wondering what he had missed.

"It's in English," she said.

"Oh, I get it. She prefers French," he said, Emma had told him of the conversations with Abella.

"Yes," she said, thinking back to her response to the Madam's request for her to speak English to them. Jeremy asked, "What do you think it means?"

"We haven't heard that they found the night manager yet," she murmured.

"We haven't," he agreed.

"So, I think he's up there with her."

"Why would he want us up there with him? He wants her to himself."

"I don't know, but I think we need to go up there. Tim?" she called, "Could you come out here?"

He did so and closed the door softly behind him.

"How's Dora?" asked Emma.

"I think she truly believes that Lottie is safe and at home, but she just wants to see and hold her." He moved to the side chair and slumped down.

"I know. Should I go into her?" asked Emma, setting aside the note for a moment.

"No." He sighed and put his head back. "She's finally resting."

Jeremy nodded at the note. "Good. Tim, could you go down-stairs and tell Inspector Levan we need some of his men sent up to the owner's apartment on the top floor?"

He was surprised, "Is something wrong?" He glanced at their room in a worried manner.

"We're not sure, but better to be safe and have the officers on the way."

"All right, I'll be quick. What do you think is happening?" Tim asked as he gathered his coat.

"We think it's the night manager who took Patrice's parents. He may have Abella," said Emma.

"But I thought they went after him in the countryside." They had told Tim the facts when they got back to their room.

"They did, but we now believe he's upstairs." Emma handed her brother-in-law the note and he headed downstairs. He walked quickly; he didn't want to be away from Dora for long. She glanced toward Jeremy, "I'll go in the elevator."

"I'll go through the passageway," he confirmed.

"I'll meet you up there."

Before he left, he grabbed her and gave her a long kiss. He stepped back, "Be careful."

"I will," she said and patted her leg where her knife was strapped. "You too."

He nodded and headed to the secret passageway.

She went out the door and made sure it was locked securely behind her. She made her way to the elevator, deliberately taking her time. That would give Tim and Jeremy time to get their individual tasks completed.

She called for the elevator and waited. It opened and she stepped in. "Top floor, please." The attendant nodded, having been told she was coming up.

As the door closed, she saw Tim exit the stairs. He gave her a quick okay symbol to let her know he had completed his task. She smiled and nodded and the doors closed. The elevator made its way slowly up to the top floor. The doors opened and William was not there to greet her as expected. The elevator operator broke into her thoughts, "Miss, you're to go in alone and I was told to take the elevator back down."

She nodded, slipped her hand into her pocket, and fingered the handle of her knife. As she made her way across the wide-open room, she called out, "Hello. Abella, I'm here."

She heard something and turned to her left. The sound she heard was a gun being cocked. A man stood there, pointing it at her. "Monsieur Alfred Remy I assume?" she asked, though she already knew the answer. When he didn't respond, she asked, "Where's Abella?"

"Oh, not to worry, she's fine," he said.

"If that's true, why am I here?"

"I asked her to get you to come up," he explained.

"Where's Abella?" she asked again, trying to delay him until Jeremy could get into the space through the secret door. She had expected him before now.

"She and my son," he said proudly, "are in the other room."

Your son, she thought. *Is that real or fantasy?* "Can I see them?" she asked.

"What for? You won't be around long," he said threateningly.

"Won't I?" she murmured and watched him fall to the ground. Jeremy stood behind him holding a mallet from the kitchen.

"About time you showed up. Grab that," she said, indicating the curtain tie.

He got the tie and they bundled the man and dragged him to a closet just off the kitchen. "Any idea what his plan was?" he asked as they closed the door.

"Maybe," she said and glanced around, drumming her fingers on her lips. "I wonder," she said and motioned to him to move into the kitchen. She moved to the vent and opened it. She wanted to know what was being said in other areas of the house.

"Do you think he took care of it?" They heard a man's voice ask.

Jeremy turned to Emma and he mouthed, "Who is that?"

"I guess your dalliance has finally led to something good," the man's voice said again.

"It's William!" Emma whispered. They both continued to listen intently.

"Papa, I didn't know you were involved with Alfred, and I didn't know about Charles and Catherine being taken."

"I did it for you, Chéri. Always for you. Otherwise, the hotels will go to Charles and there would be nothing for you."

"Papa, we need to stop." Abella pleaded. "This is my family."

"I'm your family," he said shortly. "This is all for us."

"But this has to stop. They've been found now. Why not just let them be?"

"Why?" he yelled. "Because all of these hotels should be yours but for that Emma person. We need to get rid of her or we'll lose everything."

"We?" Abella wondered if William meant only himself. Her feelings were never taken into consideration.

"I'll go check on that bungler," he said.

Emma and Jeremy stayed in the kitchen, not making a sound.

A door opened and closed. "Where is he?" William asked.

"Papa, I don't know…"

"We have to find all of them!" he thundered. "Or my plans will be for naught."

Again 'my', not our, thought Abella.

Jeremy cleared his voice and said in a low voice, "Let's get out of here."

"Wait," murmured Emma, listening intently.

"But, Papa, I think we need to stop. This is wrong." Abella pleaded.

"Girl, you will do as I say!" William said, turning his ire on her.

"No, Papa, I don't think I will this time. I'm going to notify the police. This has gone far enough."

"You're in this as deep as I am. You'll be turning yourself in."

"No, Papa, I'm not. You pulled my son into this without my knowledge."

"Yes, but you covered for me and told them it was you," he reminded her.

"I wanted to protect you," she said, miserable, knowing no one would do that for her.

"They will never believe you; they won't support you. You will go to prison and be separated from your son," he said nastily.

"They will believe me if I give them the evidence about you killing the Madam's husband," she said. Her voice had steadied.

"You wouldn't!" William shouted. Shattering glass sounded.

"I would. It's time this game was over," Abella said. The elevator sounded at that moment.

"It's the police," Emma mouthed. "Now, we go in."

The duo burst out of the kitchen as the police flooded into the room from the elevator.

Paul ran in from his room and toward his mama. She pulled him close, away from William.

Emma saw William go for the gun on the table in front of him. She quickly lunged for it and turned it on him. He put his hands in the air and waited. The police quickly took him into custody. The inspector accepted the gun from Emma.

"Can someone else tell me what is happening here?" the inspector asked, glaring at William.

He stared mutinously back without saying a word.

Jeremy and Emma started to step up to explain but were surprised when Abella cut them off. "I think I can provide what you need."

The inspector cocked his brow at her, "Would you come to the station?"

Her hands shook as she realized she could be separated from Paul. "Can we do it here?"

The inspector saw Paul clinging to her, "I think we can work that out."

Emma and Jeremy were listening. The inspector turned his gaze to them, "I'll need you two to stay also. I assume you have more information to share with me?"

"You might want to check the closet," Emma suggested.

The inspector sent her a crooked smile and turned to his officers, "Go check that room."

They went and called back, "There is a man here."

"Alive?"

"Yes."

"Bring him out," muttered the inspector. "Should I check any other rooms?"

Jeremy responded in the same tone, "No, that should just about do it."

"Is that Alfred?" the inspector asked incredulously. He had men in the country and the city searching for this man. He wiped a hand down his face and then stared at Emma and Jeremy.

"It is," Emma said.

"I'll need to know what happened here. Don't leave until I speak with you."

They nodded and watched as he moved into another room with Abella to begin questioning her.

The officers woke Alfred and when he came to, he was complaining about his head. They started to remove him, and he blurted out, "No, I belong here. This is my family."

"You can explain downtown," the officer said.

Alfred struggled, but their hold would not be broken.

Once they took him out, Emma smiled over at Jeremy, "There's always the vent in the kitchen." she suggested

He shook his head regretfully, "No, we'll wait here."

She humphed sat in a large chair and watched the door where the inspector and Abella were talking. It was a long time before the door opened. When it did, Abella and the inspector exited, and she appeared to have been crying.

The elevator signaled someone was coming up. They all watched as the doors opened; to everyone's shock, it was the Madam and Charles.

"What is happening here?" demanded the Madam.

The inspector answered, "Your daughter just explained her and her father's role in the kidnapping and drugging of Patrice, her mother, and her father."

"We can offer information to support that her father was forcing her to help him and that she wasn't aware of Paul's involvement until after the fact," said Emma firmly. "We can give you a statement."

Abella started crying again, not expecting any support.

"This is all my fault," the Madam said, "Her father never understood I wanted to be with my husband and not him."

Charles took Abella's hand in his, "Abella wasn't involved. We don't want her charged in this." Abella sank into his arms. Paul ran over to his grandmother.

Her eyes wide and hopeful she asked, "Charles, really?" They had been close until she found out about her real father.

The Madam's voice sounded imperious. "Abella, come here."

Abella would have liked to stay with Charles, but she stepped back and walked over to her mother. "Child, you should have come to me when this started."

"I should have, Maman," she acknowledged. "William said he loved me and wanted us to be his family."

The Madam appearance had changed, her head was no longer held at a regal level. She swayed on her feet. "Mama!" called Charles and Abella. They went over to her and guided her to a chair. The Madam said, "He told me the same. François was away so much when we were first married, and William was so sympathetic to a young bride."

Charles wasn't surprised; he had known about Abella's parentage long ago.

Inspector Levan spoke up, "We'll need to take everyone's statements." The Madam started to object and he said, "We can handle this privately here."

She let out a deep breath, "Thank you."

"Maman, you need to know, William killed Papa," Abella said quietly. "I didn't know."

The Madam and Charles were very quiet. The Madam finally said, "I suspected he might be involved."

Charles reacted first, "Maman!"

She reached over and patted his hand. "I had no proof but felt that William started behaving differently after your father died. He has been taking privileges he was not allowed."

Emma and Jeremy didn't want those details. The night went on with everyone giving statements.

Abella and her son were allowed to go to their bedrooms to rest. Charles and the Madam sat quietly as the police departed.

"Thank you for helping us," The Madam said, "I apologize I couldn't tell you more information on what might be happening."

"Did you know William was involved in Patrice's mother's kidnapping?" Emma asked.

"No," the Madam said honestly.

Jeremy asked Charles, "Did you know your wife and daughter might be in danger?"

"Things were happening quickly. My father had just passed away, and I was called home to take over the business. I notified Catherine to meet me here with Patrice. It was the day they were due to arrive that I was told our German hotel was having problems and I'd need to go there before my family arrived. I was suspicious of the trip and the arrival of my family."

"Who notified you the hotel was having problems?" Jeremy asked.

"I received a telegram."

"Did anyone special deliver it?" Emma asked.

"Alfred," he admitted. "I got organized and made a plan that could be in place in case something happened."

"How were we involved in your plan?" Emma asked.

"You were my backup. I recognized your name on the reservation list and moved you to the suite."

"So, it was a coincidence?" murmured Emma.

"Yes, but I told Etienne that I trusted that, if anything happened, he was to get Patrice and Catherine to you."

"I'm glad we were here to help," she said sincerely.

"We are also," he commented.

Emma thought of Etienne and said, "You might try to notify him that he can come back, the poor boy is in hiding."

"I will take care of it. He will be rewarded for helping us," said Charles.

"What about Abella? What will happen?" Emma asked.

"We have to take responsibility for much of these events occurring," Charles said, looking regretful. "Once I was born, Papa essentially cut her off from his affection."

"Yes," said the Madam. "Before that, they were always together and so similar. It just broke my heart."

"When he sent her away, I never contacted or visited her. We'll have to do better," Charles said.

"How will you do that?" Jeremy asked.

"I think we'll move in with Maman and let her get to know Catherine and Patrice."

"And Abella?" asked Emma.

"She and Paul can stay at the new hotel." He laughed suddenly and said, "She's doing a good job there."

CHAPTER 20

inally, making their way back to their room, Jeremy studied Emma and said, "You know, this is two vacations we've had weird things have happened. I say next vacation, we don't leave our room."

She smiled, and stepped into his arms, "What? Murder, kidnapping, and mayhem were too much for you?"

As he lowered his head to kiss her, he said, "Well, maybe not."

She smiled and let herself be pulled to him again. They stepped apart and continued to hold hands as they opened their door. For the first time in a week, it was quiet in their suite. It was such a relief to them both. He took the opportunity and pulled her on top of him and onto the couch.

"This is nice," she said as she lowered her head to kiss him. Just then, there was a knock on the door. "Hmm, it was nice while it lasted," she said and rolled off of him. She patted her hair while Jeremy went to the door.

Several men entered carrying trays. "The Madam thought you'd like this," one of the men said. The duo's eyes went wide at the assortment of meats, cheeses, breads, and pastries.

"Set it here." Jeremy directed them to the living room. As they were setting up, Emma went and knocked lightly on Dora and Tim's door. "Would you like to join us?" she asked when Tim answered, waving her arm behind her.

He marveled at all the food laid out, "Yes. Let me check with Dora."

A more subdued Dora came out. Emma went over to her sister and put her arms around her. "She's okay. I know she is," she mumbled into Dora's neck.

Her sister hugged her tighter.

"Will you come eat?" Emma asked.

"Yes," Dora said and held Emma's hand as they made their way to the couch.

The food was eaten, and the wine was drunk. The four sat back on the two couches. "That was good," said Tim, rubbing his belly.

"We have not had a bad meal here," Jeremy said.

"No, but we have had a lot of intrigue," said Emma. "I think we'll all be ready to head home at the end of the week."

"Yes," Jeremy, Tim, and Dora said at once.

"Will we hear what's behind all of this?" asked Tim.

"We can tell you what we know," Emma said. She and Jeremy went into detail about The Vanishing Lady case.

CHAPTER 21

The foursome decided to be tourists the next day and was joined by Papa and Abbey. They made their way to the Latin Quarter to see the church located there and wandered around the area, shopping and sampling the food.

That afternoon, they were resting from their busy morning when the inspector sent them a note asking them to meet at the Madam's that evening. They wondered if new information would be disclosed.

They made their way to the Madam's apartments at the other hotel. Tim and Dora chose to stay at their hotel and have a late dinner in the room. They dressed for the evening. Emma in the dress given to her by Abbey and Jeremy in a black jacket and tie.

They were taken up directly on the elevator and escorted into the Madam's apartment. They were greeted by a cheerful Paul. The child's mood seemed reflective of the overall group feeling.

"It looks like they're more settled," murmured Jeremy.

"And happy," said Emma. She watched Abella enter the room

with Catherine; they were laughing. Abella's bitterness seemed to have faded away.

Following them were Charles and the Madam. "We're happy you accepted our invitation. You have done so much for our family," greeted Charles.

They didn't discuss the case until after dinner. Emma asked, "What happens now?"

"William and Alfred are going to prison," stated Charles.

Emma was curious and asked, "Are you doing well with all of this?"

Abella said, "I'm doing better. Maman thinks it may be better to get some separation between us and William. We'll do that and see what the future holds."

Their evening ended and they promised to keep in touch.

CHAPTER 22

*T*heir days in Paris continued with Dora appearing to become more brittle as they passed. The four were in the lobby talking about their plans for the day. Emma said, "One last stop at the exposition, and we will finally see the cultural areas…" She tapered off, noticing a lady with a scarf wrapped around her face. *Is that the rude lady they had traveled with from New York and then again in the hotel The scarf is very familiar. But was it her? She seems taller than before.*

Two men followed her, carrying the truck that had arrived empty. *It's certainly full of something now,* she thought and watched the men struggle with it. She decided it was time to find out what was in that trunk. She moved close and stuck her foot out, tripping one of the men. He went down with a twisting motion and the trunk went with him. It crashed to the ground, breaking the clasp, with personal contents spilling out. The lady with the scarf began yelling at the men, "Pick it up!"

Before the woman could stop Emma, she pulled the top of the trunk open. There was a woman's body. *It was the wife. Then that must be…* She strode over and pulled the scarf off of 'her' and saw the husband.

"Why can't you mind your own business?" he said and took a swing at Emma. She ducked and didn't see Dora jump on his back.

"Leave my sister alone!" Dora yelled, pounding on him with her fist.

An officer in the area went to remove her. Dora responded instinctively and hit him in the eye with her fist. That act seemed to set off a large fight within the lobby. Jeremy got involved and tried to pull Emma away from the man dressed as a woman.

An army of policemen arrived and wouldn't listen to anyone; they moved everyone out to wagons and then to the station.

～

"So, is that the whole story?" asked Cole. Amazed at all he had missed. "There was The Case of the Vanishing Lady and The Woman Who Knew Too Much?"

Emma laughed, "A-ha! Finally! We could never decide on a name for Dora's case."

The group laughed in response.

"The lady in the trunk? How did you know she was in there?" Cole asked.

"I didn't," Emma admitted. "I suspected it might be the much-beleaguered husband. When I saw her in the lobby, I thought the height and weight were troubling."

"Yes, he admitted that he thought his wife planned to kill him, so he went after her first."

"Is that likely? The outfit seems planned. He couldn't have fit into her clothes."

"That's what the officers are asking," Cole said in a wry manner.

"Will I need to stay to testify?" Emma asked, knowing her family wanted to head home on time.

He laughed. "No, there were plenty of Parisians who witnessed the body in the trunk." He looked at the much-maligned group and asked, "Anyone want to go to the exposition with me?"

They laughed and said, "Yes."

As they were leaving the police station Cole stopped.

"Oh, Emma. I was asked to deliver this to you." He handed her a letter.

"Who's it from?" Emma opened the letter and read it.

"Dora! It's from Savannah!"

"What does she say?" Dora asked, walking over to her.

"She says Patrick and Lottie are doing fine. And… Ethan proposed to her!"

"How wonderful!" Dora exclaimed.

"Savannah asks if they can have the wedding at the house and if we'll help her with the details."

"Of course, we will. She didn't need to ask. When are they planning the wedding for?"

"They want to have it at Christmas in honor of when they met."

"Oh, how lovely, I love the idea of a December wedding…"

Emma and Dora's voices faded out as they walked down the street planning their friend's wedding.

CHAPTER 23

The week ended in Paris, and the foursome boarded the steamboat for their trip home. Cole took them to the train and stood with Emma while the others boarded. "Emma, could you give this to Amy?"

"What is it," she asked curiously.

He mumbled, "Some lace handkerchiefs and some pictures from the exposition. I thought she might like them."

Emma didn't react, she took the package and said casually, "That is nice. I will make sure she gets them."

"Thank you," he said. The train whistle sounded and Emma ran to jump on. She turned and waved to Cole. He would stay in Paris with his close friends Ellis and Abbey. They'd spend another month there together.

She joined the group in the carriage. "What is that?" asked Jeremy.

"A little something for Amy from Cole," said Emma with no inflection in her voice.

"That's nice," said Jeremy as he opened his book to start reading.

Dora raised her eyebrows and Emma shrugged. Tim caught that exchange and wondered what he had missed.

The trip to New York was relaxing, though Dora walked more than she slept. They disembarked and moved to the day train and then the week-long train trip. When their final stop approached, Dora had her handbag and was waiting impatiently to disembark.

They hailed a cab quickly and went to the boarding house. Dora didn't wait for it to stop and bounded down before Tim could stop her. He was close behind as she ran up the stoop. They entered and Dora started running from room to room shouting, "Lottie! Patrick!"

Tim stopped her, "Check the kitchen. I'll run up to the bedroom. Maybe she's taking a nap."

She ran to the kitchen and back to the foyer. Tim walked down the stairs and she asked, her voice strained, "Was she in there?"

He slowly shook his head. She responded by collapsing on the stairs where she stood. "My baby." Tim went to her and pulled her into his arms.

Jeremy and Emma had come in and watched, helpless how to help. She had felt sure Lottie was there.

Bang! Bang! The sound was someone pulling something up the stoop. All four went still as they watched the door open. Amy entered, talking animatedly.

Dora and Tim saw who she carried with her and ran down the remaining stairs. Dora took Lottie in her arms. Tim enveloped them and they stood together.

Amy was confused. "You're back?"

"Why don't we leave them alone?" Emma said and took Amy and Jeremy to the kitchen.

"Why don't you tell her what happened," suggested Jeremy.

Emma explained to Amy what had occurred in Paris.

"Dora should know I'd never let Lottie out of my sight," Amy said, shocked.

"We know," Emma said, "but we had no way to communicate with you." She thought of the package and reached into her bag. "Amy, Cole sent this from Paris for you."

Amy's cheeks went red and she said, "I will open it later."

Everyone came into the kitchen talking at once. Emma's gaze took in her home and her family. She commented softly, "It's so good to be home."

Jeremy reached over and took her hand in his, "Yes, it is."

HISTORICAL NOTES:

Historical Note 1: The Case of the Woman Who Knew Too Much

Lenora's brother was based loosely on William Kemmler. On August 6, 1890, he became the first person to be sent to the electric chair. After he was strapped in, a charge of approximately 700 volts was delivered for only 17 seconds before the current failed. Witnesses reported smelling burnt clothing and charred flesh, but Kemmler was far from dead, and a second shock was prepared. The second charge was 1,030 volts and was applied for about two minutes. Smoke was observed coming from the head of the deceased Kemmler. An autopsy showed that the electrode attached to his back had burned through to the spine.

Dr. Alfred Southwick, the inventor of the electric chair, applauded Kemmler's execution with the declaration, "We live in a higher civilization from this day on." While American inventor George Westinghouse, an innovator of the use of electricity, remarked, "They'd have done better with an ax."

Historical Note 2: The Case of the Vanishing Lady

Mostly considered a French urban legend set during the time of the 1889 Paris Exposition. A girl and her mother were traveling together in France. The girl left the room to get medication for her sick mother. When she returned, her mother was gone and the staff said she had never checked in.

Another version of the story was that the mother had died of the plague and the hotel covered it up by calling the girl crazy.

There are different stories -did it happen? Maybe or Maybe not. It made for an interesting story.

Notebook Mysteries

Mysteries

Books
1-2-3

KIMBERLY
MULLINS

ABOUT THE AUTHOR

Kimberly Mullins is the author of series of books titled "Notebook Mysteries". Her stories are based on historical events occurring in 1871-1890's Chicago. She holds a BS in Biology and a MBA in Business. She lives in Texas with her husband and son. When she is not writing she is working as a Process Safety Engineer at a large chemical company. You can connect with her on her website www.kimberlymullinsauthor.com.

Photo Credit: Blessings of Faith Photography

 twitter.com/kremullins_kim

Ingram Content Group UK Ltd.
Milton Keynes UK
UKHW020650130723
425033UK00017B/162/J